Rogue Lawman: Gallows Express

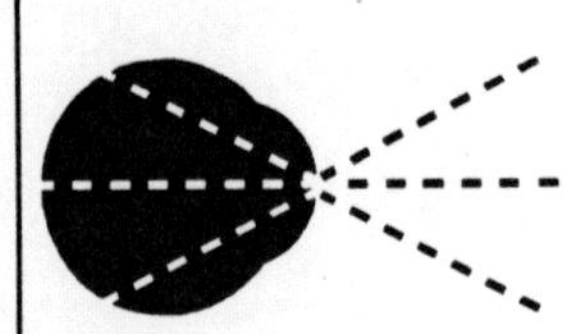

This Large Print Book carries the Seal of Approval of N.A.V.H.

ROGUE LAWMAN: GALLOWS EXPRESS

PETER BRANDVOLD

WHEELER PUBLISHING
A part of Gale, Cengage Learning

GALE
CENGAGE Learning™

Detroit • New York • San Francisco • New Haven, Conn • Waterville, Maine • London

Wheeler Publishing, a part of Gale, Cengage Learning.

Wheeler Publishing Large Print Western.
The text of this Large Print edition is unabridged.
Other aspects of the book may vary from the original edition.
Set in 16 pt. Plantin.

LIBRARY OF CONGRESS CATALOGING-IN-PUBLICATION DATA

Brandvold, Peter.
[Gallows express]
Rogue lawman : gallows express / by Peter Brandvold. — Large print ed.
p. cm. — (Wheeler Publishing large print western)
ISBN-13: 978-1-4104-4298-7 (softcover)
ISBN-10: 1-4104-4298-5 (softcover)
1. Hawk, Gideon (Fictitious character)—Fiction. 2. Large type books.
I. Title.
PS3552.R3236G35 2011
813'.54—dc22 2011031419

Published in 2011 by arrangement with The Berkley Publishing Group, a member of Penguin Group (USA) Inc.

Printed in the United States of America
1 2 3 4 5 15 14 13 12 11

FD301

For my Tin Cup pards,
Norm and Lee

1.
"You Worthless Son of a Two-Peso Whore!"

"Good citizens gathered before me now," shouted the Medicine Bow County sheriff from atop the gallows where three outlaws were about to be hanged, "let today be the first day of the end of lawlessness in Trinity Ridge!"

Not a large crowd had gathered — most folks were too afraid of repercussions from the gang of doomed men — but most of those who had braved the danger gave a hearty cheer, throwing gloved or mittened fists into the air. Their breath frosted in the chill, sunny air around their faces and red noses.

A few whores who had gathered on the second-floor balcony of a Trinity Ridge fleshpot, wrapped in blankets and threadbare mittens or moth-eaten wool coats, also yelled and hooted and stamped their fur-slippered feet.

"You got that right, Sheriff Stanley!"

screeched the drunkest of the three doves, a willowy blonde with a red scarf wrapped around her neck and a brown wool cap on her head, who looked all but devoured by her oversized, striped blanket coat. "Let this be the end of Blue Tierney's stranglehold on this county. Not to mention the son of a bitch's bastard son!"

The whore next to her had been drinking from a brandy bottle, but now the girl, a brunette with extraordinarily long eyelashes, jerked the bottle down as she spewed brandy into the air, laughing. "Claire," she scolded the blonde when she'd recovered from her paroxysm. "You're gonna get your throat cut!"

"I ain't afraid of . . ." Claire let her voice trail off when she saw Brazos Tierney, standing atop the gallows behind the sheriff, hands cuffed and ankles shackled, a hangman's noose dangling in front of his head, turn his face toward her. Tierney's face was expressionless beneath his cap of thin, curly brown hair. But his gaze was direct and sharp with menace, breath jetting from his broad nostrils and lips.

Steeling herself, Claire stepped forward, shouting drunkenly down from the balcony at the gallows, "I ain't afraid of you, Brazos Tierney. Not no more, I ain't. You're about to die, and I hope you're shittin' your pants, you worthless son of a two-peso whore!"

The crowd's din had dwindled slightly when the whore shouted the first time, but a hush now settled over Trinity's main drag, called Wyoming Street, as all faces turned to regard her skeptically. Even Sheriff Stanley turned to face her, knowing, as did the rest of the town, that it was her half brother, who tended bar in the whorehouse, whom Tierney and the two other men had brutally beaten eight days ago. Drunk and disorderly, they'd taken umbrage when Echo Lang had told them to clear out, that the party was over, the Venus was closing its doors, and all the whores were going to bed.

They'd beaten the man so badly that not even Claire had recognized Echo's face the next morning, when the undertaker had hauled him out into the early, coppery light. They'd beaten him unconscious, and then they'd cut his throat with a broken whiskey bottle.

After that, they'd all passed out only to awaken hours later in Sheriff Aaron Stanley's jail that was nearly directly across the street from the Venus. Stanley hadn't been able to believe his luck. He'd wanted to take down Brazos Tierney and his two cutthroat amigos for a long time. While he'd suspected that they were the three responsible for robbing spur train number seventy-nine from Denver from time to time, and knew they were almost constantly rustling cattle from the surrounding ranches to sell up north in Wyoming Territory, where stock detectives and brand inspectors were few and far between, he'd never had anything concrete to pin them with.

Now, he did.

And he couldn't bring himself to feel overly sorry for the beefy pimp and bartender, Echo Lang, a locally infamous lout and loudmouth. In fact, the sheriff thought Lang a small price to pay to be rid, once and for all, of Brazos Tierney, J. T. Hostetler, and "One-Eye" Willie McGee. The circuit judge had taken the train to Trinity *muy pronto* in response to Stanley's cabled summons and had sentenced the three men to be hanged before the Baldwin locomotive's broiler had been refilled with water for the return trip back to Camp Collins.

Stanley had wanted to hang the three as the judge's train pulled back out of the station, but protocol required a professional hangman be called in, a gallows be built, and a man of the cloth be present.

Well, the gallows had been built in record time, and now the three condemned men stood awaiting the hangman to tighten the nooses about their necks and for the preacher to send them off in somber Lutheran style.

Once Stanley had finished his speech, that was. . . .

He looked at the whore on the balcony. She was staring down at Tierney, one hand on the rod-iron rail, her other fist on her hip, and the sheriff had to restrain himself from chuckling at the girl's pluck, besotted as she was. He turned his head farther back to look over his right shoulder at Tierney, who was glowering back at the girl.

Stanley reached up to pull the brim of his cream Stetson lower to shield his eyes from the intense high-country sun, then thrust both his gloved hands into the air, redirecting the crowd's attention back to himself.

"As I was saying," he said as loudly as he could without shouting, "let today's hangings of these three men — men whom we *know* have been instigating illegal activities throughout not only our town and county but through all of north-central Colorado — be the beginning of the end of lawlessness.

"Let this be a warning to others of their ilk: robbing trains and stage coaches and rustling cattle, not to mention the general harassment of innocent, law-abiding citizens on the streets of Trinity" — the sheriff shook both his fists in the air for emphasis as he pitched his voice much louder — "will . . . not . . . be . . . *tolerated!*"

As his words echoed off the tall, sunlit storefronts around him, the crowd threw their hands in the air once more and cheered. There couldn't have been more than forty or fifty people out of the town's total population of three hundred forty, but the cheers went up like a roar. The town's obvious approval and eagerness to rid the town and county of the Tierney gang's evil influence made Stanley's chest lighten, easing the anxiety that had been raking cold fingers along his spine ever since he and his deputy, Matt Freeman, had led the men out here to the gallows. He'd figured Brazos Tierney's father, Blue Tierney, would make some play to save his son from the hangman's noose.

So far, however, there'd been no sign of the man or any of the men who rode for him out at his Two Troughs Ranch. Maybe Blue Tierney had had enough of the firebrand, as well.

As the cheers dwindled, Stanley's eyes swept the crowd. He was about to open his mouth to say one more thing when his eyes picked his young wife out of the crowd. Stanley frowned and closed his mouth. Janelle was the last person he'd expected to see out here today, and for a moment he thought his eyes were deceiving him.

No, it was her, all right — dressed in her old, red wool coat with the once-fashionably large buttons, red stocking cap, and thick black scarf. She was holding their year-and-a-half-old son, Jake, in her arms, the boy extending a small, mittened hand toward one of the two curs sniffing between the cracks of the nearby boardwalk fronting Herman's Drug Emporium & Candy Shop.

Stanley glanced back at his deputy, Matt Freeman — a big, mustached man in a black wool coat and broad-brimmed felt hat, holding his double-barreled shotgun in his crossed arms, a confident, proud look in his eyes. Flanking the deputy sheriff were the hangman, Amos Scudder, who'd arrived that morning from Camp Collins, and the Reverend F. Oldwin Hawthorne, who held his Bible in his large crossed hands, an oblique expression on his blue-eyed, lantern-jawed face.

"Matt," Stanley said above the crowd's low din, "tell Scudder and the Reverend to get started, will you?"

Freeman nodded and ran a wool-gloved

fist across his nose from which a drop of mucus clung. He was a big, healthy man, a former freighter, but he had been fighting a cold for the past month and the lingering, high-country winter hadn't helped. "You see her?"

"Yeah."

"Janelle don't need to be seein' this."

"No, she don't."

Stanley descended the gallows' three steps to the street and, while the hangman began placing the black hoods over the doomed men's heads, made his way around the edge of the crowd toward the back, sidestepping through the small group of unshaven ranch hands holding beers and looking bleary-eyed as they stood around the low piles of shoveled snow outside Trinity Ridge's main sporting parlor, the Venus. Janelle had watched her husband walk toward her and their son, and her usually soft hazel eyes acquired a stubborn cast as Stanley stopped in front of her.

Before he could open his mouth to speak, Janelle hefted their son in her arms and said, "Please don't do this, Aaron."

"Please don't do what, honey — for *chris-sake!*"

Seeing one of the townsmen regarding him and his wife curiously, Stanley grabbed

Janelle's arm and led her a ways back from the crowd while the boy grinned up at him and, having forgotten the sniffing curs, held his mittened hand out to his father. Absently, Stanley gave the child his finger, which little Jake gave a soft squeeze in his mittened fist.

"We talked this all out. This has to be done for the good of the town, the county. What're you doing here, anyway?" He frowned at the boy grinning up at him. "And with Jake? This is no place for a child."

"I'm worried, Aaron. I'm worried what might happen with that . . . that beast's father. I love you, Aaron, and I don't want anything to happen to you." Janelle sniffed as she fought back the flood of tears that washed over her eyes. "Isn't there any way you can just fine these men and turn them loose?"

"What?!"

Several people turned at the sound of Stanley's raised voice. He hadn't intended to speak so loudly, but Janelle was acting hysterical.

They'd talked out the significance of today's punishment over the course of several suppers in their little frame shack on the south end of Trinity Ridge, and he'd thought that his young wife had accepted his explanation. He could see now that, while she'd tried to be strong, her heart had withered. Fear had overcome her.

Thank god that hadn't happened to the six men who'd sat on Tierney's jury the other day.

"Listen, honey," Stanley said, keeping his voice down and setting his hands on his wife's slender shoulders. "I'm the lawman here in Trinity Ridge. It's my job to uphold the laws of the town and the county. If the raw element doesn't come to respect me —"

Janelle cut in with, "Raw element? You mean *killers!* They won't respect you, Aaron. They'll kill you."

"I have Freeman backing me. A sheriff couldn't ask for a better deputy."

"Matt's big," Janelle said, tears streaming down her heart-shaped face, her nose running as she squinted up at her tall, young husband, "but he can't stop a bullet any better than you can!"

"Everything's going to be fine, honey. You and Jake run along home. I'll be there in an hour or so for lunch."

"I want to go back to the ranch."

Stanley scowled. "The ranch?"

They'd left their little ten-cow operation on the west bank of Sandy Wash over a year ago, because they couldn't make a living on that parched bench, and Janelle herself hadn't wanted to raise their newborn child in poverty. Medicine Bow County had needed a sheriff, so, having been in the cavalry and having been a deputy constable for a short time when he'd first come west, he'd run for the job and been voted in.

No, Stanley thought. Janelle didn't mean it. She'd been lonely out there and afraid of attacks by Ute renegades. She was just scared and didn't realize what she was saying.

"We could go back, raise a few cows," she said now, weakly, desperately. "We'd get by. At least I wouldn't have to worry about you, Aaron. Worry about you until I just can't stand it anymore!"

Stanley drew her and the boy to him, pressed both their heads to his chest. "You go on back home, honey." He pressed his lips first to her head, then to Jake's, who reached up and tried to grab the sheriff's ear, gurgling incoherently.

Stanley stepped back, caught the boy's hand and kissed it, and gave Janelle a reassuring smile. "I'll be along soon."

He glanced over his shoulder at the gallows. All three prisoners were hooded and noosed, and the hangman stood near big

Matt Freeman to their left. The minister, Pastor Hawthorne, was delivering a prayer, facing the three doomed men. McGee was mocking him, steepling his hands beneath his chin, his shoulders jerking as he laughed.

"Go along now, Janelle," Stanley said, edging away from her and Jake. "Go home and throw a lunch together, will you? I'd love a roast beef sandwich."

Janelle stared up at him now as though she could see right through him. "He's coming."

Stanley furled his brows and stopped backing away from her. He felt a familiar hitch in his chest. *Oh, no,* the sheriff thought. *Not again . . .*

"He's coming, Aaron." Janelle's voice was low and sinister, which was the way it sounded whenever she told him about her bizarre premonitions. "I've seen him."

She nodded, her eyes bright, glassy, and certain. "He and his men are headed this way right now. They'll be here soon." Her eyes flooded with tears once more, and she pressed Jake's head to her bosom. "Oh, Aaron, please come home!"

Stanley was getting peeved. He glanced around. More people were watching him and his "somewhat unstable young wife," as the town had come to know her, giving them both strange, knowing looks.

"Janelle," he said, hardening his voice. "You listen to me, and go home. Now!"

Stanley turned away from her and walked back toward the gallows. He was glad when one last glance over his shoulder told him that she was obeying him finally and walking away, heading back toward their house, Jake looking back toward his father and grinning.

But Aaron Stanley couldn't deny the little worm of dread flicking its tail in his belly, the long, cold fingers of menace tickling his spine.

2.
"Ah, Hell"

As he made his way through the crowd, Sheriff Stanley glanced at the buildings around him, then looked down the street and into the rolling countryside beyond Trinity. Relief eased the flicking of the worm's tail when he saw nothing but the rocky, snow-dusted hills and, beyond them, the jutting purple escarpment of the Rawhide Mountains.

He stopped before the gallows where Matt Freeman stood with one foot on the bottom step, holding his double-barreled shotgun up high across his chest. "Let's get this show on the road, Matt."

The deputy nodded and looked up at the hangman, Amos Scudder, standing on the platform above him. Freeman said something to Scudder, and the wizened little man with the sunken gums nodded and started turning away, toward the wooden, brake-like lever that would drop the trapdoor beneath the doomed men's feet. He stopped suddenly when hoof thuds rose above the crowd's low din, and scowled down a near side street.

"Tierney!" someone shouted.

All heads, including Stanley's, turned to see a dozen or so riders galloping in from the north, rounding the corner of the side street and turning onto the main one, making a beeline for the gallows.

"Ah, hell," a man groaned near Stanley, and then the sheriff heard several men muttering anxiously before the sound of retreating footsteps, spurs chinging like sleigh bells. The rest of the crowd scattered like a playground full of misbehaving boys at first sight of the beetle-browed schoolmaster.

A cold stone dropped in Stanley's belly as an empty stretch of street yawned between only him, Freeman, and the fast-approaching riders. The gap narrowed quickly.

Stanley went over and picked up his Winchester repeating rifle from where he'd leaned it against the side of the gallows. He racked a shell into the chamber and lowered the hammer to half cock as the lead rider of the well-armed, hard-faced bunch, old Blue Tierney himself, reined his big gray gelding down. Tierney kept a firm grip on the reins as the sweat-lathered mount tossed its head and blew, chomping its bit.

Stanley glanced a warning at Freeman, who set his jaws and nodded resolutely as he drew a deep breath and raised his shotgun up high across his chest, raking his thumb across both rabbit-ear hammers.

"Damn," Tierney said, shuttling his gaze across the gallows and running a gloved hand down the gray beard stubbling his face. "Looks like we almost didn't make it in time!"

He glanced to the rider drawing up beside him, and the two men shared a chuckle. The other riders drew up around Tierney and this second man, who Stanley recognized as Tierney's *segundo,* Jack Wildhorn. Wildhorn was a round-faced man with a frizzy red beard that hung to his belly and a savage-looking knife scar angling across his upper and lower lips and which, when he spoke, which was rare, caused him to lisp. Cold, stupid, umber-brown eyes stared out from deep, freckled sockets.

Tierney himself was in his mid-fifties. Years of hard drinking had given him a consumptive look, pronouncing the hawkishness of his nose and eyes and drawing the chalky skin taut against his high-molded cheekbones. He was a medium-tall man, bowlegged, rangy, with the few pounds of extra weight on his slope-shouldered frame settling in his paunch. Gray-white hair curled down from beneath his hat brim to ring his ears and brush the collar of his long, blue wool greatcoat.

All the other men before Stanley wore coats of various breeds and grades of fur. A couple wore wool caps. The others, including Tierney, wore ragged Stetsons with mufflers wrapped over their heads beneath the hats, and tied beneath their chins. The knotted ends of Tierney's soiled cream scarf flapped in the chill breeze as he rested his hands over his saddle horn and looked around with a smug grin brightening his drink-bleary eyes.

"Sorry, boy," he said, directing his chin at the platform and raising his voice. "We was playin' poker late last night, and we slept in this mornin'!"

"That you, Pa?" Brazos grated out from beneath his black hood, causing the hood to suck in and out around his mouth. " 'Bout goddamn time you got here. The sky pilot done already gave us the send-off!"

Tierney chuckled and glanced at Reverend Hawthorne, who blanched at the rancher's gaze and took a half a step back on the gallows floor, near the hangman, Scudder. The executioner was also suddenly looking a tad dyspeptic as his right hand dropped slowly down from the trapdoor's release handle, and he swallowed hard.

Stanley drew a deep breath as he and Freeman sidestepped away from each other, giving themselves plenty of room to work in front of the eight riders gathered before them, the horses' breath jetting in the crisp, gold-dappled air. Had Janelle really presaged this? the sheriff absently wondered. Or was it just a coincidence? It didn't take a fortune-teller to know there was a good chance that Tierney would try to spring Brazos. Word had been going around the saloons that he was planning something.

"Look here, Mr. Tierney," Stanley said, lifting his head and putting some official steel in his voice, "I don't know what you think you're doing here today, but I gave the order that Trinity is off-limits to Two Troughs men until the day after tomorrow."

He paused for effect, and Tierney studied him with one narrowed, violet eye, half his upper lip curled back from his teeth.

"Now, your son, here — Brazos," Stanley continued, "was tried all legally by a judge and jury. Said jury found him and his two cohorts, Mr. Hostetler and Mr. McGee, guilty of murder in the first degree."

"Mr. Hostetler." J. T. Hostetler laughed behind his hood, lifting the toes of his worn, brown boots. "I like that. I'd like for you boys to call me 'sir' from now on!"

"Yeah, well, first they should think about gettin' us down off this platform," McGee said, his voice tight and testy. "And I'd appreciate havin' this rope removed from my neck. It's startin' to itch!"

Keeping his eyes on Blue Tierney, Stanley said, "You'll stay right where you are, McGee. Same with your friends. The jury has done decided their fates, Mr. Tierney. Now, before I have to arrest you for interfering in the carrying out of an officially sanctioned execution, I'll ask you to ride on back to where you came from."

Tierney winced as though he'd been stricken with indigestion. "Look, Sheriff — why don't you be a good young feller and turn these men loose? Do it the easy way? All right? I know you got a wife and a kid, and I'd feel bad as hell if I had to shoot you down like a damn dog right here in the street."

Stanley's stomach rolled, and his heart hammered, but he kept his face implacable as he adjusted his grip on his Winchester. The man before him was hard. Frontier hard. With a criminal past. And Stanley knew Tierney would kill him if he had to, and he really wouldn't feel bad at all about it.

"Look, Mr. Tierney," Stanley said. "You know I can't do that. And while, yes, you have my deputy and myself outnumbered, if you try to release these convicted felons, you're going to have a fight on your hands."

The young sheriff glanced at Matt Freeman standing about ten feet to his right, feet spread a little over shoulder width apart, holding his shotgun at once defensively and threateningly. His fingers looking thick and pink in his fingerless gloves, the deputy drew the barn blaster's hammer back to full cock.

"And you'll be the first to die," Stanley said, adding threat to his voice as his eyes held Tierney's.

Stanley heard a man behind Tierney growl, "Why, you little fuck!"

A gun exploded.

At the same time, Stanley felt as though his upper left arm had been struck by a thrown war hatchet. As he staggered to his right, he tried to keep his rifle aimed at Blue Tierney and squeezed the Winchester's trigger. A sinking sensation was added to his sudden torment when he saw the rifle jerk up to send his triggered slug high and right of his target.

Tierney's gray gelding reared as Stanley dropped to a knee, gritting his teeth against the hot, jaw-grinding pain in his left arm and upper chest. In the left periphery of his vision, the sheriff saw Freeman swing his shotgun's double bores in Stanley's direction, intending to shoot over Stanley's head at the man who'd shot the sheriff.

But then pistols popped and smoke puffed around the men directly in front of Freeman, and Matt screamed. He triggered the twin bores of his shotgun with a thunder-like explosion — the report felt like an open hand smacking the side of Stanley's head — and then the deputy screamed once more as he lowered the shotgun and staggered backward.

After that, Stanley heard only a ringing in his ears though he knew more guns were being fired. He saw the flames stabbing from barrels and saw the smoke jet from pistol maws. Horses reared and jerked this way and that, and the mouths of Tierney's men opened wide in jubilation.

Stanley felt the hot jab of at least two more chunks of lead before he got his rifle raised once more, using only his right hand while his left arm dangled uselessly at his side. He cocked the rifle one-handed and fired, watching in horror as the slug blew up dust in front of him, before he felt an incredibly huge, powerful, invisible fist slam into his chest.

Not a fist.

Looking down, he saw stuffing puff from the front of his quilted red blanket coat and then a thick red substance dribble out through the ragged hole, rolling in thick beads down his coat and across the buckles of his double cartridge belts to the street beneath him, where they licked up little curls of frozen dust.

He released the Winchester and flew back against the steps of the gallows and, no longer feeling anything, but now hearing the muffled whoops and yells and pistol pops of Tierney and his reveling men, looked up at the sky.

He saw a bird wing past. Not an eagle, a hawk, or even a buzzard. Just a barn swallow, its little wings flashing silver in the sunlight.

Odd, he thought with a startling clarity, that the last bird he'd ever see was one so benign as a common barn swallow.

And then the young sheriff's body spasmed violently as he lay there against the gallows steps. Blood welled from between his lips curled with misery. His eyes closed on the now-empty sky. And he died.

He did not see or hear his young wife screaming his name as she ran toward him while several of Tierney's men leapt from their skitter-hopping mounts to the gallows, where they began freeing Stanley's prisoners.

"Aaron!" Janelle screamed, dropping to her knees and cradling her husband's lifeless body in her arms. She pressed her chin to his forehead and cast her agonized, horrified gaze at the sky as though trailing her husband's fleeing soul there amidst the wafting gunsmoke. *"Aa-ronn!"*

She was still screaming and cradling her husband's lifeless head as the laughing riders, three now riding double, galloped back in the direction of the Tierney Two Troughs outlaw ranch.

3.
The Shortest Route to Trinity

Gideon Hawk drew his grulla gelding to a halt on the pine-stippled mountain shoulder and swung down from the saddle.

He dropped the reins and walked down a slight grade through the columnar pines and firs. Staring off across a deep canyon, he saw three riders moving Indian-file along the narrow game trail angling down the opposite ridge on which few trees grew — mostly scrub juniper with a few spindly cedars.

The riders were on the same trail that Hawk had been following.

Three men. The same three who'd been following Hawk's trail for the past hour or so, since he'd entered the central reaches of the Rawhide Mountains along the Colorado-Wyoming border. Three well-armed men, he saw now, not needing the help of field glasses to see the rifles jutting from their saddle boots as well as knife sheaths and holsters on the cartridge belts they wore on the outsides of their coats.

As the riders followed the path down the steep mountain slope and into the canyon, they looked around warily though the lead rider always returned his eyes to the trail ahead of him and on which Hawk's own sign was plainly visible, having been set there only about fifteen, twenty minutes ago. There had been several forking paths off the one that Hawk had followed, so it was likely no mere coincidence they were on Hawk's trail.

Hawk lifted his flat-brimmed black hat, ran a gloved hand through his thick, dark brown hair, then set the hat back on his head and adjusted the angle.

Turning back to his idly foraging horse, he reached under the belly to unbuckle the latigo straps, then pulled the beast's head up to slip the bit from its teeth. As the grulla went back to foraging on the gama grass jutting up from the two or three inches of ice-crusted snow amongst the pines, the Rogue Lawman, as Hawk was known much farther and wider than he wanted to be, shucked his Henry repeater from his saddle boot angling up over the grulla's right wither.

He peered through the quiet fir boughs to

watch the three riders drop down out of sight on the far side of the canyon, then racked a cartridge into the rifle's breech and lowered the hammer to half cock. He walked back across the trail, into a bowl-shaped area cut into the slope, and leaned the Henry against a boulder.

Looking around, he began gathering fallen branches and pinecones. He deposited the armload near an open patch of ground, then set about breaking the branches over his knee and arranging the pinecones and a handful of needles into a shaggy mound. Soon, he'd coaxed a small fire to life and set a coffeepot to boil on a rock in the center of the fire.

He sat down on the ground and leaned his back against the boulder, the rifle within reach of his right hand. He hunkered down inside his three-point buckskin capote and raised the collar against a chill breeze blowing up from the canyon. He was sitting there, one knee raised, the pot beginning to rumble and send steam curling thinly up from its spout, when he heard a horse blow from up trail.

The grulla had already sensed the approaching riders, and was staring up trail with its ears pricked, its eyes wide and alert. Hawk's horse lifted its head slightly and loosed a shrill whinny. One of the mounts of the approaching riders returned the greeting, and Hawk heard a muffled, slightly breathless voice say, “Up there. I see his mount.”

Hawk stared over the snapping, crackling fire at the grulla. The horse had craned its neck to watch the three riders approach from up trail, which Hawk couldn’t see for the ridge wall to his left. Also, the men were moving up a rise from the canyon floor.

He knew, though, when they were within view of the grulla, because the horse twitched its ears, widened its eyes slightly, and shook its head, at once expectant and apprehensive, though the horse, Hawk knew — he gave a bemused little snort at the reflection — was more interested in the strangers’ horses than in their human riders.

He heard the clomps of the approaching horses’ hooves and the squawk of tack, and then the first man rode out from behind the ridge shoulder, followed by the other two. All three swung their heads around warily before the eyes of the leader found the fire and, a half second later, the tall, rugged, dark-haired man reclining on the other side of the dancing flames.

The lead rider pulled his horse up in front

of the fire, stopping about ten feet back from it. The two other men pulled their own mounts up beside his and stared over the thin tendrils of wood smoke at Hawk, whose own face was implacable as he ran his keen, green-eyed gaze across the strangers.

Finally, the lead rider — a short, fat man of indeterminate age with a thick, blond beard covering his pale-complected face — canted his head to one side and curled his pug nose. "You know whose land you're on?"

"Nope," Hawk grunted, his left wrist draped across his left upraised knee. "Don't much care."

"Oh, you don't, do you?"

Hawk hiked a shoulder.

"Well, you're on Two Troughs range. And the Two Troughs owner, Mr. Blue Tierney, don't care for strangers. So you best just keep on ridin', bucko, if you know what's good for you."

Hawk let his eyes drift casually from the lead rider to the other two men — hard, cow-eyed saddle trash in fur coats and shabby hats. The one in the middle had blond hair hanging down past his shoulders while the man on the left end of the group appeared to be a Mexican with a round face, large ears, and a brushy black mustache concealing his mouth.

"Ain't this the trail to Trinity Ridge?" Hawk asked.

"It's one of 'em," said the lead rider. "There's plenty of trails to Trinity."

"Let's say you're comin' from Laramie," Hawk said in a calm, conversational voice. "What would be the shortest route to Trinity?"

The lead rider stared disdainfully across the fire at the brown-haired, green-eyed stranger, and narrowed one eye at him. "The trail you're on would be the shortest. But, like I said, the trail you're on crosses Two Troughs range. And, like I said, Two Troughs is off-limits to —"

"What would the next-shortest route be?" Hawk cut in.

The lead rider obviously didn't like being interrupted. His pug nose turned brick red, and his lips tightened, his shoulders rising and falling heavily as he breathed. The other two men looked at him, the Mexican grinning, as though eager to see how he would handle this impertinent stranger.

"The next-shortest route," the lead rider said in a tone of strained tolerance, "would be straight south from Laramie to Snakehead Butte. From there" — he swung an arm out in a hooking motion — "you head west along Buffalo Creek to Coyote Creek, then over the divide to Trinity."

"Seems to me going that way would take a whole extra day. Maybe two days."

"Mister," said the man with the long blond hair, "two extra days is a whole lot better than never makin' it at all — now, isn't it?"

He jutted his chin at Hawk, his eyes dully belligerent.

"If those were my choices." Hawk stretched his legs out and crossed his arms on his chest. "Nah, I think I'll just keep ridin' the way I've been ridin'."

Suddenly, the cool benevolence left his eyes, and they darkened to spruce. The leathery skin of his face drew back hard against his high-tapering cheekbones — the Indian features he'd inherited from his father, a now-deceased Ute war chief. "And there's not one goddamn thing you three mangy curs can do about it, less'n, of course, you wanna die hard."

The lead rider looked as though he'd been slapped across his cinnamon-bearded cheeks. He tipped his head back slightly, lifting his chin, and his eyes blazed brightly from their freckled sockets. The other two men set their jaws hard, and their own eyes turned to stone. The horse of the man with the long blond hair lowered his head, and shook it, rattling the bit in its teeth.

The challenge was there in the air between the three strangers and Hawk. They hadn't been expecting such a sudden, poker-like call, and they were all three ill prepared to discern if the man was bluffing or not. They didn't know the man, after all. But, while he was not old even by frontier standards, he was not young. And he didn't look foolhardy.

There was no mistaking the dead seriousness in his dark green gaze.

He was outnumbered three to one, and, while he had the brass-breeched Henry rifle leaning nearby and the bone grips of a Colt jutted up from the soft brown holster on his right hip, above the tucked-behind flap of his coat, he couldn't possibly reach either weapon before the Two Troughs riders bore down on him.

The question, however, was plain in the lead rider's brown eyes:

Could he?

Apprehension pinched the skin above the bridge of the man's nose and cut deep lines across his forehead. The other two men betrayed similar expressions, and first the long-haired man and then the Mex cut quick, curious glances at the lead rider. He fiddled with the bridle reins in his hands as he said, "Mister, I reckon there ain't no point in chasin' you out of here now, since you're halfway to Trinity. But so help me god, we catch you out here again, you're gonna be one goddamned sorry son of a bitch."

He glanced at the two other men, then reined his dun around quickly and angrily sunk his spurs into the horse's flanks. The horse lunged off its rear hooves and bolted on down the trail, the other two men following suit while casting Hawk angry, anxious glances over their shoulders. Hawk and the grulla watched them leave, and when they were gone the grulla gave a parting whinny, which was answered in kind.

The grulla swished its tail.

Hawk waited to make sure they were gone, and then he leaned forward and dipped a hand into one of his saddlebag pouches lying beside the fire. He pulled out a black tin cup and a small rawhide swatch, and used the swatch to lift the pot from the fire and fill the cup with coffee.

Returning the pot to the fire, he sank back against the rock once more and blew ripples on the coffee, on the surface of which several small white ashes floated.

He smacked his lips. Nothing like a hot

cup of black tar on a cold, late winter afternoon. He took another refreshing sip and narrowed one eye at the sky over the unmoving pine tops. He'd have to find somewhere to hole up in a couple of hours. Too early to stop yet. He still had a good day's ride or so to Trinity. He'd probably roll in a little after noon of the next day.

Switching the smoking cup to his right hand, he unbuttoned the top two buttons of his capote, drew the top flap down, and reached into his shirt pocket for the flier he'd picked up in Cheyenne a couple of weeks ago. He flipped it open and held it out before him, ran his eyes over the notice once more:

WANTED
TEMPORARY LAWMAN
TRINITY, COLORADO TERRITORY
INTERESTED AND QUALIFIED
PARTIES SEND LETTER OF
INQUIRY TO:
MALCOLM K. PENNYBACKER,
MAYOR, TRINITY, COLORADO
TERRITORY
BY MARCH 1, 1879

"Temporary lawman," Hawk muttered, lifting his cup to his lips for another sip.

He'd known what the euphemism really stood for even before he'd sent the good Mayor Pennybacker his query letter and been rewarded with a letter back, vaguely sketching out the situation. A town tamer was what the mayor was looking for. Apparently, the sitting sheriff of Medicine Bow County had been "killed in the line of duty" and another lawman was needed to fill his seat until another election was held. That was pretty much all that the letter had said, but something had told Hawk that the situation was dire.

No, not *something.* A rumor that had made its way from Trinity to Cheyenne. A dark bit of news in addition to the reported killings of the sheriff and the sheriff's deputy that had caused the citizens of Cheyenne to cluck and shake their heads but that had thrust a rusty dagger of remembered personal agony deep into the Rogue Lawman's heart so that he'd felt sick to his belly for a time, and weak in the knees.

Hawk glowered into the fire.

After a time, the dancing flames reflected in his darkly brooding eyes, he held the notice out in front of him. He let it drop into the flames that plucked at it like thin red fingers until the sheet turned brown at the edges, then black. The growing, eager flames reached into the paper, tonguelike, consuming it. The paper shrunk and turned black as it dwindled against the burning wood.

A few glowing, brown remnants reached up on the fire's thermals and swirled into the air for a time before dropping into the snowy brush and dissolving. But Hawk's own bitter memories did not die until, gritting his teeth, he ground a heel into the hard earth and kicked dirt and gravel onto the flames, knocking over the coffeepot.

Heaving himself to his feet, he tossed the dregs of his coffee onto the steaming flames, then grabbed the pot and emptied that, too, on the fire. He swabbed the cup and pot out with handfuls of snow that he scooped off the top of the boulder, then returned both instruments to his saddlebags.

He tossed the bags over the grulla's back, the horse watching him now curiously, wary of the man's suddenly sour countenance. The Rogue Lawman tightened the latigo strap, slipped the bit through the horse's teeth, and mounted up. He swung the horse around and booted him on down the trail, heading west toward Trinity Ridge.

He'd ridden only about an hour when he heard a distant pistol shot and a woman's scream.

4.
"Kill Me an' Get it Over with, Damn You"

Hawk was following a horse trail hugging a tree-lined creek meandering along the bottom of a long, narrow canyon.

A steep sandstone ridge shouldered on his right; a lower, less rocky ridge humped on his left. As he reined the grulla to a stop beneath some breeze-jostled cottonwoods whose leaves flashed gold in the dying light, he looked around to get his bearings.

There was another shot. A man yelled. The commotion seemed to originate from a dark notch gouged out of the ridge wall to his right and about a hundred yards ahead. As the woman screamed again, Hawk spurred the grulla into a gallop, leaving the creek trail and following another, scruffier trace off to the right, heading toward the ridge.

The sandstone wall, glowing like copper pennies now as the sun sank behind Hawk, towered over him, pocked and pitted and streaked with guano. As he and the grulla followed the trace into the fifty-yard gap in the stone wall, where shadows bled out from the ridges and large boulders strewn around him, he could hear the faint trickle of a stream. He saw a cabin ahead, abutting the box canyon's rear ridge.

Thin, gray smoke ribboned from the stone chimney climbing the cabin's south wall.

It was about a hundred yards away, so that the figures running through the scrub north of the cabin and the gray log barn looked little larger than fingers. But in the coppery-salmon light, Hawk could see the glow of the white blouse and tan skirt and long, auburn hair of the woman who was running and, judging by her screams, trying to get away from the three men chasing her.

She wasn't having much luck, and the men knew it.

They were yelling and laughing, and even from this distance Hawk recognized the three from his coffee camp earlier. The Mexican was just now catching up to the woman, grabbing her around the waist and, pivoting on his hips, lifting her high in the air. She gave another squeal, kicked at the man, and tried to club him with her fists.

"She's a spry one!" The Mexican laughed as the other two men — the tall man with the long blond hair, and the short, fat, bearded man — caught up to them.

Hawk sighed. He racked a shell into the Henry's chamber one-handed then set the rifle across his saddlebows as he urged the grulla ahead at a fast walk. The woman, still in the arms of the Mexican, flung one of her feet out and caught the fat man in the groin. The man jackknifed forward, yowling and crossing his hands over his balls.

The man with the long blond hair laughed and jumped back away from the woman's scissoring feet. The Mexican held her up tight against him, laughing and nuzzling her neck before wheeling and hauling her off toward the barn, both front doors of which stood wide.

There were four horses in the pole corral off the barn's far side, milling and swishing their tails, a couple watching the commotion with bland fascination.

The Mexican carried the woman into the barn as the man with the blond hair followed, whooping and laughing, while the fat man limped a good ways behind them, crouched forward and jutting his chin like a wedge. Hawk, who continued riding toward the barn, heard the fat man's angry, bellowing curses. As the Rogue Lawman drew closer, he could see the red rage leaching up from behind the man's light-colored beard, and then the man ambled on into the barn's dense, dark shadows.

Hawk drew the grulla up to the right of the open doors and swung down from the saddle. He could hear the woman whimpering and sobbing inside the barn, could hear the men grunting and talking in low, harsh tones, breathless as they tried to take what the woman was not compelled to give.

Holding his Henry repeater in both hands, Hawk strode through the barn doors, stepped to one side, putting the wall behind him so the light wouldn't outline him, and looked around.

As his eyes adjusted to the musty darkness, he saw shadows moving inside one of the stalls on the right side of the narrow runway. There was the sound of cloth being torn, and the woman cried, "Please . . . please, *stop!*"

One of the men laughed and said, "Look out, Kimber, or she'll sink one of them boots of hers in your oysters again!"

There were shuffling sounds, the light crunching and rustling of displaced straw, and more rips of torn clothes.

"There, now," the Mexican said in his slightly accented, breathless voice, "hold her down. Pull her dress up! *Mierda,* she's strong!"

A belt buckle clanked. It was followed by the thud of a shell belt landing in hay. The woman continued to groan and pant, but the sounds were muffled now, as though she were being held facedown in the hay on the other side of the stall partition.

Hawk's eyes adjusted quickly, and the three jostling figures defined themselves as the Mexican dropped to the stable floor with the woman. The long-haired gent was down on his knees, apparently holding the woman's head and arms down. Only his head was visible above the stall. He was facing Hawk but his chin was dipped, looking at the woman beneath him.

The fat's man's thick back was facing Hawk; he'd removed his coat and he was now sliding his suspenders off his heavy, sloping shoulders.

"Give it to the bitch, Rodriguez," the fat man grunted. "Go ahead and give it to her, and then it's my turn."

"No, it ain't your turn, Kimber!" protested the long-haired man. "You drew the shortest straw, remember?"

Hawk stepped forward. The long-haired man turned his head toward him, and he frowned as though he couldn't believe what he was seeing. The woman continued to sob and grunt and groan facedown in the straw.

"Sorry to interrupt like this," Hawk said raising the Henry to his shoulder and drawing the hammer back to full cock. "But I'm afraid I got some awful bad news."

The fat man wheeled, his bearded cheeks flushed with shock and fury.

Hawk's Henry leapt and roared, red-orange flames stabbing from the barrel. The .44 round smashed through the dead center of the man's forehead, and he flew straight back against the barn's outside wall as though he'd been lassoed from behind.

"You all just died," Hawk said calmly as he ejected the spent cartridge over his right shoulder and levered a fresh one into the Henry's chamber.

"Holy shit!" screamed the long-haired gent, straightening so quickly he lost his footing and stumbled back against the stall partition behind him.

He grabbed the Smith & Wesson positioned for the cross draw on his left hip, but his fingertips only grazed the handle before Hawk's Henry roared again, punching a chunk of hot lead through the man's chest, puffing dust from his heavy buffalo coat. The long-haired man turned a backward somersault over the stall partition and into the next stall beyond.

As Hawk's second ejected shell casing clanked onto the hard-packed runway floor behind him, he heard the Mexican curse but he couldn't see the man. Not until he'd stepped forward and looked into the stall, where the woman lay with her skirts up around the small of her back, exposing her long, pale legs and floury-white rump. She held her arms up over her head.

The Mexican was reaching over her for his holstered six-shooter but froze when Hawk said with menacing calmness, "Uh-uh." He cursed to himself, wanting to take the shot and finish him here and now. But he might hit the woman.

The Mexican froze on all fours over the woman, looking back at Hawk over his shoulder. His pants were down around his ankles. The man's black eyes shone with rage. His hand rested over his holstered .45.

Hawk kicked open the stall door, went inside, reached down, and jerked the man up by the back of his shirt collar. He rolled his eyes to the fat man who sat down against the outside wall as though he were napping except for the blood that trickled from the quarter-sized hole in his forehead, forming a large drip at the end of his freckled, pug nose.

"If you're gonna kill me, amigo," the

Mexican said through gritted teeth, "kill me an' get it over with, damn you."

"In due time, *amigo.*" Hawk stepped back and shoved him with his rifle barrel into the runway. "Outside. Move!"

The woman was shuffling around in the straw, shoving her skirts down her bare legs while looking up at Hawk in mute horror, tears and bits of straw flecking her pale, pink-mottled cheeks. Thick, disheveled tresses of chestnut hair hung down around her shoulders.

"No!" the Mexican snapped. "Right here. Now!"

"I'm going to give you a chance to run for it, you stupid bastard." Hawk grinned.

The Mexican stared at him, one eye corner narrowing. His glassy jet orbs grew even brighter with cunning, and then he reached down and jerked his pants up above his knees while shuffling out into the runway, glancing anxiously over his shoulder at Hawk. The Rogue Lawman followed him, challenge in his eyes.

When the man had pulled his pants up to his waist, he stepped outside, turning full around to regard Hawk daringly, holding his hands up to his shoulders in supplication. He glanced over at the horses, all four of which were hanging their heads over the top corral pole, flicking their ears curiously at the two men before them.

The Mex was breathing hard with desperation. "You gonna let me saddle?"

"Nope." Hawk shook his head. He snarled, *"Run!"*

He raised the rifle and narrowed an eye as he aimed down the barrel, lovingly caressing the cocked hammer with his gloved right thumb.

Fear flashed in the Mexican's eyes. He started to say something, but then he whipped around and dashed straight out in the sage and rabbit brush.

When he was fifteen yards from Hawk, he glanced over his shoulder, then turned forward again, put his head down, and began sprinting in a serpentine pattern. He glanced back, grinning with more and more confidence the farther he ran from Hawk and the Rogue Lawman's aimed Henry repeater.

Fifty yards, sixty . . .

The Mexican glanced over his shoulder, his mustache rising as he grinned.

Hawk squeezed the Henry's trigger.

Boom!

The Mexican continued running, but he no longer weaved. He ran off to the right through the sage and cedars, his arms sort of flapping and his legs growing wobbly, his stride shortening. He tripped over a rock, twisted around, and piled up in a heap on his back.

Hawk stared out across the sage, watching for movement in the Mexican's body. As he did, he ejected the spent cartridge and seated fresh. The Mexican was still, one ankle propped on a flat, white rock, arms stretched nearly straight out from his shoulders.

A sound rose behind Hawk, and he swung around quickly, automatically. A soft gasp escaped the woman's lips, and her eyes widened at the rifle before she jerked them to Hawk's face.

The Rogue Lawman slid the barrel sideways, then set it atop his shoulder. The woman continued to stare at him, a wary curiosity in her gaze. Hawk tried to speak but found himself mesmerized by the girl's beauty — a ripeness of figure, an evenness of facial features, and an inexplicable aura, an earthy naturalness radiating from her eyes.

She wasn't much over twenty, he guessed, her face oval-shaped and perfect, her cheeks light-complected though touched evenly and lightly by the western sun. Her almond-shaped eyes were a rich, lustrous brown, a shade darker than the chestnut hair that was piled loosely atop her head with rich tresses falling free about her shoulders. One lock curled out from behind her lower back to rest across her belly, the flatness of which was accented by the pleated wasp waist of her lilac day frock.

The bodice was torn, and she held the ragged flaps across her breasts, the inside curves of which shone beneath her arm. Her other hand was holding her torn riding skirt closed at her left hip.

Her full lips opened, and she frowned at Hawk as though she, too, were intending to speak. But then she looked past him into the field beyond, glanced at him once more, curiously, skeptically, maybe with revulsion, then swung around and, awkwardly holding her clothes together, walked toward the cabin. Her watched her go, her long thick hair jostling down her slender back that flared to rounded hips and long legs, the hem of her skirt sliding across her high-heeled, green canvas boots.

When she opened the cabin's rickety wooden door, stepped inside, and pulled the door closed behind her, Hawk lowered the rifle to his side and looked around.

The barn had a vacant look about it, with few furnishings inside, and weeds grown up around its stone foundation. A rain barrel was tipped onto its side. In spite of the woman's presence, the cabin had the same run-down, abandoned look, its roof missing more shingles than it boasted, and one window shutter dangled toward the ground by a single nail. The only horses in the side paddock were the three geldings that the three Two Troughs riders had been riding earlier, and a sorrel mayor.

Hawk looked at the cabin again. Thick smoke curled from the chimney, as though the fire had been stoked. If the woman lived here, she likely lived alone. But Hawk couldn't imagine one so young and beautiful living way out here, much less alone. Her lilac day suit was store-bought, and not the customary attire of a ranch woman unless she were heading for church or town.

Hawk let the questions evaporate. Whoever she was and what she was doing here alone was no business of his.

Leaning his rifle against the open barn door, he went in and grabbed hold of the fat man's ankles and dragged him a good ways into the brush behind the barn. He rolled the man into a shallow ravine, then tramped back to the barn for the long-haired gent and gave him the same treatment. When he'd rolled the Mexican, whom he'd shot through the base of the neck, into the ravine with his partners, he stepped back to rest his hands on his knees, catching his breath.

Having no intention of wasting time and energy on burying such men, he walked back to the barn where the grulla was waiting patiently, reins dangling. He slid his repeater down snug in his saddle boot and turned to regard the cabin once more. Smoke still lifted from the chimney, same as before, but now the plank door was open and propped back against the cabin wall with a rock. He thought he could smell the inviting aroma of boiling coffee on the cooling air.

No sign of the woman, though. Since he didn't know if he should take the propped-open door as an invitation, he decided he wouldn't and, grabbing the grulla's reins, swung up into the saddle. He rode out to where a lone cottonwood jutted up from a small hollow in the middle of the box canyon. There were rocks and cedars, plenty of protection, so he deemed the place a good place to camp.

The rosy sun was down behind the purple western ridges, and night was coming on fast, a sharp, knifelike chill threading the breeze.

Hawk built a fire while there was still some light left, however weak. Before he had time to put coffee on, and when he'd just begun unsaddling his horse, he heard footsteps moving toward him. He reached for the rifle but aborted the movement when he smelled the subtle but distinctive smell of female growing on the air around him.

5.
Schoolteacher

Hawk had the brow strap of the grulla's bridle in his left hand as he watched the woman walk up to the edge of the hollow. She'd put her hair up and secured it with a tortoiseshell comb trimmed in silver, though a loose mane hanging down her back blew about her shoulders in the breeze. She wore buckskin gloves and a man's wool coat that did not go with her dress.

She regarded Hawk with a puzzled frown then glanced at his fire, the flames torn by the wind. "You're welcome to the cabin," she said, clutching her arms with her gloved hands and giving a shudder. "Going to be cold tonight."

Hawk tossed the bridle over a deadfall log. "I'll be fine out here."

She shook her bangs out of her eyes. "The cabin . . . it's not mine. Just a line shack I use when I'm traveling this way. I've never . . ." She let her words trail off and acquired a consternated look, as though unsure how to proceed. "I've never run into trouble here before."

"Two Troughs," Hawk said, reaching under the grulla's belly to unbuckle the latigo straps.

"What's that?"

"You're on Two Troughs range." He tossed his head in the direction of the ravine into which he'd rolled the dead men. "Those were Two Troughs riders."

The woman hiked a shoulder and slid a lock of hair from her left eye with her hand. "I haven't much cared whose range this was. The cabin's always been available when I've passed through, so I've stayed here. The Two Troughs bunch is an outlaw outfit, anyway. Can't see that they'd have much need for a line cabin."

She paused, canted her head toward the yard. "It has a good stove, and I have some supper cooking." She glanced at the coffeepot he'd set on the ground, its top tilted up. "And I have a big kettle of coffee, too."

"No, thanks," Hawk said, lifting the saddle from the grulla and giving the woman his back. "Like I said, I'm fine out here."

She regarded him, puzzled, for a time. As Hawk reached into his saddlebags for his pair of braided rawhide hobbles, she hiked a shoulder, turned away, and started back toward the cabin. Hawk watched her go, holding the hobbles in one hand. He looked down at them, pensive.

It was going to get cold tonight. And he hadn't tasted a woman's cooking, aside from café fare, in a long time. . . .

He tossed the hobbles in his hand, then slid them back into a saddlebag pouch. He returned his coffeepot to the pouch, as well. He tossed the saddle atop the grulla and slipped the bridle over its ears.

When he'd kicked dirt and rocks on his fire, he grabbed his rifle, mounted up, and put the horse up and out of the wash. Looking toward the cabin, he saw the woman stop on the small front stoop, the handle of the open door in her hand. She looked toward him, and continued looking toward him until he was halfway to the barn. Then she went on into the cabin and closed the door.

Hawk led the horse into the barn where he unsaddled him, gave him some grain and a good rubdown with a scrap of burlap, then turned him out into the paddock off the barn's opposite side with the others. There was fresh water there and some hay in the crib.

The hay told Hawk that, despite their being an outlaw band, the Two Troughs crew was likely using the place. Possibly infrequently, but he'd have to keep an eye out tonight for more riders from the main headquarters, though he doubted any would be out at night, unless they were moving stolen stock, and he'd seen no sign that the main headquarters was anywhere near.

The three he'd killed were likely making their way back from Laramie after a few days off to chase whores and play cards, or somesuch.

His rifle resting on one shoulder, his saddlebags and war sack draped over the other, he closed the barn's front doors, then made his way over to the cabin, the windows facing him now showing a weak lantern glow. There was only a little green light left in the sky, and he guessed the temperature was around forty and dropping fast.

He tapped on the door with his rifle barrel and waited. Presently, footsteps sounded, there was the metallic knocking of the latch being tripped, and the door slid toward him. The woman stood there, arching her brows. "Change your mind?"

Hawk shrugged.

She looked him up and down, and there was that wary, disapproving look in her eyes again. Then she turned away from him, and he took that as his permission to enter, so he did. Drawing the door closed, he looked around, taking it all in quickly — the one-room, twenty-by-twenty-foot cabin with a fireplace in the south wall over which a small iron pot was suspended and dribbling rich, dark juices down its sides and sputtering in the glowing coals below.

There were three cots, a few shelves of airtight tins, a few more holding utensils over a dry sink against the back wall, a square kitchen table that had been scarred and burned so many times, the initials carved into it crusted with old food, that it looked like one massive, elaborate tattoo.

There was also a black coffeepot in the fire. The woman grabbed a leather pad off the hearth and used it to carry the pot over to the table. She grabbed a tin cup off a shelf, looked inside as though to make sure it was clean, jerked her eyebrows up as if deeming it as clean as anything else around here, and filled it from the pot. She slid the cup to the door side of the table, coffee spilling over its sides when it caught in a gap between the warped planks.

As she returned the pot to the fire, Hawk eased his war sack and saddlebags down on the floor beside the door, leaned his rifle against the wall, and removed his hat. The woman came back to the table where a half-filled cup of coffee sat beside a book that lay facedown and open, over a mess of crumpled papers like those torn from a child's school tablet.

"I have a rabbit stew cooking," she said, looking down at the table as she smoothed her torn but crudely mended dress beneath her and sat down. She wore a loosely woven sweater over the top of her dress, concealing the torn bodice, and she leaned forward on her elbows now, pressing her hands to her temples.

She kept her eyes down, and her voice was thin as she said, "Please, sit down. You're making me nervous, standing there."

Hawk hadn't realized he'd been staring at her. But of course he had been. Any man would stare at such an attractive creature, especially one so unexpected in such a remote, rough-hewn place. He tried to brush the remembered image of her long, creamy legs and round rump from his vision, and cleared his throat.

"Obliged."

He looked around, saw the woman's coat hanging from a hook under a broad-brimmed leather hat. There were three more vacant hooks, and he hung his hat on the one farthest from the coat then shrugged out of his capote. He hung that on another hook, then, running his hands back through his thick, wavy dark brown hair, kicked a chair out across from the woman and sagged into it.

He placed a hand on his cup, feeling awkward and half wishing he'd stayed in the cottonwood hollow. The woman continued to stare down at the table, kneading her temples with her long, pale fingers. She had only one ring, a diamond-shaped turquoise stone set in gold on the middle finger of her right hand. No wedding band.

"Name's Hawk," he said tentatively, glancing at her across the table and lifting the cup to his lips. He blew on the surface and sipped the hot, invigorating liquid.

"I guess my nerves are frayed."

"You all right?" Physically, she looked fine. Sometimes, though, the mental scars were slow in surfacing but even more severe.

She nodded.

"I heard a couple of pistol shots," Hawk said.

She didn't say anything. The only sound was the sputtering of the pot on the flames and the crackling of the flames themselves.

Finally, she sat back in her chair, and her large, brown eyes found him and held his gaze. The glowing lantern on the table shone in them brightly. “I saw them ride up, invited them into the cabin, told them I had plenty of food. None of them said anything.”

She shivered with remembered fear and looked at the door behind Hawk. “They just came in, looking hungry as wolves though it wasn’t food they were after. They came around the table, two on one side, the big man on the other. Somehow, I got away from them, ran through the door. One of them fired. To frighten me, I think.”

She crossed her arms on her chest, lowered her chin, and wrapped her hands around her shoulders. “Then they caught me.”

She closed her eyes. Quietly but evenly, without emotion, she added, “I’ve never been so frightened. I’ve lived on the frontier a long time, and that’s never happened before.”

He saw that the side of her right hand, starting beneath her little finger, was scraped and bloody. Hawk sipped his coffee, then slid his chair out, rose, and slowly reached over and wrapped his hand around her wrist.

She looked up at him, frowning, but did not resist when he drew her hand down on the table. Sitting back down in his chair, he slid her sweater and the sleeve of her dress up her forearm, slowly revealed the scraped and bloody skin to which a few small, white thorns and bits of sand clung.

"I didn't even notice," she said, looking down at her hand. "It's only now beginning to hurt."

"Hang on." Hawk rose and went over to his war sack. He returned to the table with a whiskey bottle and a clean red bandanna. He sat down in his chair and placed the bottle on the table. Removing the cork from the bottle, he poured some whiskey on the bandanna, then took her hand in his left hand and looked up to see her eyes studying him.

"This'll burn," he warned.

She drew the corners of her long mouth down, and nodded as though he'd told her something she was well aware of.

He began swabbing her hand. She jerked her arm suddenly, when the cloth first touched the scraped and badly chafed skin, but she kept her hand on the table, putting a little pressure on his fingers.

"What's your name?" he asked her.

"Regan Mitchell."

Hawk nodded as he worked his way up the underside of her forearm, gently dabbing at the cuts and removing the grit and broken cactus thorns.

He turned the bandanna over and splashed more whiskey on the other side. "What're you doing out here by your lonesome, Regan Mitchell?"

"Teaching school." She winced as Hawk dribbled a few drops of whiskey into the longest of the gashes, running about six inches toward her wrist from her elbow.

Hawk raised an eyebrow at her. "Out here?"

"Over in Fairfield. A little mining camp. I teach reading there one day every two weeks. I ride out across the mountains from Trinity, ride back the next day. I usually stay the night here." She turned her mouth corners down once more. "I doubt I'll do it again, though. Don't think I'd sleep."

She looked across the table at him while he refolded the cloth and dampened it again from the bottle. "I do appreciate your help, Mr. Hawk. But . . . what you did . . ." She let her voice trail off in bewilderment, regarding him again like a rabid dog that had just wandered into her camp. "I can't condone cold-blooded murder."

"It was cold-blooded?"

"Yes, I would say it was cold-blooded!"

"I like to think in terms of practicality."

She winced again as he laid the cloth

down on her arm but kept her exasperated gaze on the Rogue Lawman's passive, chiseled features. "You might have asked them to stop. I would have felt fine about their mounting up and riding away. That seems practical to me."

Hawk glanced up at her, pointedly narrowing one eye. "Would you really? Would you have felt safe knowing three rapists were roaming these hills?"

"I would have taken extra precautions to avoid them next time."

"And what about the next beautiful woman they ran into? What if she didn't know what they're capable of?"

"Mr. Hawk," Regan Mitchell said, her voice pitched low in shock at his attitude, "what you did was against the law. It's called murder."

"Are you going to turn me into the authorities? If, that is, there were any authorities to turn me into out here."

She lowered her gaze to the arm he was continuing to clean with the cloth. "No. Of course not. But the point is . . ."

"Then you're a party to murder." Hawk raised his eyebrows at her and, removing the cloth from her arm, which was thoroughly cleaned, leaned back in his chair.

She returned his look, suddenly indignant.

"That's taking it rather far, isn't it?"

"When it comes to killing savages," Hawk said in his low, resonate growl, "I believe in taking things to the extreme. Those men would have taken turns raping you, Miss Mitchell. And when they were finished, they probably would have cut your throat and tossed your naked, bloody body into the same ravine in which they're lying now, awaiting the carrion eaters."

She turned her head away sharply, closing her eyes, her beautiful face bleaching. Hawk stood and rummaged around in his war sack once more, returning to the table with a small ball of clean white gauze wrapped around a stick. He set the linen onto the table, then fished a barlow folding knife out of the pocket of his black denim trousers, sat down in his chair once more, and cut off a three-foot length of the gauze.

She'd crossed her arms on her chest, draping her long fingers over her shoulders as she stared blindly at the cabin wall to Hawk's left, where there was nothing but a five-year-old feed store calendar. He held his hand out to her.

"Your arm —" Hawk looked at her. "It is Miss Mitchell, isn't it?"

"I don't know many married schoolteachers — do you?" Her voice was low but clipped, cold. She lay her arm on the table again, turned so that the abrasions faced upward. "Who are you, Mr. Hawk? What are you doing out here? Obviously, you're not a cowpuncher."

Holding her hand with his free one, Hawk wrapped the gauze around her arm, starting at her elbow, overlapping it neatly.

He grinned. "I'm your new lawman, Miss Mitchell."

She stared at him, lines of incredulity cutting into her forehead. "You must be joking."

Continuing to wrap her arm, he said, "Sheriff Gideon Hawk. At your service."

6.
"That's Insanity, Mr. Hawk"

Hawk set her arm on the table, then pressed the end of the gauze firmly against the underside of her wrist, tamping it secure.

"Oh, no," Regan Mitchell said, holding her injured arm in one hand and sinking back in her chair, giving Hawk that horrified stare once more. "This is terrible."

"I appreciate the vote of confidence." He got up and returned the gauze to his war sack.

"The town council's fliers. You're answering one of those, aren't you?"

"I reckon you could say that."

"Have they hired you?"

"Not yet. My interview or whatever you want to call it is tomorrow."

She stared at him but at the same time her eyes darted this way and that in their sockets, and her face turned even paler than before.

Hawk came back to the table, sat down,

and splashed some whiskey into his half-empty coffee cup. He held the bottle up. "Join me?"

"No, thank you," she said with a distracted air. She glanced at the pot suspended above the fire. "The stew should be ready."

She walked over to the fire and grabbed the rawhide pad.

"Here," Hawk said, rising. "Let me do that."

"I'm fully capable —"

"I'm sure you are."

Hawk took the pad out of her hands and looked down at her, towering over her. She stared up at him with those liquid brown eyes, and he tried to ignore the tug in his loins.

Christ, what a beautiful woman. And she was *all* woman. He had another mental image of her long legs and creamy round rump beneath the skirts shoved up around her waist, but a quick, fiery jab of shame shouldered the image aside and put a damper on his carnal hunger. God, he was little better than the men who'd attacked her. . . .

"But, please," he said. "The pot's heavy, and" — he glanced at the arm that she'd now covered with the sleeves of her dress and sweater — "you're not at full strength."

She let her eyes drop from his face and

they seemed to stray of their own accord across his broad shoulders and thick, wind- and sunburned neck around which a green bandanna — almost the same green as his eyes — was knotted.

Quickly, she turned her head away from him and said in a sharp, sarcastic tone, "Have it your way, Mr. Hawk."

She went back to the kitchen, plundered a couple of shelves for two tin plates and some silverware, and set them on the table. When Hawk had set the steaming pot down on the table's end, she refilled their coffee cups.

Hawk lifted the lid from the pot and gazed down at the chunks of meat and potatoes swimming around in a rich, dark gravy glazed with small pools of copper-colored fat. The smells were heavenly, and it reminded Hawk of the supper aromas wafting around his once intact and happy home, Linda shuffling stove lids around while his boy, Jubal, set the table and jabbered about fishing or school or the little horses he carved from wood.

"You bring the rabbit from Trinity?"

"I shot them just today, on my way back from Fairfield."

She reported this with a faintly haughty air, sitting down in her chair while smoothing her skirts against her legs. She glanced at the old Spencer rifle leaning against the wall behind her. It was an old, rusty carbine with badly weathered fore- and rear stocks; Hawk had assumed it had gone with the cabin.

"Two rabbits. You must be a good shot."

"My father taught me well." She used a large spoon to dish the stew onto her plate.

"A hunter?"

"No." She shook her head, kept her lips primly pursed, making sure that while they were having a civil conversation, she did not care for him nor approve of his new job in her hometown. "He was a wild-horse trapper. A mustanger. I grew up in eastern Colorado, where we hunted all our food. I was the only child, and after my mother died it was up to me to provide for the table."

Regan slid the steaming pot toward Hawk and finally looked at him from beneath her pretty, thin brows. "And town was a two-day ride from the ranch."

"You did right well for yourself, then. And your father." Hawk had dished himself a plateful of the aromatic stew spiced with salt, pepper, and wild onions. "And tonight, for me."

She glanced at him quickly, with faint

suspicion in her eyes.

"I meant only the stew, Miss Mitchell."

She flushed and looked down at her plate as she speared a chunk of the rabbit meat with her fork.

"Tell me, Mr. Hawk," she said after they'd eaten for a while in silence, swallowing and looking across at him, "are you what one would call a 'town tamer'?"

Hawk glanced from beneath his brows at her. "I reckon if Trinity needs taming, I'll tame it. Why do you ask, Miss Mitchell?"

"My father had the gyspy in him, so we've bounced around the frontier a bit. I've run into town tamers before. I don't mind telling you that I care nothing for the breed at all."

Hawk continued to eat, letting her continue without prompting.

She swallowed a bite of food, sipped her coffee, and wiped her hand on the cloth she was using for a napkin, her eyes crossing slightly, beguilingly, as she gazed across the table at him. "The towns I've seen that needed taming were much worse off after the so-called 'tamers' had moved in and gotten a so-called handle on things. The way they handled the lawlessness was merely to add to it. Unsanctioned killings by both the gun and the hang rope." She shook her head in disgust. "It was vigilantism run amok."

"To my way of thinking," Hawk said as he continued eating, "vigilantism run amok means that innocent people were killed. The right kind of vigilantism should merely punish the guilty whom the traditional law for whatever reason was unable to throw a loop around. Usually, it's because of bureaucratic loopholes or the squeamishness of the traditional lawman that this happens. Or the sheer number of the badmen in relation to the good."

He looked up at her. She was staring back at him, holding her fork midway between her plate and her mouth, which hung partway open in awe of what she'd heard.

"Rest assured, Miss Mitchell." Hawk sipped from his coffee and wiped his mustache with the back of his shirtsleeve. "When the number of badmen has been reduced in Trinity to the point a traditional lawman or lawmen can keep the lid on, I will be very happy to turn in my sheriff's badge, and ride on." He sipped from the coffee cup that he held in front of him with both his large, weathered hands. "I certainly do not intend to 'run amok.' "

She set her fork down and kneaded her temple. "What you are so casually trying to rationalize, Mr. Hawk, is lawlessness upon lawlessness. The two do not add up to law-*fulness.* Besides, it's the most grievous of transgressions against the Constitution."

"What do you hold more dear — the rights scribbled on a scrap of paper, or the rights of individual Americans who are trying very hard to live decent, respectable lives but who've fallen prey to untamable brigands who kill our lawmen and laugh at the laws those men were trying to uphold?" Hawk shook his head. "It's a far different country out here, Miss Mitchell, than the one in which the Constitution was penned. You were raised out here, so you know that as well as I do."

"That's insanity, Mr. Hawk. I find myself sitting here, listening to a madman."

As though he hadn't heard that last — he had, but only vaguely, not having allowed himself to hear clearly and to think about it, because he'd suffered such doubts about himself before — Hawk set his cup down and picked up his fork. "I do, however, admire your ideals." He raised his eyes to hers and smiled. "Romantic as they are."

She shook her head again as she sank back in her chair, leaving a good bit of food on her plate, her coffee cup steaming weakly before her. Absently, she rubbed the arm that Hawk had wrapped for her. "Blue

Tierney and that son of his have brought more trouble than Trinity even realizes. . . ."

"What happened there?" Hawk asked, setting his fork down on his empty plate, feeling a faint prickling at the small of his back.

"You don't know?"

"Only that the sheriff was killed when he was trying to hang some prisoners, and that the mayor of the town and the town council need someone to regain control before another permanent lawman can be seated."

When she only looked at him, puzzled, he splashed some more whiskey into his coffee cup and held the cup up in front of his chin. Regan looked down at her plate, considering it for a time, then, apparently deciding that she could not let good food go to waste, picked up her spoon and began eating. She ate quickly, the way a man would eat, though she was far from mannish, as though to get it out of the way.

"Blue Tierney, head of the Two Troughs gang, and his men rode into town that morning," she said, dabbing at her mouth with her napkin between bites. "I wasn't there but I heard later, saw the blood around the gallows."

She swallowed a mouthful of food as though with difficulty. "Tierney's men shot the sheriff, Deputy Freeman, and the hangman. They left Pastor Hawthorne alive . . . because he'd dropped to his knees and lost control of himself. Sobbed and begged for his life, poor man. I hear he's been only half a man ever since, resigned his position in the Lutheran church, and now frequents one of the saloons."

She swabbed the gravy from her plate with a last chunk of potato and popped it into her mouth, casting Hawk a look, one brow arched, that said she was finished.

Hawk sipped his coffee. His hands shook faintly. Probably, she hadn't noticed. He swallowed the lukewarm liquid heavily spiced with whiskey and ran his hand across his mustache. "What else?"

Regan beetled her brows at him. "You mean . . . the sheriff's wife? Janelle?"

No, Hawk thought. Ah, shit. No. It hadn't been merely a grisly false rumor that had made its way to Cheyenne on the lips of bored drummers and wandering punchers.

Hawk took another sip of coffee, felt his gut tighten, and swallowed. He dipped his chin weakly.

"I guess that's the most tragic part of all this," Regan said softly, sadly, using the pad to lift the coffeepot.

She offered the pot to Hawk, who shook his head, impatient to hear the dreaded story, then refilled her own cup and set the pot back down between them. Absently, she raised the wick of the lantern in the middle of the table, against the deepening night shadows that seemed to grow like malevolent living creatures from the walls trimmed with stretched animal hides.

"Killed herself."

"How?"

She looked at him, her perplexity deepening, then canted her head to one side, brown eyes boring into him. "You heard?"

"Tell me how the sheriff's wife killed herself."

Regan flattened her hands on the table, on each side of her empty plate, and stared down at the left one as if seeing something hideous there in her knuckles. Her voice thickened; her eyelashes fluttered and grew wet.

"The morning after her husband's funeral, she suffocated their little boy with a pillow."

She paused, keeping her eyes on her left hand. Her upper lip quivered for a moment, and a single tear, golden in the lamplight, slid down from her eye and across her smooth right cheek. "Then she walked up to the business district in her nightdress and hanged herself from the gallows that had been built for her husband's prisoners."

There was a sudden clank. It took a quarter second for Hawk to realize that he'd let his cup slip from his hands. It bounced off the edge of his plate, spilling coffee and whiskey, and rolled off the edge of the table where it hit the floor with another, duller clang.

"Shit," he wheezed, staring dumbly down at the cup where it rolled to rest about four feet from the table.

He heard a gasp. He looked across the table at Regan, who'd leaned back in her chair and covered her mouth with one of her hands. She stared across the table at him, her eyes bright and sharp as javelins.

"Oh, no," she breathed, her soft, even voice belying the horror in her gaze. "You're that Rogue Lawman from Nebraska!"

7.
That Rogue Lawman from Nebraska

Hawk drew a deep breath of the cool night air as he pulled the cabin door closed behind him and blew it out at the stars guttering like sparks from a blacksmith's forge in the velvet black bowl over the canyon.

He hadn't started out to be that Rogue Lawman from Nebraska. Just a workaday lawman, albeit a federal one, with a beautiful young wife, Linda, and a boy to raise. "Three-Fingers" Ned Meade had taken all that away from him, starting with the boy whom the lunatic outlaw had hanged one stormy Nebraska night from a tree topping a hill just outside of Hawk's hometown, near the creek where Hawk and his young son, Jubal, had fished summer nights and weekends.

Hawk stepped off the stoop and into the yard. His breath frosted in front of his face. He walked a little ways out, absently kicking stones and looking around, making sure all was quiet, that no other riders from the Two Troughs had shown up. When he'd circled the cabin, he went over to the barn and checked on the horses, two of which were down on their sides, asleep, while two others stood head to tail, still as statues. Hawk's grulla stood off in a rear corner, facing the low, ragged-topped ridge to the north where several coyotes were having a yipping contest.

There were also the occasional, distant, eerie wails of a stalking bobcat. The horse flicked its tail every time it heard the screech. Horses hated bobcats, their fiercest enemies.

Hawk watched the horse for a time, standing there by the corral with one hand absently draped over the butt of the horn-gripped Colt .44 holstered high on his right hip. He had a silver-chased Russian .44 positioned for the cross draw on the opposite hip. Two hand irons often came in handy in his line of work.

Which was?

He chuffed caustically at the question. Killing was his line of work. Anyone and everyone who found themselves in the lamentable position of being the bereaved father turned Rogue Lawman's prey. It had been that way since the prosecuting attorney had taken a bribe and turned Jubal's killer free. Hawk had hunted and killed the attorney. Then he'd stalked and killed Meade's outlaw gang, saving "Three-Fingers" Ned for last. And then he'd just kept right on hunting because that's what he was good at. Sometimes, for his own private satisfaction, he wore his old deputy U.S. marshal's badge upside down on his chest.

To him, that's what the laws of justice on the frontier had become. Topsy-turvy. Upside down. When badmen ruled, all bets were off. Sometimes, good lawmen just had to turn rogue to do any good. And while Hawk had gotten a lot accomplished in the past few years, there was still much work to be done.

And that flier he'd seen in Cheyenne had pointed him to his next job. A good lawman had died. His wife had killed herself — *hanged* herself — and their boy was dead. She might have pressed the pillow to the boy's face, but it was her husband's killers who'd really killed the child. Killed her, too.

Killed them all.

Now, it was Blue and Brazos Tierney's turn to go down hard. . . .

Hawk ground his jaws together angrily though he felt a comforting sense of firm resolve as he checked out the barn, inspecting the place by match light, then went back into the yard. He righted the overturned rain barrel, sat on it, hiked a boot on a knee, and dug into his coat pocket for his makings sack.

He could smell the piñon pine wafting from the cabin's brick chimney. The woman had stoked the fire to heat water for a sponge bath. That's when Hawk had decided to make himself scarce, give her time to bathe and get into bed.

He'd offered to sleep in the barn, but she'd said — and they were the first words she'd spoken after realizing who he was from the magazine and newspaper articles she'd read — "Don't be silly. There's a warm fire in here, nothing but the late winter chill out in the barn."

He hadn't protested. In spite of her disapproval of him, he liked being around her, smelling her, seeing the light shine in her hair. He was a man, after all. He still loved Linda, but she was dead. Sometimes his involuntary cravings for a woman were all he had to remind himself that he was still alive.

He smoked the cigarette and listened to the coyotes. The stars sparkled more and more brightly as he watched them. The cold pressed against him.

When he'd finished the smoke and figured he'd given the woman enough time to crawl into her nightclothes, he field stripped the cigarette stub, raised his collar against the chill, evacuated his bladder, and headed back to the cabin. He opened the door slowly, then, seeing the long hump on the cot against the cabin's far wall, stepped in and closed the door quietly behind him, easing the locking bar into its steel brackets.

The lamp on the table was turned low, so most of the light came from the leaping flames in the hearth against the wall to Hawk's left. Like tiny, orange fingers, the evanescence danced in Regan's hair that spilled across the saddlebag pouch that she used for a pillow. She lay facing the wall, two wool quilts drawn up to her neck.

She spoke suddenly in a beguiling, strangely intimate tone: "There's wash water on the table. I heated it fresh, Mr. Hawk."

A battered fry pan sat atop the table, curls of steam rising from the dark water inside.

"Much obliged."

Hawk doffed his hat and removed his coat, placing both on the wall pegs. Removing his neckerchief then rolling up his shirtsleeves, he moved to the table and stopped suddenly, frowning deeply.

Regan turned her head to speak over her left shoulder. "I found the horse on the floor. It must have fallen from your saddlebags."

Hawk reached out and plucked the wooden carving off the table. It was the black stallion that Jubal had carved a few days before the boy had been murdered by "Three-Fingers" Ned. From an oval-shaped base against which its rear feet were set, as though atop a rocky ridge, the horse flung it front legs high in the air, hooves clawing at the sky. The lantern light rippled off the jet-black mane and expanding nostrils. The black eyes shone with wild vigor.

"A very accomplished piece," said the woman, still glancing at him over her shoulder. Her tone was faintly inquisitive.

Hawk caressed the horse with his thumb. "My boy."

Regan said nothing but only lay staring at him over her shoulder. At length, she turned her head back toward the wall, and the cot creaked beneath her shifting weight.

Hawk ran his thumb across the carving once more. "Here you go, Pa," the boy had said when he'd finished the piece after working on for it for nearly seven nights in a row, after his homework had been completed. "What do you think?"

Hawk had been amazed, of course. As Regan had said, it was an accomplished piece of art. It was even more amazing, given Jubal's trouble with school and the agonized hours that he and Linda had spent on his homework. Try as he might, the boy had only managed to make Cs and Ds. But give him a piece of wood, and he could turn it into a living, breathing horse, bear, or wildcat in a matter of days, sometimes only a few hours. A poet in wood, Linda had remarked to Hawk as they both sat watching the boy work at the kitchen table of their little, frame house in Valoria.

A tear had dribbled down along the sides of her long, fine nose. Hawk had reached over and, smiling tenderly, wiped the tear away with his thumb. Now Hawk felt a tear slither out of his right eye and make a cool wetness on his cheek.

He closed his hand over the horse, giving it a gentle squeeze, then reached down for his saddlebags, set them on the chair he'd sat in earlier, and returned the horse to a pouch.

"I'm sorry about your wife and child, Mr. Hawk."

Her soft, consoling voice, barely audible above the popping, crackling fire, caused another couple of tears to roll down Hawk's cheeks. He nodded quickly, silently, as he dragged a towel and a sliver of soap out from inside his saddlebags, then set to work briskly washing his face and the back of his neck and scrubbing the trail dirt from his hands.

When he was finished, he stripped down to his long-handles, draping his clothes over the back of a kitchen chair, then climbed into the cot abutting the front wall, across the sleeping area from Regan Mitchell. He glanced at her as he arranged his blanket roll at the head of his cot for a pillow.

He glanced across the room.

Her long body lay still beneath her blankets, the firelight continuing to glisten in her rich, curling hair that hung down over the side of the cot to nearly the floor. He couldn't tell if she was awake. He couldn't see her eyes. Her shoulders rose and fell slowly.

"I suppose we might as well ride on to Trinity together," she said suddenly, startling him. "Since we're both heading the same direction, I mean."

Hawk lay his head back against the blanket roll and crossed his arms on his chest. "Don't see why not."

He felt his mouth corners rise. He liked

the woman. No man could be blamed for wanting to spend time with her.

"All right, then. Good night, Mr. Hawk."

"You might as well call me Gideon."

"Good night, Mr. Hawk," she said with mild reproof.

Hawk sighed. "Good night, Miss Mitchell."

He closed his eyes, and for a time he fought the remembered nightmare images from his past. But he'd become a good warrior, and after twenty minutes or so, the snapping of the flames, the quiet moans and sighs of the night breeze, and the sporadic yips of coyotes lulled him into a deep, dark sleep.

Hawk rose early the next morning, while Regan still slept, and went out to feed and water the horses. When he returned to the cabin, she was up, had the fire stoked, and was warming what remained of last night's stew for breakfast.

They ate and then cleaned up and put their gear together in silence. It was almost, Hawk thought, as though they'd slept together the night before. A shy awkwardness lingered between them.

He found, however, that he couldn't keep his eyes off of her. At least, he couldn't help stealing glances at her whenever he thought she wouldn't notice. The morning light shone brilliantly in her hair, revealing red and copper highlights. It bathed the smooth skin of her cheeks and neck so that it glowed like ivory.

Her brown eyes were bold and frank, he noticed in this new light. Sultry and beguiling beneath stern, brown brows. While her body and attire bespoke a conservative young frontier woman, her expressions were rife with a tomboy's spirit. He liked that. It was like the spirit of a wild mare. While he'd been attracted to her from the first moment he'd set eyes on her, now he was doubly so.

And he didn't like it. No, he didn't like it at all.

She had her mind made up about him, and she wasn't the kind of woman whose convictions were easily swayed. That was all right with Hawk. He had no time for her. For any woman, for that matter.

Oh, he enjoyed a bedroom frolic from time to time, as did any man, even a man devoted to the memory of his dead wife. But Regan Mitchell was not the kind of woman a man took to bed for a single night's pleasure. Even if he did manage to bed her, he thought with another devilish snort, it would come at a hefty price.

"What was that, Mr. Hawk?"

Hawk looked at her as he finished buttoning his three-point capote over the sheepskin vest he wore with the leather side out. His ear tips warmed. Had he snorted aloud that time?

"Huh?"

"I thought you said something," she said from her cot, where she was gathering the last of her gear into her saddlebags. She had her wool coat on, the collar raised to her neck, and she'd donned her man's tobacco-brown, broad-brimmed felt hat. Her hair tumbled down over her back almost to her rump.

"Nope." Hawk set his rifle on his shoulder, draped his saddlebags and war sack over his other shoulder, kicked the door wide, and headed out. "Gettin' late, Miss Mitchell. Let's get a move on."

He tramped over to the corral, and Regan Mitchell was close behind him, ready to go. She saddled her horse with the expertise Hawk would have expected of a girl who'd been raised on a wild horse ranch. She was gentle, but her movements were fluidly assured and she did not pull her punch when her white-stockinged roan drew a lungful of air as Regan was about to tighten the latigo straps.

Hawk watched the beautiful, self-assured, though somewhat haughty, woman out the corner of his eye. He didn't realize, however, that she was tossing inquisitive, faintly incredulous glances his way, as well.

When they both had their horses rigged, Hawk opened the gate, and they led the mounts outside. He left the gate open so that the dead riders' mounts could leave or stay as they pleased — other Two Troughs riders would likely pick them up — and then he and Regan swung up into their saddles, and Hawk let the young woman lead the way out of the canyon and westward toward Trinity.

They rode in silence, crossing several jogs of hills and traversing a shallow canyon. The ground was dusted here and there with a recent snow, and crusty snowdrifts clung to the north sides of hillocks and ridges and stream banks. The sun was so bright that it was hard to look at the sky, which was as blue as a summer lake, but the air was cool. Probably not very far above freezing, Hawk figured, judging by the ice-fringed springs they passed.

"Mr. Hawk," Regan called unexpectedly as they started into broken country, sandstone ridges towering around them.

"Yes, Miss Mitchell?"

She reined the roan to a halt suddenly atop a barren bench angling from the base of a rocky ridge, curveted the mount on the trail, and regarded Hawk seriously.

Hawk checked the grulla down about twenty yards behind her, at the base of the bench, and waited.

She jerked the roan's head up with one hand on her reins. "Nothing's going to bring them back, you know?"

Hawk returned her gaze, his brows lifting a straight ridge over his eyes. "I know that, Miss Mitchell."

She reined the horse around and galloped off down the other side of the bench.

It wasn't much later, when they were traversing a narrow canyon, that Hawk spied a flickering shadow along the ridge to his right. Regan had stopped her horse to inspect the bottom of the canyon, as though not quite remembering how she'd crossed it before. Hawk turned his attention to the ridge, his right hand automatically falling across the brass-plated butt of his Henry repeater, which jutted up from its boot under his right thigh.

"This is always a little confusing," Regan was saying to his left and at a slightly lower elevation. "There are two old horse trails through here, and I can't remember . . ."

She let her voice trail off. Hawk wasn't listening, anyway. He was running his gaze along the ridgeline, where the shadow flicked again suddenly and he caught a glimpse of two silhouetted legs and a hat before the man dropped into a nest of some rocks about a hundred feet above him and Regan.

A second later, the sun glinted off the end of a rifle barrel as the maw angled downward and slanted back in Hawk's direction.

"It's the right one there," Regan said suddenly, pointing.

Smoke puffed from the rifle's maw. At the same time that the thundering report reached Hawk's ears, the slug tore into a stony thumb jutting out from the ridge wall just above his head, peppering him and the grulla with rock dust.

Regan gasped.

There was the distance-muffled rasp of a shell being levered quickly into a rifle breech. Hawk knew he didn't have time for the Henry, so he left the rifle in its boot, kicked his boots out of his stirrups, and, twisting around to his left, heaved himself out of his saddle and directly into Regan.

The woman groaned as Hawk's much larger, heavier body bulled her out of her saddle. She grunted when they hit the ground together, Hawk managing to maneuver his body beneath hers to cushion her fall. His own impact with the ground, however, set up a clanging in his ears, and he saw four horses instead of two lunge up trail and away from him just as he heard another echoing rifle blast.

Strands of Regan's hair screened his face, slipped between his lips. She pushed up on an elbow, looking around, dazed, stretching her lips back from her teeth in pain.

"Get down!" he rasped, feeling the bullet singe the side of his boot before tearing into the ground beside it.

8.
Rance Harvin

Hawk shoved the woman down the steep grade toward the rocky canyon floor as the rifle barked three more times in quick succession.

The Rogue Lawman winced, expecting the bullets to hammer the ground around him or *into* him, but a quick glance up the rocky ridge told him the bushwhacker was trying to shoot his and Regan's horses. Vaguely relieved that he heard no screams as both mounts galloped around a bend in the canyon wall and out of sight — and likely beyond the reach of the shooter's rifle — Hawk turned to see Regan glancing back at him from behind a low upthrust of rock down the incline about twenty yards away.

"Come!" she called, stretching an open hand toward him. "What're you doing? *Hurry!*"

As he heard another shell being racked into the shooter's rifle breech, Hawk rolled off his right elbow and, grinding his boot heels into the gravel, heaved himself down the grade. He scampered on all fours, then rolled three times.

The ground was churned up behind him by another bullet, and the rifle report flatted out around the canyon, but now Hawk was below the brow of the incline. Wincing at the aches in his back and rib cage, he twisted around behind the scarp while at the same time grabbing Regan and giving the woman an unceremonious pull across his own body to his right side.

"I said keep your damn head down!"

"Goddamn you!" she barked.

Another bullet smacked the side of the scarp a few inches above Hawk's face, and as the rifle's report thundered over the canyon, Hawk snapped his own head back behind cover, brushing painful rocks shards from his cheeks.

"You're one to talk," the woman snapped at him, crouched beside him on her hands and knees, hair dusty and disheveled, her cheeks coated with grit. "Who the hell is up there, anyway? More Two Troughs men?"

Hawk slipped both pistols from their holsters and thumbed back the hammers. "How the hell should I know?"

"My god — they probably found the bodies you left in the ravine."

"Lady," Hawk said, grinding his teeth as he returned her acrimonious gaze, "I'm beginning to wish I'd let them roll *you* into that ravine."

She shook her head and edged a peek around Hawk and the scarp, trying to get a look up the ridge. "My rifle's with my horse. I suppose you left yours in your scabbard, as well."

"Sorry — I reckon in the heat of the moment I decided that getting you out of the line of fire was more important than having my rifle." Hawk laughed once without humor and pressed his shoulders back against the scarp, turning his head to survey the ridge.

Two more bullets thundered into the other side of the upthrusting rock. Shards flew in all directions, some arcing up and over the formation and raining down on Hawk and Regan's hats. The explosions of the rifle followed on the heels of the bullets.

"Henry repeater, I'll bet," Hawk mused aloud, running his tongue across his chapped lower lip. "Just like the one I left on the grulla. What I wouldn't do to get my hands on a long gun now."

"He's certainly out for blood."

"Whatever gave you that idea?"

"What're we going to do?" Regan looked down the grade and into the rocky-floored canyon beyond. "I suppose we could make a run for it."

"He'd ride us down. Besides, I don't run *from* dry-gulchers. I run *to* them."

"Jesus!" she swore, surprising him again with her blue tongue. He didn't think she'd uttered foul language even when she'd been in the goatish clutches of the three Two Troughs men. "I certainly wouldn't want to offend your sense of male honor and bravery. You know — it never ceases to amaze me how simply *stupid* men are. And we women must *rely* on you!" She gave a loud groan of hopeless frustration, balling both of her small hands into fists.

Hawk poked his head out from behind the scarp. When he drew no fire, he jerked his Colt up and triggered two shots toward the hollow in the rocks about ten feet down from the ridge, where he'd seen the shooter settle. He balled a cheek in dismay when he saw his slugs spike up dust from rocks a good fifteen yards short of his target.

He drew back as the rifleman triggered two more quick shots, and then one more.

"You can't be serious," Regan exclaimed. "You don't actually think you're going to be able to hit him way up there with a short gun, do you?"

"I just thought I'd give it a shot," Hawk said, suddenly weary of the woman's presence. Beautiful, she might be. But he was realizing what an authentic pain in the ass she was. He ground his teeth as he said, "I don't think I could hit him with a rock from this distance, either."

Silence descended over the canyon and the jutting outcroppings that shone like old pennies in the crystalline, late morning sunlight. Hawk pressed the back of his head against the scarp, sizing up the situation while ignoring the burn in his right calf, where the shooter's bullet had grazed him, and the blood he could feel dribbling down inside his boot.

"If we're not going to make a run for it," Regan said tensely, "what do you propose doing, Mr. Hawk?"

He slipped his Russian .44 from the cross-draw holster on his right hip, flipped it, and extended it to her butt first. "Take that in case he comes down here, but don't waste any shots on him."

"Did you learn your lesson?"

"Stow it," Hawk growled, flipping open the loading gate of his Colt. He removed the two spent shell casings and replaced them with fresh from his cartridge belt.

Spinning the cylinder, he pushed away from the scarp. "Sit tight."

"What're you going to do?"

"I'm going to work my way around him."

Moving straight back away from the scarp, keeping the formation between him and the bushwhacker, Hawk tramped at a crouch down the incline, loosing gravel in his wake and holding one arm out to keep from losing his balance on the slippery terrain.

"Please don't get yourself killed, Mr. Hawk," she admonished behind him. "I honestly don't want to be stranded out here, afoot, with that gun-handy bushwhacker."

"Keep your frillies on," Hawk said as he reached a narrow ridge that hugged the lip of the canyon.

"I'll thank you not to talk about my *frillies,* Mr. Hawk," she said, the demand punctuated by another short burst of rifle fire from the ridge.

Hawk negotiated the trail along the lip of the canyon for a good fifty yards, crouching, keeping his head below the shooter's line of sight. He was relieved to find a notch that bore into the ridge and quickly took it, stumbling over rocks and shrubs that choked the cut, as the growing pain in his right calf made it difficult to walk.

The shooter's continued, sporadic rifle fire

provided Hawk with bearings as he moved around to the ridge's backside. When he'd gained a nest of rocks at the base of the ridge, he waited until he heard another short burst of fire, then, glad that the man hadn't decided to leave his position for a better angle on the scarp behind which Regan was hunkered, Hawk started climbing the ridge.

Amidst the rifleman's sporadic, booming shots, Hawk heard a hollow, more distant crack, like that of a triggered pistol. He'd never heard his Russian .44 fired from a distance, and from behind a ridge, but something told him Regan was triggering the piece.

Hawk paused, his heart thudding. Had the shooter moved on down the ridge, threatening her? The thought had no sooner swept across Hawk's brain than he heard the rifle blast twice more from just above him. Hawk continued moving slowly as he heard another pistol shot, and then another.

Then the reason for Regan's shooting dawned on him.

The rifleman was trying to leave his nest, and she was trying to keep him pinned down in spite of the pistol's short range. . . .

She'd fired three shots. She had only three more. Hawk had to hurry to be within accurate range with his own shooting irons before the bushwhacker left his position. He ran, ignoring the burn in his calf, nearly straight up the ridge. The grade was steep. He scissored his arms, pumped his knees, breathing hard, sucking large draughts of air through his mouth.

Regan fired a fourth shot.

Hawk took several more strides. The ridgeline was ten more strides away. . . .

Regan's Russian popped again. The bullet ricocheted off rock on the other side of the ridge, whining. She must have been shooting high enough, coming close enough to her target, that the rifleman wasn't willing to take a chance that she wouldn't hit him.

The ridgeline was five yards away when Regan triggered her last shot.

Hawk's right boot came down on a rock. The rock rolled out from beneath him, and he dropped to his hands and knees with a grunted curse. He rose once more, grunting, breathless, his boots clomping and scraping on the loose gravel that carpeted the ridgeline.

A shadow moved above him. He caught only a glimpse of the man's hatted, coated figure silhouetted against the broad sky behind him, when Hawk threw himself to his right.

The man's rifle barked loudly, the bullet screeching out over the ridge behind Hawk.

The Rogue Lawman rolled off a shoulder and pushed up on an elbow while rocking the Colt's hammer back and then firing quickly, aiming by instinct.

Pow! Pow! Pow!

There was a sharp grunt. The rifleman lowered his rifle. His spurs raked the ridge crest with a dull ring, and then he sagged backward, letting the rifle drop at his feet with a metallic thud.

He disappeared like a giant bird taking wing after prey in the canyon below.

Hawk heaved himself up, wincing again at the burn in his calf, feeling a good bit of cool liquid in his right boot. Holstering the .44, he plucked several sharp goatheads and bits of gravel from the heels of his hands, then continued up to the ridge crest. Not allowing himself to be skylined, he took three strides down the opposite side of the ridge, and stopped beside a cracked boulder, and stared down into the canyon below.

Nearly two hundred feet away, at the bottom of a narrow talus slide, the rifleman lay piled up at the hem of Regan's skirts, who stood gazing down at the man, holding Hawk's empty Russian down low in her right hand. The pistol's silver chasing was bright in the sunlight.

She lifted her head to gaze up at Hawk.

She must have left her position behind the escarpment lower down the slope to shoot from several yards above the ridge's base. Giving her bullets a better chance of keeping the bushwhacker pinned down while Hawk stole up on the bushwhacker from the other side of the ridge.

Hawk ran the back of a dusty coat sleeve across his sweaty forehead. "Crazy damn woman."

It was almost as though she'd heard him. She continued staring up the incline at him, one hand on her hip, with what he assumed, though he couldn't see her clearly from here, was a hard-jawed look of defiance.

Hawk chuckled as he lifted his hat from his head, ran a hand through his hair, and headed back up and over the ridge to look for the dry-gulcher's horse. "Pity the poor bastard who lands her."

He found the horse in a little hollow cut into the side of the mountain. It was cropping jimsonweed and lapping at water dribbling out from a spring deep in the rocks. It was a tall, cream gelding with a brown-spotted rump. The horse was ground-hitched but it sidestepped, tail raised, when it saw a stranger moving toward it. It rippled its nostrils and shook its head at the smell of blood in Hawk's boot.

The Rogue Lawman grabbed the horse's reins and swung up into the saddle before the mount had followed through on its impulse to flee, and got it under a tight rein before walking it down along a game path and into the notch canyon carved into the ridge. The horse was high-stepping and snorting in confusion, likely wondering who this strange-smelling man astraddle it was, and where its owner was, when Hawk turned the beast out of the notch and headed west toward where he'd left the woman and the horse's dead rider.

As he approached the bottom of the ridge, where the dead man lay, Regan was moving toward him from up trail, riding her own mount while leading Hawk's grulla by the reins.

She had a smugly satisfied look on her face. They stopped ten yards away from each other, the cream swishing its tail but more interested in the strange horses than the dead man sprawled amongst the rocks up the ridge a ways.

"That was a fool thing to do," Hawk said, swinging down from his saddle.

"He was trying to leave his cover," Regan said. "I probably saved your life. So we're even now."

"You oughta listen to what a man tells you. Especially one who knows his business." Hawk winced when he put weight down on his right foot.

"How bad is it?" Regan frowned down at his calf. The dark stain, about the size of a man's palm, shone on the outside well of his right boot.

"There's a nice little scratch in there, but I'll make it." Trying not to limp — Hawk had developed the hunter's as well as the prey's revulsion of weakness — he climbed twenty feet to where the bushwhacker lay sprawled against the side of a boulder. The man lay across the slope, on his side, one cheek resting against his outstretched left arm, legs tangled.

He'd lost his hat in the fall — a tall man with long, coarse gray hair tumbling down from a pink pate. A strange-looking hombre, Hawk thought. Not tall, but skinny, and he wore no gloves on his bony, white hands. His fingernails were untrimmed, and they curved down over the tips of his fingers like hard, yellow talons.

He wore a duster over a vested serge suit and a collarless, white shirt that had likely been crisp before his tumble down the ridge. A gold watch lay near his belly, connected to a vest pocket by a gold-washed chain.

The flaps of his duster were thrown back, revealing that the man wore no sidearm. At least none that Hawk could see. He might have a hideout weapon under his vest, but there appeared no telltale bulge.

Blood oozed down from the three holes in his chest, staining the sand and rocks beneath him.

"All three heart shots."

Hawk looked down the slope to where the woman sat her saddle, staring up at him coldly.

"Nice shooting, Mr. Hawk. That's Rance Harvin, in case you're wondering."

"Never heard of him," Hawk grunted.

"Apparently, he's heard of you. Harvin's a professional killer, Mr. Hawk. A regulator. Roams this area, from Wyoming on down to Lyons, culling work from the larger ranchers, mine owners, and saloon proprietors. He rides through Trinity quite often, spends a day or two before moving on. A rather distinctive-looking gentleman."

She lowered her voice slightly. "Or, at least he was." She quirked her mouth corners grimly. "Someone with money, apparently, doesn't want you taking the lawman's job in Trinity."

Hawk reached down, grabbed the dead man by his vest lapels, and hefted him over his shoulder. "Yeah, well," the Rogue Lawman said with a grunt as he started down the ridge, "I just love being welcomed with open arms."

9.
Trinity Ridge

Trinity Ridge sat in a broad bowl between the Laramie Mountains in the north, the Never Summer and the Snowy Ranges in the west, and the Mummy Mountains to the south. Several low mesas and bluffs surrounded the town, hemming it in from the broader valley beyond. Regan informed Hawk that one such ridge in the southeast, which earlier pioneers had called "Trinity Ridge" due to its being capped by three columnar rock formations, had given the town its name.

Farther east was mostly the open country of the North Platte headwaters, spotted with low bluffs including the famous Steamboat and Signature Rocks, and shallow canyons, with the Bozeman Trail stamping it from north to south, and the Overland Trail from east to west.

Because of the surrounding mountains, Trinity was out of the way commercially.

When in a few years the gold pinched out of the nearby bluffs and streams, it wouldn't exist as anything besides a supply camp for area ranches. But now it was joined to the Union Pacific tracks by a semi-regular spur line, and it was connected to Laramie and Camp Collins by a weekly stage line that hauled a few passengers now and then, and, of course, the mail.

The town appeared relatively healthy, Hawk thought as he and Regan Mitchell rode along its broad main street sheathed in well-maintained, false-fronted business buildings with here and there a private home fronted by a leather-seated buggy and flanked by a hay barn and corral. Quiet, too. Now. Without a lawman around to keep a tight rein, the nights were probably another matter.

Trinity appeared comprised of a good six or seven plotted blocks. The entire town, including original log cabins and adobe-brick shacks arranged willy-nilly on the fringes, probably occupied close to a square mile.

Hawk, leading Rance Harvin's cream by its reins, and Regan passed a church. Hawk was vaguely looking around for an undertaker's shingle, as he'd like to rid himself of the dead regulator he'd tied belly down across the man's own saddle. He'd have left the man where he lay along the slope of that ridge, but the killer had obviously been hired by someone to kill Hawk before the Rogue Lawman could reach Trinity and pin a badge to his shirt.

And he wanted to make sure that the man — or men — knew what they were up against. Moreover, bringing Harvin's carcass back to town was Hawk's own way, albeit a semiconscious one, of telling the killer's employer that he could kiss Hawk's ass.

"Other end of town," Regan said, reading Hawk's mind. "Hy Booker buries the dead in these parts. Maybe you and he could go into business together."

Ignoring the woman's comment delivered in her customary cold monotone, Hawk reined the grulla to a halt in front of the Poudre River House Hotel, which sat in the middle of town and on the main street's — Wyoming Street's — north side. It was a big, three-story, white-clapboard building with a long row of front windows on the first floor. A big, beefy young man in coveralls and wool watch cap was sweeping the roofed front porch.

"I was due here an hour ago for a meeting with my prospective employers." Hawk turned to Regan and offered a dry grin.

"Been a pleasure, Miss Mitchell. Maybe see you around again sometime."

"Tell me, Mr. Hawk — does the mayor know who you are?"

"You mean — does he know my reputation? I wouldn't know. I signed the letter I wrote him. See no need to hide behind an alias anymore."

Regan glanced at the hotel and shook her head in disgust. "They oughta know better." She glanced at Harvin before pursing her lips and dropping her eyes to Hawk's right boot. "You really oughta have that leg of yours looked at, Mr. Hawk."

"As soon as I know if I'm stayin' or not."

"Dr. Blackman's office is just on the other side of my house." Regan canted her head to indicate a small, frame house down a side street intersecting Wyoming Street to the south and a similar structure just beyond it and with a sign attached to a post in the front yard.

"Nice place you have, for a schoolteacher," Hawk said.

"Well, then," she said with a sigh by way of parting, neck reining her horse away from the hotel but stopping suddenly when the hotel's front door squawked open.

Hawk swung his head toward the hotel, where a short, older gent with badly disheveled gray hair stepped onto the porch. He was followed by three other men — all well-dressed and conservative-looking. Hawk's interviewers, most likely. Members of the Trinity Town Council. The three were casting wary, slightly befuddled looks at the dead man hanging over the cream gelding. The last man came out — the youngest of the three, though he looked to be in his late fifties, early sixties, and walked with a limp. He closed the heavy, green door behind him, and the beefy young man with the broom turned toward him and the newcomers, his dull eyes finding the horse carrying Rance Harvin.

"Oh, my," said the first man, adjusting his spectacles as he walked down the porch a ways to get a good look at the dead man, whose head and arms hung down that side of the cream.

The others shifted around behind him, the youngest man smoking a cigar and stopping near the door to regard Hawk with bemused eyes.

The older gent with the wild gray hair shifted his gaze from the dead man to Hawk, his ragged silver brows arching over his bespectacled eyes. "You must be Mr. Hawk."

Hawk nodded soberly and glanced back

at the dead man. "And this here, I'm told, is Rance Harvin."

The four councilmen all looked at Harvin once more, then raked their gazes to Hawk before shuttling curious looks at Regan Mitchell, who sat her roan facing the hotel, both her gloved hands clamped over her saddle horn. Hawk said by way of explanation, "Ran into each other along the trail."

Regan said in a faintly sneering tone, "Someone else, apparently, didn't want Mr. Hawk joining the ranks of Trinity's illustrious citizens. Someone even more vehemently opposed to his presence than even myself, because they tried to have him killed."

Hawk gathered that the woman had previously vocalized her opposition at the city council meetings to the town's hiring a town tamer. He was surprised these old gents had even allowed a female to partake in the formal debates that had obviously taken place.

Before any of the councilmen could respond to the woman's statement, she reined her horse around and booted it down the cross street, heading home. Hawk glanced back at her, vaguely admiring the way her thick hair bounced along her slender back, as well as the sand in her character, before turning to the councilmen.

"I do apologize, Mr. Hawk," said the wild-haired man, shuffling over to the top of the porch steps while the others flanked him like bashful schoolboys. "Apparently the rougher element got wind of your coming — gossip spreads fast in a town the size of Trinity — and did something to try and prevent it. My guess would be it was one of the shadier saloon owners who had Harvin awaiting your arrival. Impossible to prove, of course."

He glanced at Harvin again, and scowled. "I guess it is a good indication of what you'll be up against . . . if you're offered the job, that is, after we've chatted a bit. And if you decide to accept."

"Yeah, well, I've been shot at before, Mister . . ."

"Oh, pardon me." The gray-haired gent flushed with chagrin. "I'm the mayor of Trinity — Malcolm Pennybacker." He introduced the other three men as Benjamin Learner, Romeo Pike, and, the youngest of the four who was smoking the cigar at the rear of the small pack — Carson Tarwater.

Each man nodded as his name was mentioned, and then Pennybacker turned to the big man holding the broom on the porch,

"Reb, take Mr. Hawk's horses to the livery stable, will you. And deliver Mr. Harvin to the undertaker, Mr. Booker."

The big man opened his mouth but tried several times before he was able to spit the words out like peach pits, "You got it, Mr. Mayor."

He smiled bashfully, eagerly, then carefully set his broom against the hotel's front wall and approached the Trinity mayor, wiping his big, red hands on his coveralls. The mayor dug into his pants pocket and clanked a couple of coins into Reb's open hand.

"Thank you, Mr. Mayor," the big, sweet-faced stutterer said with effort, stumbling on every word.

"Don't drink that all up at the Venus, now, Reb," the mayor cautioned the big man, who hurried down the porch steps. "Joe Lundy will want you back here to finish up your chores before you start patronizing the drinking establishments — understand?"

"Oh, no, sir, Mr. Mayor. I mean . . . I'll be right back here to finish up my chores, Mr. Mayor."

Hawk tossed the big man the reins to Harvin's horse, and then his own. He slipped his rifle from its saddle boot, swung his saddlebags and canvas war sack over his left shoulder, and stepped back away from the grulla.

The big man hurried up the street, jerking the cream and the grulla along behind him.

Harvin's head and arms bobbed stiffly down the cream's right side, his legs doing the same over the left saddle fender. Several people on both sides of Wyoming Street stopped to gawk at Reb's grisly cargo. As the wind of the young man's passing wafted against him, Hawk thought he'd detected the sour stench of beer on Reb's breath, mixed with the smell of chewing tobacco.

Inwardly, he smiled.

"That's Reb Winter." Mayor Pennybacker tapped his temple with an index finger to indicate Reb's obvious limitations. "Odd-jobber. Dependable when he doesn't have his head in a beer bucket." Having noted Hawk's slight limp, he looked down at the Rogue Lawman's right boot and frowned. "Do you need to see Doc Blackman, Mr. Hawk? Before we get down to business?"

Hawk shook his head and mounted the porch steps, and all four men stepped back, retreating as though from a bobcat that had wandered out of an open cage, sudden looks of apprehension on their faces. "I'll get looked at later, if needed. At the moment, I could do with a plate of food and a beer."

"That can certainly be arranged," Pennybacker said, turning and following the other three men into the hotel, glancing back and up over his left shoulder at the Rogue Lawman following and towering over him. "The Poudre River is the best-appointed hotel in town, and its kitchen fare rivals any found in either Cheyenne or Laramie. The owner, Joe Lundy, moved up from Denver, where he managed the Larimer Street Saloon."

"Nice to know," Hawk said, wincing a little at the burn and lancing pain in his right calf.

He thought the wound had dried up, as he couldn't detect any more fresh blood in his boot. He'd have gone ahead and seen the doctor, and gotten the wound sewn up if it needed it, but he didn't want to be seen running to a sawbones first thing after pulling into town. Most wouldn't think much about it, but sometimes the unconscious impressions were the most powerful.

He had no idea who might be watching. He'd show no sign of weakness to possible adversaries.

When they were inside the lobby's dark foyer, with the varnished stairs climbing the rear wall beyond, and the desk to the left, Pennybacker turned to Hawk, tipping his head back to give the man the slow up-and-down. "You're certainly a tall man — aren't you, Mr. Hawk?"

Adjusting his round, wire-rimmed spectacles, he turned to the dark-haired, middle-aged woman smiling superciliously behind the desk. "Louise, would you please have Joe fix a plate for Mr. Hawk? And have an ale drawn, as well?"

The woman shifted her icy blue eyes to the Rogue Lawman, her face looking waxy in the light angling through the hotel's front windows, her thin lips long and red. She wore several pounds of jewelry about her neck and on her wrists and fingers. "So you're Mr. Hawk," she said in a tone to match her expression.

Not waiting for a response, she said through the same varnished smile to Pennybacker, "Of course, Mayor," and stepped out from behind her desk to make her way through the councilmen and Hawk, striding into the dining room ahead of them, her purple brocade skirt trimmed with large, gold-stitched flowers swishing about her legs and ample rump.

"Not everyone approves of town tamers, Mr. Hawk," Pennybacker explained, holding his head up close to Hawk's shoulder and glancing after Louise Lundy. "But the Lundys want Trinity reined in as bad as all the other respectable business folk in town."

"Except Miss Mitchell, obviously."

Pennybacker scowled and cleared his throat. "Yes, well, she'll come around, too. This way, Mr. Hawk," the mayor said, indicating the broad, arched doorway on the lobby's right side through which the other councilmen were following Mrs. Lundy.

The dining room was all but deserted. There were only two afternoon diners — two elderly ladies sitting at a small table against the far wall, near the broad field-stone hearth that resembled the inside of a dragon's mouth and filled the room with wisps of blue smoke and the aromatic tang of piñon pine.

Nearer the room's entrance, there was a lounge area outfitted with a leather couch and two deep, overstuffed chairs surrounding a coffee table. On the table were several brandy snifters and two cigars smoldering up from cut-glass ashtrays. While three of the councilmen took the seats they'd apparently occupied earlier while they'd waited for Hawk's arrival, Pennybacker stood around hemming and hawing nervously, polishing a fist with a palm, not sure where to put Hawk since the prospective town tamer was about to dine.

Hawk took the decision out of the mayor's hands by kicking a chair out from the small, round, white-clothed table that abutted the front wall, within conversational range of the councilmen. He dropped his rifle, war sack, and saddlebags on the floor at the base of lime-green wainscoting.

Hawk doffed his hat as he stood in front of the table, looking out the long row of clean windows before him, dropping his hat on the table and running his hands through his hair. He looked up the street to his right, started bringing his eyes back toward the hotel, then shuttled them up the street again.

His gaze held on a large wooden platform about a block away. It was partly concealed by the shadows of the tall buildings on the south side of the street, so that when he'd glimpsed it earlier he'd thought it the loading dock of a mercantile or feed store. But as he scrutinized it now, the three steps leading up to the main platform from the right, there was no doubting its significance.

"That it?" Hawk canted his head to indicate the platform.

"Say again, Mr. Hawk?" Pennybacker said, shuffling up beside Hawk with a painfully administering air and crouching to look out the window.

"Up the street there . . . That the gallows?"

Pennybacker cast his gaze in the direction Hawk had indicated and nodded. "Yes, that's the gallows."

"Where the sheriff was shot?"

"Yes, it is. It is at that. Where Tierney and Jack Wildhorn and their Two Troughs gang rode in and freed Tierney's son."

Both continued to study the gallows over which the shadow of the southern buildings lay. The nooses had been taken down, but Hawk could see where they would be strung from the scaffold's overhanging beam. He felt a dry knot in his throat and tried to clear it as he asked, "And where . . . ?"

His mouth turned to dust, his tongue a scrap of parched leather, and the words dried like a single drop of water in sand. One of his own nightmare images flashed in front of his eyes — Linda hanging from the cottonwood tree in their backyard in Valoria, her body looking so pale and fragile there in her nightclothes, her lower jaw hanging slack — and Hawk blinked several times to sweep the memory away.

He felt his head go light, his body sway forward. He placed a hand on the table before him to steady himself while staring straight out the window, his jaws hard, his expression dark and grim.

"I'm sorry," the mayor said, looking up at the taller man skeptically. "What was that last, Mr. Hawk?"

"Nothin'."

Hawk knew the answer to the question. There'd been no reason to ask it. Regan had told him that the sheriff's wife had hanged herself on the same scaffold on which her husband had died. After killing their child . . .

Hawk shook his head and narrowed an eye, suppressing such thoughts and images that lanced his core and spread a hot, oily liquid up the back of his neck and head. "Just speculating aloud."

"You look like you could use a drink, Mr. Hawk."

Hawk looked over his left shoulder. A young man had come with a tray, and he was holding the tray out toward Hawk while the wild-haired mayor smiled up at the prospective town tamer witlessly, perhaps with a little concern in his own drink-bleary eyes.

Hawk took the beer schooner off the tray and, sagging into his chair, sipped the foam off the top of the glass before taking a deep gulp. He'd taken one more draught, downing half the coffee-colored brew that owned a rich, hoppy tang, when the young man returned with a steaming, oval-shaped plate piled high with thick slices of roast beef and potatoes smothered in gravy, and an extra small dish of spinach boiled with ham.

"Thank you, thank you," Hawk said with relief as the young man set the plate before him. Hawk's stomach expanded and contracted at the delightful smells wafting up on the steam and diluting the grim recollection.

The young man indicated Hawk's glass. "Another, sir?"

"Don't mind if I do."

When the young man had gone, Hawk draped a napkin over a knee, shrugged out of his coat, rolled up his shirtsleeves, and got down to business with fork and knife. He glanced to his left, saw the mayor and the councilmen looking stiff and awkward as two sat on either end of the couch and two in the chairs fronting the couch and angled to face the coffee table.

"Don't mind me," Hawk said. "You men have questions to ask, go ahead and ask."

He kept the men in the corner of his left eye as he shoveled food into his mouth, chewing and swallowing hungrily and washing down every second or third bite with a swig of the hoppy ale. The men looked around at each other, silently conferring, before the youngest of the four, Carson Tarwater, who sat on the right end of the couch facing Hawk over the coffee table, blew a long plume of smoke into the air, and said, "So, Mr. Hawk . . ." He narrowed his eyes in bemused speculation. ". . . You're him."

"What?" Hawk said, holding a forkful of food in front of his mouth. "You thought I'd be taller? Or shorter?"

10.
"The Tierneys Must Be Stopped"

Carson Tarwater had a haggard face pitted from what appeared a long-ago bout with smallpox. Still, it was a regally handsome countenance, broad of cheek and wide of jaw tapering to a resolute chin, with dark-brown hair graying at the temples and swept back from a prominent widow's peak. The man stretched his long, thin limbs. He dimpled his clean-shaven cheeks.

"I must say I didn't know what to expect. Some of the illustrated newspapers, I'm told — don't read the trashy things myself — make you out to be a hero of the common folk whom the laws of the frontier are incapable of fully protecting against the badmen running rampant everywhere."

The man's slow, pleasant voice betrayed a soft southern accent. "Others, a hard-nosed criminal. A kill-hungry pistolero so tormented by the deaths of his family that he kills and keeps on killing merely to fill the void in his tortured world."

Hawk slid the forkful of meat and potatoes into his mouth and sipped his beer. "You have an opinion yet?"

"I'm leaning toward the latter."

Hawk stopped eating to arch a puzzled brow at the man, who stared back at him, cheeks dimpled.

Mayor Pennybacker shifted in his chair left of the couch. Leaning forward, he set his snifter on the end of the coffee table, rested his elbows on his knees, and entwined his short, bony fingers.

"You see, Mr. Hawk," he said, "Carson here is the one who suggested we hire a town tamer. When we received a response from you, he was quite pleased."

"I know what it takes to bring civilization to the frontier," Tarwater said. "You see, I left my ranch in Texas to join the Confederacy. When I returned, carpetbaggers had moved onto my land, stolen all my horses and cattle — mavericks it had taken me six years to brand. My wife even married one of the Yankee devils. I couldn't get those men off my property or to return my woman. Words, of course, wouldn't sway them. And while I'd fought hard in the war with General Hood, I'd lost my stomach for bloodletting."

He pinched his broadcloth trousers up at the knee, revealing a wooden ankle rising from a wooden foot painted to resemble a black shoe. "As well as my foot."

"Blue Tierney must be stopped." This from one of the two men who had not yet spoken — Romeo Pike, a rotund, jowly, dark-skinned man who obviously had some Spanish or Mexican blood. "Him and his son must be stopped, Mr. Hawk. They run wild throughout the county, rustling, claim-jumping, attacking the Poudre River Transport line, whose stages run once, sometimes twice a week through Trinity and often carry payroll pouches for area mines and ranches. They're badly hurting my business." He flushed slightly and glanced around at the other men. "All of our businesses. They must be stopped . . . at no risk to the good folks of Trinity, of course. . . ."

"What do you do, Mr. Pike?" Hawk asked, chewing slowly now that his stomach was finally getting full.

"I run the transport company and U.S. Post Office, kitty-corner from the hotel." Pike nodded at the front window.

"He's not the only one getting hurt, Mr. Hawk," Tarwater said. "It's hard on my business, too. I have the tack and feed store over by the undertaker's. And I do some horse selling." He glanced at Mayor Pennybacker. "You wanna tell him what they did to you, Mayor?"

The Trinity mayor shifted around uneasily and lowered his watery eyes to the coffee table, off of which he scooped his brandy snifter with both hands and rolled it between his palms. "They found my granddaughter down by the creek last summer." He grimaced and thumbed his spectacles up his nose. "Brazos and several other men abused her terribly." He glanced up at Hawk, and a hardness entered the man's gaze. "She's . . . a simple girl, Mr. Hawk. A child in a young woman's body. And now. Now, you see, she's carrying a child. She's being cared for by the Sisters of Saint Theresa's in Cheyenne."

The mayor threw his snifter back, draining it.

Hawk set his fork down softly, staring at his plate. He wasn't sure if it had been the mayor's story or the food he had so quickly consumed, but he was suddenly no longer famished.

Silence descended on the room. The only sounds were the mutterings of the old women sitting along the far wall, sipping tea, and the occasional clatter of a pan or stove lid in the kitchen. The fire popped and crackled.

"I run Learner Freighting," said the other man who had remained silent till now as he sat on the other side of the coffee table from the mayor. "Two Troughs riders harass my wagons almost weekly. Last month, apparently to celebrate Tierney's springing of his son from the gallows and killing Sheriff Stanley and his deputy, Matt Freeman, they ran one wagon and four mules into a canyon. The skinner, mules, freight, and wagon — all lost."

"Not to mention . . ." Romeo Pike looked around and let his voice trail off as though chagrined.

Hawk turned on his chair to face the men and set the boot of his bullet-troughed calf onto his knee to get some weight off of it. He winced as he said, "Not to mention what?"

A brief, uncomfortable silence. All the men looked down or askance except for Tarwater, on whose haggardly handsome face a bitter smile quirked.

The mayor said quietly, "The preacher. Pastor Hawthorne. He was there . . . on the gallows. He didn't take the shooting well."

Tarwater snorted unabashedly and puffed his cigar, staring out the windows flanking Hawk. "I'll say he didn't."

Benjamin Learner shook his head as if the current topic offended him. "Our trouble now is not only with Tierney's men, though they've been running wilder than usual since they killed our lawmen. But other men — wild drifters and general ne'er-do-wells — run lawless here, too. Like packs of wild dogs, coming and going, doing what they please, taking what they please. It's gotten so that decent men don't dare patronize the saloons and whorehouses anymore after sundown."

This evoked muffled laughter from the other men in the room. Hawk even gave a snort as he dug inside his sheepskin vest, which he wore with the leather facing out, for his makings sack. Learner's face turned red.

Slowly, quietly, Hawk shaped a cigarette. With a sigh, he stuck the quirley between his teeth, scratched a lucifer on his right holster, and touched it to the quirley. Puffing smoke as he returned the makings sack to his shirt pocket, he said, "How much you gonna pay me?"

"Thirty a month," the mayor said.

They all looked at Hawk, waiting.

He shook his head as he drew a lungful of smoke. "Might not be here that long. I want a thousand dollars when I have both Brazos and Blue Tierney hanging from that gallows out there. Along with the other two men Tierney sprang. By that time, I'll have the town back on its leash."

"Hanging?" Tarwater was incredulous. "We don't need to go through all that again. Kill 'em! That's what you do, isn't it, Hawk?"

"I do what needs to be done," Hawk shot back at the man. "Since Stanley wanted them hanged, and he died trying to see them hanged so the town could take comfort and satisfaction in the law being upheld, I'm going to hang them."

Tarwater laughed as he clapped his hands once and sagged back on the sofa, lifting his natural foot with false glee. "How ironic. Soon as we bring the bastard to Trinity, the Rogue Lawman's going straight!"

Hawk blew smoke through his nostrils and eyed the man grimly. "I don't see what difference it makes how I clean up your town, Mr. Tarwater. As long as it's cleaned up."

"I have to agree with Mr. Hawk," said the mayor. "We'll let him do it his way."

"Tell me, Hawk," Tarwater said, crossing his leg with the bizarre-looking wooden foot over the other knee, his cigar sending smoke curling toward the ceiling. "Why no alias? They tell me you used to ride by the name

Hollis. George Hollis."

Hawk shrugged. "Once everyone learns your alias, there's really no reason to go on using it, now, is there, Tarwater?"

Of course, he could come up with another name. But, frankly, Hawk was tired of the charade. It was easier for bona fide lawmen to track him now, under his real name, but he simply no longer cared. He gave little consideration to his reasons, but what it boiled down to was that he no longer cared if he lived or died.

"Those are my terms, gentlemen," he said. "Take it or leave it."

He took another deep drag off his quirley, then dropped the stub in his empty ale schooner. Rising, trying to put the brunt of his weight on his left foot, he scooped his gear off the floor, draping the saddlebags over his back. He rested the Henry repeater over his shoulder.

"I'll let you talk about it. I'll be upstairs."

"Hawk," Mayor Pennybacker said when the Rogue Lawman was nearly to the door. He cleared his throat as he regarded Hawk from around his chair back. "We've already talked about it. The job is yours, on the terms you've laid out. When Reb returns from the undertaker's, I'll have him show you to the sheriff's office."

Hawk studied the men and nodded slowly. "One more thing before I get down to business. I'll need the names of the men who were freed from the gallows when Brazos was freed."

The men glanced around at each other. Finally, the mayor stood, turned to Hawk, and said with a solemn air, "J. T. Hostetler and 'One-Eye' Willie McGee."

"They come to town often?"

Pennybacker glanced at Learner, as though the freighter with the impeccable gray hair and matching gray suit would be more qualified to relate what happened in Trinity's saloons after sundown.

"Almost every night," Learner said tensely. "They're close friends of Brazos. All three come to town almost every damn night though they haven't been seen since Blue and the other Two Troughs riders rode in and sprang all three."

"All three ride together, huh?"

"Usually." Mayor Pennybacker glowered as though thinking about his granddaughter. Darkly, he added, "They're all hardened killers and rapists, Mr. Hawk. And they're very brash. It's most likely you'll be seeing at least Brazos and his partners in town again before long."

Hawk thought about that, shifted the

saddle on his shoulder. "All right."

He turned and headed into the lobby to register for a room with the persnickety and obviously disapproving Louise Lundy. The woman said nothing to him as she gestured at the register book, silently instructing him to sign after he'd paid a week's rent in advance. When he'd set the pen down and picked up his key, he caught her studying him with an odd, faintly incredulous air. She quickly looked away.

Puzzling.

The puzzle was solved, however, when Hawk reached his room on the second floor, turned the key in the lock, and nudged the door open with his rifle barrel. The shadowy room was hammered with sunlight from beneath a half-drawn shade on the front wall, opposite the window.

Hawk kicked the door closed. Then he froze. The familiar female scent was his first warning.

No, she couldn't be here.

How could she be here?

He whipped around, raising the Henry and aiming one-handed from his right hip.

He could see little more than her silhouette sitting in the armchair upholstered in purple velvet, her back to the window. Her thick hair tumbled down her shoulders in rich, golden waves. She had hiked a high-topped black boot onto a knee, very unladylike. Her cream, concho-banded Stetson was hooked over the other, upraised knee. Her rifle leaned against the wall beside her, near her saddlebags.

"Goddamn," Hawk growled, grinding his back teeth. "How in the hell did you get here?"

"Mrs. Lundy looks respectable enough, but even her churchgoing fingers snapped up the two double eagles I wagged in front of her face. And turned over your room key."

"You crazy bitch."

"Nice to see you, too, Gid."

Hawk let his war bag and saddlebags slide off his left shoulder and hit the floor with a thud. His pulse hammering in his temples, he strode forward, held the rifle out from his hip with both hands. Loudly, resolutely, he levered a live cartridge into the chamber and held his finger taut against the trigger.

"That was a nice stunt you pulled back in Arizona. Killing Ironside, those lawmen . . ."

"Well, look at it this way," Saradee said, sticking the rolled quirley between her full lips, her white teeth glinting against the oval-shaped shadow of her face, and ran her tongue across the paper cylinder to seal it. "They died in the line of duty. Their families can be proud."

Hawk held the maw of the cocked repeater two feet away from her forehead. "You crazy bitch."

She fired a lucifer on the side of the marble-topped washstand to her left and touched the flame to the quirley. Puffing smoke, her lilac eyes touched his, and he felt a fire burn in his belly. It licked down toward his loins, setting the raw male need ablaze.

Christ, she was beautiful. And deadly. If some horned spirit residing in the farthest, darkest reaches of hell had wanted to send a beautiful siren to tease and torment Hawk beyond what he'd already been through, that demon could have done no better than this round-hipped, full-breasted succubus in men's dusty trail garb seated before the Rogue Lawman now.

Cold sweat beaded behind Hawk's ears as he stared down at her fine-nosed, lightly tanned face.

"You're starting to repeat yourself, Gideon."

Saradee held the smoking cigarette away from her velvet pink lips and flicked a bit of chopped tobacco from a corner of her mouth with a long, tapering finger. Her eyes crossed slightly as she stared mockingly down the barrel of the cocked Henry.

"And we've been through this before, as well. You're forcing me to repeat *myself.*" Slowly, enunciating every word clearly, and seeming to enjoy making her tongue work enticingly between her rich lips, she said, "Go ahead and pull the trigger . . . or set the rifle down, Gideon, and let's enjoy each other's company for a while, huh?"

11.
"Why Torture Me?"

Hawk kept the rifle aimed at Saradee's head. "Why'd you do it?"

"Kill the rangers? Why, because I couldn't bear to part with, you my friend. Sergeant Ironside's death was inadvertent. He was simply in the line of the Gatling gun's fire."

"They had me outnumbered and dead to rights. And they had every right to kill me." Hawk depressed the Henry's hammer, lowered the barrel, and turned away from the delectable blonde sitting there with a boot hiked on a knee, casually smoking her cigarette. "You should have let it shake down. Why torture me?"

Hawk set the Henry down against the wall beside the door.

"Because their killing you would torture me, lover."

Hawk sagged onto the bed and doffed his hat. He rested his elbows on his knees and took his head in his hands, brusquely running his knuckles over his head, mussing his hair. He remembered the scene there at the end of that lonely canyon in western Arizona, when he and Ironside and Saradee had killed the *contrabandista,* Wilbur "Knife-Hand" Monjosa, and the five rangers had moved in on him unexpectedly.

They'd been sent by an old friend, Gavin Spurlock.

No, Spurlock was not merely a friend. Gavin had been like a father to Hawk. He'd given Hawk his first job as a deputy U.S. marshal out of Yankton, Dakota Territory, when Hawk had returned from the bloody battlefields of the Civil War. Hawk's own father, an old Ute war chief who'd fallen in love with Hawk's mother, a pretty blond immigrant girl named Ingrid Rasmussen, had died when Hawk was still a child. The chief had many wives, and Hawk had been one of many children, so the chief hadn't paid much attention to his half-breed offspring.

For all practical purposes, Hawk had been fatherless, and he'd grown up fast, mostly on his own though he'd spent a few years with his mother's brother and sister-in-law on a farm in western Kansas. But his uncle had been a hard, unemotional man, not at all like a father. Gavin Spurlock, however, had taken Hawk under his fatherly wing, given him a job, and made him an expert at it. He'd also given the young veteran cavalryman a place to call home, a place to, as Spurlock had said, "sink a taproot," which Hawk had done when he'd married Linda and fathered Jubal.

Gavin Spurlock.

The name burned on a saber of a fiery guilt across Hawk's brain, and Hawk heard himself groan as he pressed his knuckles against his temples. When he'd gone rogue, he'd become in essence a traitor to the one man he respected most in the world — a venerable chief marshal who held no laws more sacred than those laid out by the Constitution of the United States of America.

That's why, last year in the desert, Spurlock had sent the rangers to assassinate Hawk after the Rogue Lawman had fulfilled the mission that Spurlock himself had given him — ironically, to locate and assassinate the kill-crazy renegade, Wilbur "Knife-Hand" Monjosa, who'd murdered Spurlock's blood son, Andrew.

But Saradee had managed to crawl into the wagon in which perched the deadly Gatling gun and taken all the rangers down in one long savage blast of .45-caliber bullets. Then she'd ridden away, leaving Hawk dumbfounded on hands and knees, staring aghast at the carnage before him — so many innocent men dead because of him. And the man he respected most had not only tried to kill him but become a vigilante himself, in ordering Hawk's assassination.

"Ah, Christ," Hawk said.

He heard Saradee chuckle. He felt a tug on his right boot, and looked down to see her kneeling on the floor before him.

"Let me get your boot off, Gid. You got an owie here," she said in a little girl's voice, canting her head to inspect Hawk's bloody pant leg. She jerked the boot up off the floor, and Hawk winced as, applying steady pressure on the heel and toe, she worked it down his leg.

His calf, he realized now, felt hard and swollen, but when Saradee gently rolled his cuff up his leg, he saw through the broad blood stain only a shallow furrow carved across the outside of his shin. Saradee inspected it closely.

"Not bad, 'specially for you," she said, looking up at him, her breasts pushing out from behind her hickory blouse that she wore unbuttoned far enough that Hawk could get a good view of her deep, dark cleavage in which a small, silver crucifix nestled. "Saradee'll have it cleaned up in no time."

"Forget it."

"Don't be that way, lover."

"Don't call me that."

"But, Hawk." She spread her lips, and they rose up slowly at the corners, showing her teeth and dimples. "That's what we are. Whether you like to believe it or not. Now, I ain't sayin' it's love. Nor that I've been any more loyal to you than you've been to me — a woman's got her needs, after all. But I reckon I'd walk a long ways across a snowy prairie or a hot desert just to have you hold me in those big outlaw-lawman's arms of yours."

She leaned against his knees and ran her hands up and down his thighs; he could feel the warmth of her palms through his pants, and it set up a tingling in his crotch. She giggled delightfully, as if she could feel what he was feeling.

"There's just somethin' about an upside-down lawman that makes a girl turn all to jelly inside."

"Saradee," Hawk snarled, curling his upper lip at her. "Get the hell . . ."

He let his voice trail off when someone knocked on the door. Automatically, he closed his right hand around the Russian's walnut grips.

"Easy, lover." Saradee chuckled, rising, strolling over to the door, her round rump giving her tight, black denims a good stretching, and pulling the door open wide.

She grinned as a stocky Chinaman in a blue silk smock came in hauling a copper tub in his meaty hands.

"Bath, please," the man said, glancing at Saradee, his dark eyes glowing with natural male delight at the girl's curvy frame swathed in skintight trail duds. "You, Miss — bath, please?"

"Yes, please, please," Saradee quipped, gesturing. "Sit right there, please, Chang."

"Me no Chang." The Chinaman shook his head seriously as he set the tub down in the middle of the room, on a deep, Oriental rug with woven green leaves against burnt umber. He tapped his board chest proudly and grinned, showing several silver teeth. "Me Baozhai!"

"Yeah, well, whatever your name is," Saradee snarled, narrowing her eyes at the man impatiently. "Just fetch the damn water, and make it hot! Can't you see I have a man bleeding to death over here?"

"Oh, blood no good! Blood no good!" Baozhai said, shaking his head as he glanced at Hawk's bloody calf. "Blood stain rug!"

He shuffled quickly out the door, sandals slapping the rug and then the wooden floor of the hall.

Saradee crouched down beside the chair she'd been sitting in earlier and fished a bottle out of her saddlebags. There were two water tumblers on Hawk's washstand. She poured bourbon into each, handed one to Hawk, who still sat on the bed, scowling at her, then sat down in the chair. She sipped the whiskey, then, while the Chinaman made several trips with hot and cold buckets of water with which he filled the tub, she busied herself with more whiskey and building and smoking a second quirley.

Hawk sipped from the glass she'd given him. His heart beat persistently, slowly against his breastbone as he stared at her, and she met his gaze with a smug one of her own.

Why couldn't he kick her out of his room? Out of this town? Out of his life?

Moreover, why couldn't he kill her?

God knew he'd vowed to drill a bullet between her pretty breasts countless times before, ridding himself and the world of the kill-crazy blonde — a notorious long rider and killer both here and in Mexico — once and for all.

But when the Chinaman had finished filling the tub, which sent steam snaking toward the stamped tin ceiling, and left after Hawk had tossed him a silver dollar, the Rogue Lawman was reminded of why he hadn't shot her. She threw back the last of her whiskey, exhaled the last puff of smoke through her nostrils, and slowly undressed before him. And then she knelt on the floor beside the bed, removed his second boot and then his cartridge belt and guns. Soon his pants and shirt were off, and his long-handles lay strewn about his castoff boots and pistols.

She lowered her head between his knees and worked her magic on him — slowly, excruciatingly — like she always had before, until he was grinding his toes into the rug and fairly ripping up the mattress with his fists.

When she'd finished, she ran the back of her hand across her mouth, straightened those long legs, her heavy breasts with swollen nipples swaying across her chest, and stepped into the hot water. She stood there for a time, copper-colored steam tendrils snaking about her knees and long-muscled thighs. She returned his smoldering gaze as she hastily knotted her yellow-blond hair atop her head, and then sank slowly into the water.

"Come on, Gid," she said huskily. "Join me." She stretched her lips and lowered her chin slightly, cupping her breasts in the palms of her hands. "Stop fighting me. I'm one battle you're never gonna win. You know it, and I know it."

Her teeth glistened white between her fleshy lips.

Loins heavy, his pulse thudding slowly in his temples, Hawk stepped into the tub with her, cupped her breasts in his hands, hearing her sigh, and ground his lips against her neck, devouring her.

The soft caress of the woman's hair, the soft, wet kisses of her probing lips were still on the Rogue Lawman's body when he woke later from a nap, buried deep in the bed's sheets and quilts and down-filled pillow.

Before he'd climbed into the tub with Saradee, thus beginning two hours of pure, carnal bliss in the charms of a beautiful demon for which he knew he would sometime in the future pay a hefty price, Hawk had built a fire in the room's potbelly stove.

He looked at the stove now, over the tub around which the rug was still saturated with soapy water. The coals lay flat in the stove's grate, glowing dully.

Out the window, long afternoon shadows were spreading amidst shafts of salmon light angling over the tall false building fronts on the street's opposite side. Pigeons cooed from the tops of the facades, their bullet-shaped heads and tapering bodies silhouetted against the green-lemon sky.

Hawk drew a deep breath, raked his hands over his face. Time to inspect his new office digs. He wondered why Reb Winter hadn't knocked on his door. Had Saradee told Mrs. Lundy that Hawk shouldn't be disturbed?

He smiled grimly at the ceiling. Of course she had.

He glanced to his right, expecting to see her long body humped beneath the quilts beside him, her blond hair splayed across the pillow. But she wasn't there. The covers were thrown back to reveal the wrinkled mattress sheet. Her pillow still bore the dent of her head and a single strand of blond hair.

Hawk frowned. Disappointment nipped at him. It was followed by a keen wave of shame.

After Arizona, he hadn't wanted to see her again except to kill her. But he hadn't killed her. Instead, he'd bedded her. Enjoyed every joyous carnal moment that he'd toiled between her writhing legs. He could still feel the scratches her fingernails had raked across his shoulder blades and buttocks.

Hawk sat up, dropping his feet over the side of the bed. A dull throb in his lower right leg reminded him of Rance Harvin's bullet, and he looked down to see the calf that Saradee had deftly cleaned with whiskey and then wrapped with gauze after their bath . . . while doing other things to him that he would likely remember on his deathbed with the same bite of chagrin he felt now.

He'd enjoyed her. He'd enjoyed every minute of her. And he'd likely enjoy her again, next time she blew in like a wisp of sweet-smelling pine, a shrieking, yellow-fanged witch in the body of a flaxen-haired Saxon queen. . . .

A floorboard squawked in the hall. Hawk lifted his head from his hands, eyes glinting with apprehension. The floor squeaked again, and he reached down for his horn-gripped Colt and cocked the piece as he strode naked to the door. He placed his hand on the knob, waited a second, then drew the door open quickly, thrusting the pistol into the hall.

Reb Winter jerked with a start and pressed his broad back against the hall's opposite, wainscoted wall, his watch cap in his hands. His eyes were wide and fearful in his round, boyish face. He tried to say something but didn't get more than two full words out before Hawk depressed the Colt's hammer, lowering the gun.

"Hang on."

He closed the door and dressed in clean clothes from his saddlebags and war sack. When he'd donned his hat and buckled his shell belt around his hips, Reb was still waiting for him in the hall.

"So, you're gonna be the new lawman?" the big, rawboned kid asked Hawk, his eyes shy, his big, red, work-callused hands nearly ripping the brim of the watch cap he worried against his chest.

"For a while."

"You really that *Rogue Lawman,* I heard tell about?"

"I reckon I am. How 'bout that tour of the sheriff's office?"

"Hot-diggidy-ding-dong damn!" the young man said, spittle flying across his fat lower lip as he fired the words out like bullets from a half-jammed Gatling gun. "Right this way, Mr. Hawk!"

"Call me Gid, Reb."

The younker snorted delightfully, mashed his hat onto his head, and took improbably long strides toward the stairs. “Right this way, Gid!”

12.
Reb

On the street, Hawk followed the stuttering youngster, Reb Winter, westward, noting the curious, sometimes cautious glances tossed his way from both men and women alike.

Three blocks beyond the hotel, they walked up the three steps of the gallery fronting the jailhouse, which was apparently one of Trinity's original buildings, constructed as it was of adobe with the ends of straw protruding from the walls. The back of the place was built of stone. The front door was constructed of split pine logs. It was scarred and sun-silvered, and the knob was rusty.

Reb Winter fished around in a pocket of his coveralls for a key on a large steel ring, and jammed the key in the door's rusty lock. It took considerable jerking and grunting, the kid cursing under his breath, before the bolt opened with a rusty scrape and a click. Reb sighed, swabbed sweat from his brow with the back of his wool shirtsleeve, pushed the door open, and ducked inside.

"Here's your office, Gid." Reb stopped to one side of the doorway, glancing around at the dusty, rough-hewn office, then tossing his head at the door at the rear. "The cell block's through there." He blinked and screwed up his face before he could manage: "Sheriff Stanley . . ." He blinked hard as he fought the words through his lips. "Wh-when he had prisoners, he always hired me to haul-haul-haul 'em food and to swamp out their cells, haul s-s-slop buckets an' such. I'll do the same for you, G-Gid."

"Obliged, Reb."

"Well, here's the key." Reb gave the ring to Hawk. "If there's n-nothin' else you need, I reckon I'll h-h-head back to the hotel. They'll be needin' wood split for the s-supper stoves."

"Appreciate the help, Reb."

"Let me know if you need anything else, Gid."

"Thank you."

The young man lumbered on out of the sheriff's office and drew the door closed behind him. Hawk stood near the potbelly stove in the middle of the room, flanked by a box half filled with split wood, and looked around. The office was like other such offices he'd seen about the West. Sparsely, simply furnished with a desk, a map of the county on the wall behind it — in the building's right rear corner — and a dozen or more wanted posters nailed to two old doors, which in turn were nailed to the room's walls around the desk.

A large bobcat hide was stretched across the back of the front door. A gunbelt with an old Schofield pistol hung from the square-hewn center post near the stove, beneath a nail from which another key ring hung. There were two keys on the ring, and when Hawk had tested out the keys, he discovered, as he'd suspected, that one fit the door to the stone cell block while the other one worked in the locks to all five cells that lined the narrow rear corridor.

There was a one-by-one-foot window in each cell, barred and with shutters closed over the bars from the inside. The cell block was almost eerily dark, the only light being that from the late afternoon sun pushing around the sides of the shutters or slithering through cracks in the ancient stone walls.

Hawk left the cell block, hung the cell block keys on the hook above the Schofield, and walked over to the desk.

It was actually two desks — the main oak

one abutting the east wall while a secondary desk, made of what appeared to be the bed of a small farm wagon, angled off of it, forming the short leg of an L. Both desks were a mess of papers — wanted circulars, pink telegraph flimsies, letters from other lawmen and judges, writs, tax bills, and court documents of all shapes and sizes.

There was a moldy half of a meat and cheese sandwich poking out from a scrap of waxed paper, and a half-smoked cigar lying beside a box of kitchen matches. A box of .45 shells protruded from a pigeonhole it shared with a small knife-sharpening stone.

The usual fare of a local lawman's office.

There was a green Tiffany lamp on the desk, betraying a woman's influence. Hawk's eyes slid away from the lamp and dropped to an oval daguerreotype beside it. His gaze held on the picture of a young family — a handsome, young, mustached man in a brown suit and bowler hat seated in an upholstered arm chair and flanked by his standing, pretty, young wife in a conservative day frock, stylishly embroidered and with a ruffled neck and sleeves.

The girl was a brunette, probably not much over twenty. She had a generous mouth and soulful eyes. Her hair had obviously been curled for the picture. It hung down from a small, flowered hat consisting of the same material as the dress.

The young man's left arm supported a small child. A toddler. Probably not much over a year old. The boy was dressed in a little sailor's outfit, and his big eyes were rolling off to the side, probably following a cat or something else in the photographer's studio. They were slightly blurred.

Likely a Laramie or Cheyenne studio photo, Hawk thought. The family picture had probably been made not long ago, in celebration of the couple's starting a family in the form of a handsome baby boy.

The young parents looked proud.

With his thumb, Hawk brushed away a cobweb that a spider had spun from the shade of the Tiffany lamp to the daguerreotype. He felt a thickness in his throat, and he sagged down into the swivel chair behind the two desks arranged in an L before him, and heaved a bereaved sigh. He stared at the picture for a long time, until he could bear the eyes staring back at him no more — so full of vain optimism and foolhardy dreams, they were — and then he turned to the office's front windows.

At the same time, he gave a violent start, closing his hands over the arms of the chair. It took him a moment to realize that he'd just heard a gun blast. Another blast followed, and then several more, and Hawk was out of his chair and reaching for the Henry he'd set against the front wall.

Hooves pounded, men whooped and hollered and shouted, and amidst the snapping and crackling of pistols and rifles, slugs hammered woodenly into buildings and awning posts. One thudded into the sheriff's office door just as Hawk reached for the knob. He hesitated, then pulled the door open quickly, and racking a shell into the Henry's chamber, he stepped onto the office's weathered gallery.

"Get the hell outta the damn street, pilgrim!" a man shouted to Hawk's right, where several horses were dancing and prancing in front of the small stone building whose large wooden sign identified it as the TRINITY BANK AND TRUST CO.

It sat a block away from the sheriff's office, between a drugstore and TARWATER'S TACK & FEED on Wyoming Street's opposite side. Hawk quickly counted five men, two continuing to fire rifles from their saddles while three dismounted. Two of the three stormed into the bank with pistols raised high while the third held the reins of his and two other horses, and whooped and hollered and waved a big, silver-chased pistol around, ordering men and women off the street.

"This here's a holdup!" one of the mounted men shouted from behind the neckerchief covering his mouth and nose. "And if you don't wanna get a bad case of the lead poisonin', I suggest ya haul your mangy asses off the *street!*"

One of the apparent bank robbers — a tall man clad in a green duster and high-crowned hat astraddle a stocky Appaloosa — triggered a shot toward an elderly, stoop-shouldered gent in a green visor and arm bands looking out the door of a small law office to Hawk's right. The man ducked his head with a startled yelp as the bullet tore a dogget of wood from the doorframe above his head, and lurched back into his office, screeching, *"Robbery! Robbery!* The bank's bein' *rawwwwbbbbbed!"*

"You got that right, ya old codger," the man on the Appy roared, laughing, as he triggered a slug through the law office's door.

For Hawk, the shot was muffled by the bulk of the sheriff's office as he strode down the opposite side of the building from the bank, casually shouldering his cocked Henry rifle. When he reached the rear of the jail-house, he heeled it west along the flanking alley, past the back of the law office and the log cabin abutting it, in which the attorney no doubt resided. Hawk stopped at the rear western corner of a land company office and edged a look up the side of the chinked log hovel toward the main street.

He was a little west of the bank, which was good. The bank robbers were all milling directly in front of the bank, still yelling and howling crazily, laughing and triggering their pistols to keep the good citizens of Trinity off the street and out of their way and to think twice about trying to become heroes.

Hawk could see a horse's tail waving, and dust billowing, but that was about it.

Still, he stayed close to the side of the land office cabin as he strode south toward Wyoming Street, the sounds of the skitter-stepping horses and the men's howling and shooting growing louder with every step. Near the front of the cabin, off the corner of the roofed porch fronting the place, he dropped his hat in the dirt, and crouched behind a rain barrel.

There was a patch of dirty, icy snow beneath his boots, and he ground his heels into it for adequate purchase.

From here, Hawk had a good view of the bank robbers — two mounted, one on foot and holding the reins of his own horse and the horses of the two men who'd gone inside the bank. From inside the bank, female screams rose amidst angry shouts and a single pistol blast. Meanwhile, Hawk rested the barrel of his Henry over the top of the rain barrel and pressed his cheek up against the stock, narrowing an eye as he lined up the bead at the end of the barrel with the V-notch atop the receiver.

He set both on the chest of the man facing the street astraddle the Appy and squeezed the trigger.

Boom!

As the bullet slammed into the robber's chest, he sagged back in his saddle, his eyes growing so wide in shock and exasperation that Hawk could see the whites around the irises. He threw his arms out to both sides, releasing his rifle.

Before the Winchester hit the ground, Hawk drew a bead on the other mounted rider fronting the bank and squeezed the trigger. The slug plunked into the side of the man's head, just above his left ear, spraying bright red blood over the bank's narrow boardwalk and against the stone wall beside the double front doors.

The second robber lost his black hat and dropped his rifle. As his startled steeldust wheeled and twisted, the man flopped down the horse's right side. He would have tumbled to the ground, but his left boot got hung up in its stirrup, so his lifeless, hatless body flopped across the cantle of his saddle as the horse, shrieking, galloped west along Wyoming Street, heading for the high and rocky.

Hawk ejected the smoking shell casing from the Henry's breech. It arced over his right shoulder and thumped into the snow at his boots as he racked a fresh cartridge into the chamber.

Now the man who'd been standing and holding the reins of the three horses, having released the reins when the contents of the second man's skull had painted the front of the bank, triggered his pistol straight out from his shoulder.

Calmly, Hawk noted the smoke and flames stabbing from the barrel of the man's Remington, and then the slug ripping into the corner of the land office above and left of Hawk's head. He didn't so much as flinch as he pressed his cheek once more to the Henry's stock and applied deadly pressure to the trigger, leaving the man with the pistol writhing and flopping around on the street in front of the bank, as though he'd been dropped from a high cliff.

The three horses he'd been holding scattered, one inadvertently kicking this last downed man's head with its right rear hoof.

From inside the bank, a woman screamed. A man shouted. A pistol popped. In the relative quiet that fell over Wyoming Street in the wake of the gunfire and the cacophony of the fleeing horses, boots thumped and spurs chinged. A woman sobbed.

In the bank's open doors, a broad-chested man in a cream duster appeared, holding a young woman in a cream dress in front of him with one arm while holding a cocked pistol to the girl's head with his other hand. He and the girl stepped out onto the boardwalk.

Another, taller man also dressed in a bandanna mask and duster stepped out behind him then shuffled to one side, crouching over the rifle he held straight out from his right shoulder.

"Hold your fire, Mr. Whoever the Hell You Are!" ordered the broad-chested gent who was using the girl as a shield. "You squeeze that trigger one more time and this girl here's gonna have an extra hole in her head."

"Don't shoot!" This from a man just now ducking out of the bank — a rotund gent in a long buffalo coat and a crisp, high-crowned, Montana-creased John B. Stetson hat. He pointed at the girl and the bank robber. "That's my daughter in that killer's arms!"

Hawk slid his eyes back to the two bank robbers and the girl.

The broad-chested man stretched a savage grin and canted his head toward the man standing in front of the bank. "You heard him. That's Mr. Boatwright. Owns the Burnt Creek Ranch. This here's his daughter — the plain-faced one, Miss Jane. Not the purty one, Miss Callie. But I think it'll piss burn Boatwright, just the same — won't it, Mr. Boatwright? — to see his daughter's plain-faced head rollin' around in the dirt of Wyoming Street."

Hawk kept his rifle aimed at the man's head and growled through clenched jaws, "Let her go, or I'll kill you."

The broad-chested man's fleshy, mustached face turned brick red, and his blue eyes spat fire. "You drop that hammer, you'll likely kill me, amigo. I see how you can shoot. But my finger here's wrapped tight around the trigger of my Smithy, and I'll pop a slug through this child's brain plate, sure enough!"

"Mister," shouted Boatwright stepping

down from the bank's boardwalk and thrusting a demanding finger at Hawk. "You lower that rifle and let these men go. I demand it!"

The man with the rifle and with a pair of bulging saddlebags hanging over his left shoulder was backing slowly eastward along Trinity Street, apparently heading toward three horses hitched in front of a small adobe cantina a half a block away. He had his chin dipped low, mean yellow eyes riveted on Hawk. The lower half of his face was painted umber by the sun going down behind the Rogue Lawman while his forehead was shaded by his broad hat brim.

Hawk slid his Henry at the man, and drilled a .44 round through the tongue of purple shade licking down from the man's hat.

The man triggered his own rifle into the front of the land office cabin flanking Hawk as he went down hard on his butt before flattening out on his back, bending his knees and shaking his boots as though he'd been struck by lightning.

13.
The Mays Gang

"Jesus Christ!" shouted the broad-chested bank robber, who'd swung a quick look at his suddenly dead partner. "What'd I tell you, you crazy son of a bitch? You got wax in your ears?"

Hawk quickly levered a fresh shell into the Henry's breech.

"Stop! Stop!" Boatwright walked out farther into the street, holding his gloved hands to his head as he shuttled his horrified gaze between the lone living bank robber and the dead man who continued to shiver and shake and grind his boot heels into the half-frozen street. To Hawk, he said, "Lower that weapon and let this man go! He'll kill my daughter, you arrogant fool!"

"He's got that right, mister," shouted the broad-chested bank robber, the wide-eyed girl sobbing in his arms as the man half-dragged her backward, her high-heeled cloth half boots catching on the man's scuffed toes. "I'm gonna shoot her now — now, you hear? Less'n you toss that Henry down in the street!"

Hawk said, "You let her go, you'll live. You continue to hold her, you're gonna die. It's as simple as that."

Hawk expected Boatwright to try to intervene again and was vaguely surprised when the rancher stood in shocked silence in front of the bank, turning his head from Hawk to the bank robber then back again. Silence had fallen over the street so that the girl's hushed sobs and grunts as she struggled in the bank robber's arms sounded like distant screams.

"I'll kill her," the bank robber said, holding his position now in the middle of the street. "I swear I'll kill her. Mr. Boatwright, you tell him."

Boatwright switched his horrified gaze between the bank robber and Hawk.

The bank robber looked back at Hawk, who narrowed a hard green eye as he stared down the barrel of the cocked Henry. Fear dampened the exasperation and fury in the broad-chested man's eyes as he stared back at the Rogue Lawman, a nerve in his sunburned right cheek twitching.

"Good lord," he said softly, barely audible above the girl's groans. "You aim to kill me no matter what I do — don't ya?"

Hawk lifted his mouth corners slightly, but his eyes remained granite-hard.

There was another sound. The sound of dripping water. Hawk glanced quickly down to see urine dribbling down the side of the man's right boot, forming a yellow-brown puddle that lifted tendrils of pale steam from the street. Hawk lifted his gaze to the man's face, saw the bald-assed fear in the man's pale blue eyes, and knew he had to move now or the girl would die.

He flicked a glance behind the man — a quick look as though at someone trying to flank the bank robber. Just as the man began to turn his head around and give a little slack in his trigger finger, Hawk's repeater leapt and roared.

The bank robber jerked his head back and let both his arms fall slack to his sides, triggering his Smith & Wesson into the ground at his feet and blowing up a dogget of ice-crusted mud and half-melted snow. The girl screamed, bolted to her left, got a foot tangled with one of the backward stumbling bank robber's, and fell in a heap.

Blood leaking from the hole in his right cheek, the bank robber stood stock-still, gaping at Hawk as he flicked his thumb weakly across the hammer of the Smithy while feebly trying to raise the gun once more for a shot. Hawk quickly ejected the spent cartridge, seated a live one, and finished the bank robber by slamming a .44 bullet through the dead center of the man's chest.

"Jane!" intoned the rancher, Boatwright, as he bolted toward his daughter. "Oh, for chrissake — are you all right, honey?"

The girl sobbed as she continued to lie on the street while her father knelt beside her, placing a hand on her back while glaring up at Hawk, his lips set in a hard line beneath his gray-brown, handlebar mustache. Hawk automatically released the lock on the Henry's loading tube, beneath the forestock, and began feeding fresh shells to it.

Instead of more gunmen, however, he saw a good dozen people lining the boardwalks up and down the street, staring toward him and the dead men and the Boatwrights warily. A couple of horsebackers were riding in from the east — three men in rough trail garb — and they were slowing their horses as they came within fifty yards of the bank, staring stiffly, curiously over the bobbing heads of their ranch ponies.

Hawk saw Reb Winter standing out front of the Venus House, near the ghostly-looking gallows, and he beckoned the young man. Reb tramped toward him, grinning shyly but also with boyish delight at the dead man as he approached.

"That was sure some fine shootin', Gid!"

Hawk locked the sixteen-shooter's loading tube as he continued to gaze around at the milling crowd, a low hum rising along both sides of the street as the growing nighttime crowd began discussing the recent robbery attempt and shootings.

"Reb, will you take these men over to the undertaker?" He glanced up the street, in the direction of the sprawling, stable-like shack hunched beneath a large sign announcing HY BOOKER, BLACKSMITH AND UNDERTAKING SERVICES. "Here's for your trouble." He flipped the big lad a double eagle. "Tell Booker that in return for burying these fellas, he can have their horses and guns and other valuables on their persons. Any other valuable besides stolen money, that is."

As Reb eagerly set to work dragging the broad-chested man eastward by his ankles, Hawk lowered his rifle and started up the street.

"Look here!"

Boatwright was striding up behind Hawk while a woman who'd probably been shopping in the ladies hat shop just east of the bank tended his daughter. Hawk turned sideways as the rancher in the long buffalo coat stopped before him. He was nearly as tall as Hawk, and the handlebar mustache gave him a regal flourish.

He squinted his eyes angrily, his leathery cheeks flushed with fury.

"Who in the hell are you, and what right do you think you have to endanger my daughter's life like that?"

"I didn't endanger it, Mr. Boatwright," Hawk said, digging behind his sheepskin vest for a cheroot. He canted his head toward the man Reb was dragging away. "He did. I saved it. Don't bother thanking me, though. Comes with the territory."

Hawk bit off the end of his cigar and strode away toward the sheriff's office, ignoring all the lingering gazes being cast his way from up and down both sides of the broad main street.

The sun dropped behind the Wind River and Medicine Bow Mountains, and the velvet night spread across the sage- and rabbit-brush-carpeted knolls and low mesas of the broad valley in which Trinity nestled.

The pianos in the town's saloons and rustic fleshpots pattered noisily, as though in accompaniment to the coyotes yipping from the surrounding, star-dusted hills. Traffic on the street was confined mainly to foot traffic, though horseback riders came and went infrequently.

Hawk had set a hide-bottom chair on the jailhouse's gallery, and he sat out there now, bundled in his three-point capote against the descending, high-country cold. He had a fire going in the office's wood stove, and a pot of coffee chugged away atop it — fuel for his night's vigil over the town. Until he got Trinity back on its leash, he wouldn't be getting much sleep.

That was all right. He didn't need much sleep these days. . . .

He held his rifle across his knees in his gloved hands as he sat kicked back in the chair, boots crossed on the gallery's spindly pole rail. A tall, thin-shouldered man came down the street from his right, angling toward the whorehouse that called itself the Venus, where a thin crowd of men had been coming and going since sundown. There were a couple of other pleasure parlors in Trinity, but the Venus seemed to be doing the best business this evening.

Men looked at him askance as they came and went, probably wondering who the man was sitting on the jailhouse porch with a rifle in his lap. Most probably knew and had probably heard about the dance out front of the bank earlier, as well. Maybe that's why he hadn't heard any signs of trouble in town.

At least, not yet. The night was still young. And the liquor and women would flow until well after midnight. . . .

As the tall man passed the jailhouse and approached the Venus, the front of which was partly obscured by the gallows standing between it and the sheriff's office — a great platform sitting there darkly, ominously, as if in silent testimony to Hawk's presence here — a couple of the shadows standing around outside the place said, "Evenin', Reverend."

Another man said, "You sure you wanna go in there, Reverend? Why don't you go on home? Just don't seem right. . . ."

"Get out of my way!" boomed a stentorian voice.

The Venus's front door opened, showing a wedge of orange lamplight and causing the sounds of the piano being played inside to grow momentarily louder before it closed. A couple of the men standing outside chuckled but mostly without mirth, it seemed.

Shambling footsteps sounded to Hawk's left. Tightening his grip on the Henry, he glanced in that direction to see a bulky figure in a flat hat moving toward him along the various boardwalks lining the north side of Trinity Street. He knew Reb Winter's gait well enough to know that it was the young handyman approaching now, holding something before him in his hands.

"Evenin', Gid."

"Reb, how you doin' this evening?"

"Oh, all right, I reckon," the young man said, having as much trouble as usual in getting the words out. "I brought you a plate of food from the Poudre River House. Seen you sittin' out here, and figured you was gettin' hungry."

"That I am, Reb." Hawk reached behind him to lean his rifle against the front wall of the jailhouse, then accepted the oilcloth-covered plate that the big man held toward him. "Much obliged. What do I owe you?"

"Mr. Lundy said it's on him. Sort of a welcome-to-Trinity present, I reckon. He done heard about what you did out front of the bank, and I reckon he's one of them who's right happy we finally have us a lawman who'll brook no bullshit from the likes of the Jethro Mays bunch."

Reb chuckled with childish glee.

"Mays was the name, huh?"

Reb nodded. "They used to do a lot of thievin' in this area, but Sheriff Stanley and his deputy, Freeman, run 'em out. They musta heard Stanley was dead. . . ." He chuckled again. "But hadn't heard he'd been replaced yet."

Hawk wondered if they *had* heard that Stanley had been replaced, and hired Harvin to kill his replacement before he got to town. He'd likely never know the answer to the question, however, so he let it go.

"You liked Stanley, Jed?" Hawk asked as he dug into the food.

Reb nodded. "He was a good man. Fair and honest. Sure wish he coulda run the Tierneys outta the county, like he run the Mays Bunch out." The big younker ran a hand across his nose then gestured at the half-open door. "You want me to pour you a cup of coffee to go with that?"

Hawk nodded as he swallowed another bite of the venison liver and onions. "I'd be right obliged."

When Reb had brought Hawk his coffee, he excused himself, saying he had to get back to the hotel where Mr. Lundy was butchering out a fresh-killed antelope for stew the next day.

Hawk thanked the boy again for the food and coffee, and when Reb had lumbered off, Hawk continued to shovel the succulent liver into his mouth. He didn't care for beef liver, but he loved the taste of fresh venison, especially when it was only lightly fried in butter and smothered in onions and fried potatoes, like it was here.

He'd finished his meal and taken his plate into the office, where he'd refilled his coffee cup, then sat back down again in his porch chair. He'd make a few rounds again soon, but he'd fortify himself with another cup of the piping-hot coffee first.

Reaching into his shirt for a half-smoked cigar, he froze the movement when he saw a dark-clad figure moving toward him from the other side of the street. The figure approached the porch, and Hawk saw the mass of auburn hair tilt back as she lifted her head.

The light from the doorway behind him showed a young woman in her early twenties with a blanket wrapped around her shoulders. The bottom of the blanket flapped around a pair of nice, bare legs and the incongruous tops of brown stockmen's boots. He could tell that her shoulders were bare and that beneath the blanket she was wearing little more than a pink corset and camisole edged in black lace.

She stopped at the bottom of the steps, set a boot heel on the bottom step, and lifted a smoldering quirley to her lips, sucking in a lungful of tobacco smoke. She seemed nervous as she stared eastward along Trinity Street, which had become lit with clumps of burning oil pots and torches suspended from poles and awning posts.

"Can I help you, miss?" Hawk said, pulling the cigar from his shirt pocket and sticking it into his mouth.

The girl turned toward him and blew a long plume of smoke at him. She had a long face with a straight, clean nose and the discerning, faintly jaded eyes of a working girl. Her hair, which appeared naturally curly, tumbled down around her shoulders. The light from inside the sheriff's office revealed dark brown eyes and a mole on the girl's dimpled chin.

"Maybe," she said, showing a crooked front tooth. "Maybe not." She sucked the quirley again quickly and blew the smoke out. "I heard what you did over to the bank earlier."

Hawk stared at her, waiting, scratching a lucifer to life on his right-side holster.

"Look," she said, "I heard over at the Venus, where I *work,*" she emphasized, rolling her eyes, "who you are. Some lawman gone rogue. And that you're right handy with a gun. I also heard you're our new sheriff. Well, I got a favor to ask."

14.
A Favor

The girl from the Venus stared up at Hawk, awaiting some response.

Hawk drew on the cigar, blew smoke out over his boots crossed on the pole rail. "I'll help if I can, miss. What do you want me to do?"

"My friend Claire works over at the Venus with me. It was her brother, Echo Lang, who Brazos Tierney and his pals murdered that night Stanley arrested 'em. While they was still passed out. Anyway, Claire thinks Brazos is gonna come in and kill her. And I'd really, really appreciate it if you'd go over there and try to reassure her that you won't let him do that." She blinked and stared at Hawk with subtle beseeching. "And that you're gonna go out there to his pa's ranch and kill the son of a bitch."

"I didn't say I was gonna go out there and kill the son of a bitch," Hawk said, staring at his cigar coal. "What I intend to do,

Miss . . ."

"Call me Cassidy."

"What I intend to do, Miss Cassidy, is fulfill Sheriff Stanley's wishes of bringing him in here to Trinity and to hang him from that gallows that was constructed just for him and his pals Hostetler and 'One-Eye' McGee."

"I don't understand," Cassidy said, shaking her head. "Why don't you just kill 'em?"

Yes, why? Hawk thought vaguely. That's what he would have done under normal circumstances. But he seemed to have tucked the young sheriff Stanley and the man's wife and child into a special, sweet place in his otherwise dark heart. And despite his doubts that the law had much practical application out here on the wild frontier, he felt a deep-seated urge to honor the man's memory as well as that of his family by fulfilling Stanley's desire to hang Tierney and friends legally.

Hawk would finish the job that Stanley had started, in Stanley's honor, though he had no illusions that he could really bring peace to the area without employing his usual, more practical methods.

"Rest assured, Miss Cassidy, Brazos Tierney will hang. And he will cause no more trouble for you or your friend Claire or anyone else around Trinity."

"Yeah, well, would you mind telling that to Claire?"

Hawk frowned at her curiously.

"You see, Claire's locked herself in her room." Cassidy tossed her head to indicate the Venus on the other side of the street. "With a bottle, an opium pipe, and a gun. She won't come out. Afraid Brazos'll get her."

"Why is she so certain Brazos has it in for her?"

"Because when Stanley was getting ready to hang Brazos and his pards, she yelled somethin' smart at him from the balcony up yonder. You shoulda seen the look he gave her."

Cassidy slowly shook her head and took another quick puff off her cigarette. "After Brazos gives someone that look — that marble-cold, dead-eyed look — why, their life ain't worth a pound of dried mule shit. Besides, he never did like Claire. Always had it in for her and Echo. Said they was uppity. Always said he was gonna kill 'em both one day." Cassidy gave a fateful snort. "Well, one down . . ."

Hawk stared out over his boots at the Venus, the front of which was now lit by several flares and a couple of burning oil pots on the second-floor balcony. The buzz of male conversation rose from the front stoop, and Hawk could see the hatted silhouettes there, here and there the umber glow of a drawn cigarette.

Hawk dropped his boots down off the porch rail. "Reckon this would be as good a time as any to start introducing myself around town." He gained his feet and shouldered his rifle, rolling his cigar to one corner of his mouth. "Lead the way, Miss Cassidy."

"Sure do appreciate it, Mr. Hawk." Cassidy turned, and holding her blanket closed across her bosom, began retracing her steps toward the whorehouse. "Mrs. Ferrigno's a right patient lady, but I'm afraid she's fixin' to give Claire the boot, since she ain't been bringin' in any money for nigh on two weeks now."

Hawk followed Cassidy around behind the gallows. As he approached the Venus's porch, which was missing several planks and generally sat askew on its low stone pilings, the three men there broke their conversation off abruptly.

Cassidy turned the knob of the front door and grunted as she shouldered the door open, its bottom raking across the warped pine puncheons, and a moment later Hawk found himself in the whorehouse's dingy foyer. He could hear conversation through the cracked plaster walls around him, smell tobacco smoke and liquor as well as the cloying sweet aromas of marijuana and opium.

"This way, Mr. Hawk."

Cassidy hung her blanket on a hook near the door — the heat of the place was almost stifling, likely so the girls could run around half-clad without catching colds — and started up the stairs at the far end of the hall. Cassidy's dress was short, with accordion pleats and paper flowers sewn into the hem, her legs long and well-turned.

They were halfway up the stairs when Hawk heard a loud pounding, and a woman's husky voice yelled, "Claire, goddamnit. I'm tired o' this shit! You open up this door right now. You got a job to do, girl!"

Hawk followed Cassidy down the musty second-floor hall. The air here was a potpourri of perfume, tobacco, and strong tanglefoot, as it was downstairs, but up here there was also the unmistakable musk of sweat and sex. A door opened to Hawk's left, and a man stepped out awkwardly, nearly running into the Rogue Lawman. Hawk's gaze met that of Carson Tarwater, and the latter man's lips spread in a bemused smile, his eyes glassy.

"Ah, I see our new sheriff has finally made his way over to the best whorehouse in town." Tarwater glanced at Cassidy. "And you couldn't have chosen a more delightful hostess, Mr. Hawk."

Hawk glanced at the girl, who stood with one hand on her hip, smiling proudly. "He ain't here for business, Mr. Tarwater. At least, right now he ain't."

The girl raked a quick, coolly appraising glance up and down Hawk's tall, lean frame, then jerked her thumb over her shoulder, toward a door at which a heavyset woman in a nondescript sack dress stood, leaning against the wall with a look of disgust on her pinched, haggard face. "The new sheriff's come to see if he can't coax Claire out of her room."

"Good luck," Tarwater said. "I doubt that girl's going anywhere until she sees first hand the bone-cold, limp-dicked carcass of Brazos Tierney." The councilman pinched his hat brim to Hawk and Cassidy. "Good night." He waved at the heavyset woman. " 'Night, Mrs. Ferrigno!"

"Good night, Mr. Tarwater. Hope you had a good time."

Tarwater shuffled down the hall and started limping down the stairs, his voice echoing in the narrow stairwell as he replied, "Beats the hell out of marriage — I'll guarantee you that!" He laughed drunkenly as his wooden foot clomped on the steps.

Hawk followed Cassidy over to the door where Mrs. Ferrigno stood. The woman extended a plump hand with short, pudgy fingers bulky with cheap rings. "I'm the head o' this household, Mr. Hawk. Thanks for killin' Jethro Mays. My whole life savings resides in that bank, and I intend to retire in another year or two and live the good life in San Francisco. As a society woman!" She laughed raspily, then canted her head toward the closed door. "Think you can get her outta there? Claire's my best girl, but I don't run a hotel for nonworking whores."

"Let me give it a shot." Hawk stepped up to the door, tapped his knuckles against the center panel. "Miss Claire? It's Gideon Hawk, the new sheriff of Medicine Bow County. Look, I know that Brazos Tierney has his sights set on you, but I want you to know you have nothing to fear. Tierney is finished."

From behind the door, Hawk heard a gasp. There was the low squawk of a bedspring, a light tread on the floor. The lock clicked and the door opened a foot. A girl whose head came up to the center of Hawk's chest stared up at him through the gap.

"You're him?" Her eyes were wide, eager, expectant. *"Him?"* She thrust an open magazine up against the gap in the door. "The Rogue Lawman who deals justice throughout the West with blood and thunder? Who stops thieves, killers, and rapists cold with hot lead fired from the barrels of his Colt .45s?"

Hawk looked at the magazine, saw an inked sketch of a black-clad man on horseback wearing a flat-brimmed black hat very much like Hawk's, firing a rifle from his shoulder at three ugly hombres firing back at him from behind rocks and a tree stump. The rider's face was broad and determined, teeth gritted, while the men who were obviously owlhoots looked horrified and desperate.

"Only one Colt," Hawk said. "And it's a .44, not a .45. The other's a .44 Russian made by Smith & Wesson. I've always preferred a .44 to a .45 though the .45 sounds better to the penny-dreadful scribes, I reckon."

The petite blond girl, clad in a stained flannel housecoat and pink slippers, stared through the gap at him. "You *are* him."

"It's him, Claire," said Cassidy. "He's

gonna kick Brazos Tierney out with a shovel. Same with his old man and the whole rest of his gang. You got nothin' to worry about, sister. Now, will you please go back to work?"

"So you don't get thrown out!" added Mrs. Ferrigno forcefully.

Claire continued to stare up at Hawk in hushed awe.

"You really think you can handle all them by yourself?" she asked.

Hawk glanced at the illustrated magazine hanging limp now in her hand. "You've read of my exploits," he growled, narrowing one eye with the steely menace of his magazine likeness. "What do you think?"

Slowly, the girl's lips spread. The smile grew until it reached her blue eyes, and they danced in the light from the hall's two bracket lamps.

She shuttled her gaze to Cassidy and Mrs. Ferrigno flanking Hawk. "I'll come out when Hy Booker's got him in a pine box and ready to plant. Anybody tries to enter this room till then" — she held up a pearl-gripped, .36-caliber pocket pistol with her other hand and narrowed her resolute eyes — "gets a gutful of this!"

With that, she slammed the door. The locking bolt clicked home.

"Goddamnit, Claire!" roared Mrs. Ferrigno.

Hawk removed the cheroot from his teeth and turned to the madam. "Not to worry," he said, shouldering his Henry. "I'll have her out of there soon."

Both women stared up at Hawk with wide-eyed expectation.

"You promise?" asked the madam.

Hawk nodded and headed off toward the stairs.

Mrs. Ferrigno called behind him. "You want a free poke?"

Hawk stopped and glanced back.

"Cassidy's free at the moment," the madam said.

Cassidy flushed and crossed her arms on her low-cut corset.

Hawk ran his eyes up and down the young girl's exquisite frame. "Got a long night ahead," he said, returning the cheroot to his mouth. "Maybe some other time."

Cassidy lifted her eyes to his, her thin brows beetled indignantly.

Hawk headed on down the stairs.

15.
A Visit with the Stanley Family

You had to walk up the side of a low, tabletop mesa to reach the cemetery sprawled amongst cedars and three tall firs lined up on the other side of a picket fence badly in need of fresh paint. Once inside the gate that hung askew from a single rusty hinge, it wasn't hard to locate the Stanley family's final resting place.

They were the three freshest graves, mounded with iron-red dirt and chunks of sandstone to discourage predators. Two large mounds on either side of a smaller mound. The headstone announced STANLEY in a broad arc, with the names AARON, JANELLE, and LITTLE JAKE below. Their birth and death dates had also been chipped into the stone, the sheriff having died two days before his wife and their fifteen-month-old baby.

Someone had ringed the Stanley family plot, which was fronted with rabbitbrush and a single mountain sage plant, with fist-sized rocks. Hawk stepped over this make-shift border to set a handful of paper flowers he'd purchased earlier from the Trinity Mercantile Company on the baby's grave. He stepped back then and folded his hands across his cartridge belt, but he'd be damned, try as he might, if he could conjure a single prayer.

Oh, the remembered words were there, but when he tried to bring them up from his chest they turned to a chalky powder on the back of his tongue. Staring down at Jake's grave, he remembered his own boy. His heart swelled and a knot formed in his throat, but he bit back the emotion that threatened to overcome him, and set his hat on his head.

"I'll get 'em" were the only words he could find, and he was almost surprised to hear even those escape his lips as he turned away and adjusted his hat against the angle of the rising sun.

It was a cold morning. His breath frosted in front of his face, lit by the golden light of late dawn.

He spied movement out the corner of his right eye, and he turned to see a dark figure slumped beside a rock on the west side of the boneyard. A large, gnarled, pale hand reached out from under a ratty brown blanket for a whiskey bottle standing on a flat rock. Hawk couldn't see the man's face, but he saw that the gent was wearing black broadcloth trousers and side-button half boots. The trousers were of good quality, but they were stained and torn, revealing washworn, white balbriggans underneath.

The man grunted and grumbled as the hand slid out to the edge of his reach, a good two feet from the bottle.

Hawk walked across the graveyard, meandering around the rock-mounded graves and tufts of rabbitbrush until he stood over the tall, thin man sprawled on his side next to the boulder. The man's knees were drawn partway up to his chest. He had a long, cadaverous face and mussed iron-gray hair and sideburns, and he was squeezing his eyes closed in frustration as he continued to reach for the bottle in his semi-sleep.

Hawk squatted beside the man, grabbed the bottle off the rock, and sniffed the lip. He made a face as the stench of the coffin varnish, likely brewed behind one of Trinity's less reputable saloons with a good dose of strychnine and rattlesnake venom, assaulted his nostrils and burned his lungs.

"Here you go," Hawk said, setting the bottle down beside the large hand whose blue veins bulged like knotted rivers on a relief map. "Nothing like a little hair of the dog."

The man grunted, turned his head slightly upward, and half opened one eye. "Who in the devil's blue hell are you?"

"Hawk. You stay out here all night, Reverend?" He saw the frayed, soiled paper collar around the man's thin turkey neck, beneath the collar of a dark blue dress coat.

The preacher looked around briefly, trying to open a second eye. Since the light was obviously too painful for his whiskey-battered brain, he gave up on the second eye and trained the half-open other one on Hawk, growling from deep in his rheumy chest, "What's it to you?"

"Seems to me it'd be warmer in the parsonage."

Hawk fished around in his brain for the man's handle. Recalling the name and remembering seeing the sky pilot heading for the Venus the night before, on what was apparently one of a series of brothel rounds for the Lutheran minister, he added, "Don't you think you'd be better off in your own bed, Pastor Hawthorne?"

The reverend scowled at the interloper, rose onto an elbow, poked the lip of the bottle between his own lips, and took a long pull. The whiskey bubble jerked back and forth, making gurgling sounds.

Lowering the bottle once more, the man gave a loud, liquid sigh and smacked his lips.

"Whoever the hell you are, kindly vamoose and let a man sleep!" The man set the bottle down on the rock then rested his head on his arm and closed his eye, wriggling around as though to make himself more comfortable against the frosty earth.

Hawk gave a fateful chuff as he straightened. When the man froze to death out here one of these nights, if he made sleeping in the graveyard a habit, the undertaker wouldn't have far to carry him. Hawk moved off through the graves once more and headed on back down the side of the mesa via the unkempt, switchbacking trail.

He was rounding a protruding shoulder of the formation when he saw Reb Winter straddling a sorrel gelding near where Hawk had tied his grulla to an aspen branch. The young man wore a scarf under a battered, floppy-brimmed hat, and a blue wool coat too tight across the chest and shoulders. The scarf covered his ears and was tied beneath his chin.

An old Springfield rifle hung from his saddle horn by a braided rawhide lanyard.

Lifting his eyes to Hawk, Reb ran a mittened hand across his nose and grinned sheepishly.

The Rogue Lawman stopped. "What're you doing here?"

Reb reached down to pat the stock of the Springfield hanging down over his right stirrup fender. "I come heeled in order to give ye a hand, Gid."

"I don't think so."

"Huh?"

Hawk continued on down the side of the mesa. "Go on home, Reb. I appreciate the offer, but I ride alone." He'd had Reb give him directions to the Two Troughs Ranch while enjoying flapjacks and ham in the Poudre River House's dining room before sunup. "I done told you that already."

"Ah, come on, Gid. I'll be your deputy!"

Hawk grabbed his reins off the aspen and swung into the leather. "Like I said, boy — I appreciate the offer." He gave the rawboned young man a hard, uncompromising look.

"Ah, shit!" Reb punched his saddle horn. "You think I'm a dimwit, just like everyone else around Trinity. But just cause I can't speak as good as most folks don't mean I'm softheaded. With my daddy's old Springfield, I can shoot the eye out of a runnin' jack at a hundred yards!"

It took nearly a full minute for Reb to get all that out, and he basted the mane of his sorrel with spittle while doing it.

Finally, he punched his saddle horn once again and neck reined the horse around. "Everyone thinks ole Reb's only good fer runnin' groceries or splittin' wood — that's what they think of ole Reb!" he bellowed, booting the sorrel into a lunging lope toward Trinity bathed in westward-slanting shadows and sparkling morning sunshine, smoke from breakfast fires rising and flattening out over the rooftops.

Hawk watched Reb's broad back grow small as the younker loped angrily back to town, sulking. Hawk liked the kid, and he hadn't meant to hurt his feelings, but he didn't want to put him in harm's way. It was a crazy, perilous trail the Rogue Lawman rode, and he could grab the cat's wrong end just any old time. He didn't want to take anyone else with him when he saddled that cloud.

He reined the grulla around and clucked it east, tracing a broad circle around the outskirts of Trinity.

The only person who knew that he was heading out to Two Troughs today was Reb, and the boy had vowed his silence. Hawk knew that Reb would keep his word in spite of his bluster. The ladies at the Venus knew that Hawk would be handling Tierney's men soon, but they didn't know exactly when. He didn't want anyone who might be in league with the outlaws spilling the beans and alerting them to Hawk's visit.

He was only one man against a dozen or more seasoned killers, and he wanted the element of surprise on his side of the table. Of course, he wasn't sure what he was going to do with it. He figured he'd come up with something by the time he'd reached the outlaw lair.

He usually did.

East of Trinity he branched northward on a secondary trail, mostly a horse trail with wagon furrows marking the brittle yellow grass and sage on either side of it. He rode up and over several ridges before, with the sun climbing and gaining intensity, he had to stop and remove his three-point capote, which he wrapped around the soogan he'd tied behind his saddle.

He let the grulla drink at a narrow creek winding around the base of a high, rock-strewn ridge wall, and he himself sipped the tepid water from his canteen, then continued on into country gradually growing higher and more rugged, with deep canyons slashing the land and pine-covered mesas tilting toward him like giant, broken tables.

Old snowdrifts still patched the north sides of slopes. In the brassy sunshine, he could hear the glassy murmur of melting water seeping downhill.

Here and there he spied the pale blue of a crocus — the high country's first spring wildflower — amidst the dull browns of bromegrass and needle grass. Robins flitted amongst cedars and pines. Squirrels chitted. Hawks gave their ratcheting cries.

As Hawk rode up a mountain shoulder, he caught a whiff of wood smoke and checked the grulla down abruptly. From just beyond a rise about fifty yards ahead, at the edge of a fir forest, gray smoke unfurled skyward. Hawk slid the Henry from its saddle boot and heeled the grulla ahead, resting the rifle across his saddlebows and lifting his head to see over the rise as he approached it.

When he'd ridden a ways up the incline, he checked the grulla down once more, and furled his brows, his green eyes going hard and dark as he raked his gaze across the small, makeshift day camp before him. Cursing to himself, he gigged the grulla up and over the rise and reined the horse to a halt near the cream stallion with charcoal markings on its rump tethered to a fir branch just beyond the fire.

The horse's fawn-colored saddle sat loosely on its back, the latigo strap dangling. The horse's bridle bit was slipped so it could graze freely on the bluestem that was greening up around it.

Hawk pointed the rifle out from his right thigh. "Funny how you always seem to know where I'm headed. Even funnier how you always seem to get there first."

"Coffee?" Saradee lifted the steaming tin cup in her gloved hand and grinned over the brim.

"What're you doing here?"

The blonde leaned back against the deadfall fir behind her, drawing her shoulders in and pushing her breasts out until they audibly strained the rawhide drawstrings of the black leather vest she wore. It seemed to be all she wore on her high-busted torso. Her arms were long, slender, lightly muscled and slightly tanned, one wrist adorned with braided, henna-dyed leather.

"Oh, I don't know." She sighed, poking her hat brim back off her forehead and blowing ripples on the surface of her coffee. "I guess I just had the urge to join you on a good, old-fashioned rapscallion hunt."

She folded her pink lips over the lip of the

cup, drew a sip of the hot liquid into her mouth, and swallowed, canting her head to meet Hawk's disapproving gaze.

"I don't need any help."

"I disagree, lover. If it's Blue and Brazos Tierney you're after, you're probably gonna need a whole cavalry. You really oughta look a little more grateful that you at least have me on your side." She hiked a shoulder. "I figure if we're gonna die, we might as well die together."

She smiled, white teeth flashing in the sunshine.

Hawk caressed the Henry's trigger with his index finger. "Why do you taunt me like this?"

"Like what?"

"Like followin' me around, showin' up on my trail, showin' up *in my hotel rooms.*" Hawk's voice was the growl of an enraged, frustrated dog. "Christ, I had my fill of you in Arizona."

"Careful not to hurt my feelings, lover."

"What's it gonna take to get shed of you once and for all?"

"Oh, I don't know," Saradee said with her maddening insouciance. "If you'd hang around a while, I'd probably get tired of you and ride off on my own, sooner or later. Maybe if you just professed your love for me . . ." Her eyes turned smoky and a slight flush rose in her exquisite, lightly tanned cheeks.

The wind tusseled her hair, which hung straight down her shoulders to caress her breasts bulging at the outside edges of her vest. Hawk felt the old pull of her deep in his belly, and he turned away in the old, familiar revulsion, gritting his teeth.

"Goddamn you, Saradee."

"He's already damned us both, lover." She paused. When she spoke again, it was in a different tone altogether. "And you know what else?"

Hawk turned his head to her, frowning curiously. She was staring over his right shoulder, beyond the valley directly behind him and into the next valley over, beyond a low, pine-stippled rimrock. "I think three of Tierney's riders are slipping past you. Headin' to town."

Hawk reined his horse around and reached into his saddlebags for his spyglass. Wrapping his reins around his saddle horn, he raised the telescoping glass and adjusted the focus.

Gradually, three riders swam up out of the murk and into his sphere of magnified vision. He couldn't see much, as the three were a long ways off, but he could see sunlight winking off spurs and hardware.

His heart thudded in his temples.

He was close to Two Troughs. Which meant those riders were likely Tierney's men. Cold fingertips walked up and down the Rogue Lawman's spine when he considered the possibility that one of those riders could be Brazos Tierney himself.

And that all three could be the men he was hunting. . . .

Heading for the Venus.

"Shit!"

At the same time that he reached back to drop the spyglass back into his saddlebag pouch, he rammed his heels into the grulla's flanks, galloping back in the direction from which he'd come.

"Hold on, lover," Saradee yelled behind him, lurching to her feet and kicking dirt on her coffee fire. "You're gonna need help! Wait for me!"

16.
"Hold on — I Ain't Finished Yet"

Hawk saw black smoke rising from the center of town and unfurling above the rooftops bathed in midday sunshine, and his heart leapt into his throat.

But then, as he continued urging the grulla ahead, he saw that no buildings were burning. The flames seemed isolated — maybe a large trash fire — though that didn't mean they'd stay that way. He rode on into town, heading west along Wyoming Street where people stood on the boardwalks abutting both sides of the trace, switching their wary gazes from him to the gallows between the sheriff's office and the Venus whorehouse, and back again.

Hawk checked his grulla down and stared hard-jawed at the gallows cloaked in a shimmering veil of orange, leaping flames. As he gigged the reluctant horse ahead, he could feel the flames and hear the resin popping and sizzling in the green lumber, hear the frenetic sounds of the hungry fire eating away at the wood. Black smoke rose and whipped like flags in a heavy wind. Horses tethered at the hitch racks fronting the Venus sidestepped and jerked against their reins, casting fearful glances at the burning platform behind them.

Hawk saw Mayor Pennybacker and Councilman Learner standing on a nearby street corner, both men looking grim. The Rogue Lawman rode over, shucked his repeater from his rifle boot, and snarled, "What the hell are you standing there for? Have a bucket brigade ready in case that fire spreads."

He swung down from his saddle and dropped his reins in the street. Fast hooves thudded, and he turned to see Saradee trotting up behind him, her white stallion fighting the bit and tossing its head at the conflagration. Her eyes bored into the fire and danced with glee. She shook her head like a hot-blooded filly looking for a fight, and chuckled.

"You really can't blame them, can you? I'm sure the sight of that hangin' platform brought back many unpleasant memories."

"You still here?" Hawk racked a live round into the Henry's chamber and strode on up the steps of the Venus's front porch. He pushed inside and stopped in the dingy foyer as Mrs. Ferrigno moved down the stairs ahead of him, grunting and muttering, her eyes bright with fear and fury. In her arms was Cassidy, head lolling from side to side. The brunette had a split lip and a cut above her right eye, which was swelling up and turning purple.

The rotund madam in a sloppy, pink dress dropped down into the foyer, and her jaws were hard as, sidling past Hawk, her eyes bored into him. "I thought you was gonna take that killer down, Mr. Hawk. Your promise to Claire was as empty as a tin rain barrel in the Arizona desert."

She spat the last two words at him harshly then continued out the door. Saradee held the door for the woman. When Mrs. Ferrigno was gone, likely heading for the doctor's, the blond pistolera came in and stood behind Hawk. The Rogue Lawman had stopped at a doorway in the foyer's right wall. In the papered room beyond, five men sat around a round table.

Four of the men Hawk did not recognize, but one was Reverend Hawthorne, who'd apparently roused himself from the cemetery for a card game in the whorehouse. Two of the other four fit the descriptions of "One-Eye" Willie McGee and J. T.

Hostetler. Willie McGee, who wore a black eye patch and needed a shave, plucked a brown paper cigarette from his snaggly teeth to bark, "Reverend, if you got that ace o' diamonds I been lookin' for, I'm gonna be one piss-burned son of a bitch!"

"Maybe won't toss any more donations into the collection plate, eh, Willie?" said the man sitting to McGee's right with a laugh, his back to Hawk, a battered black hat tipped back on his thin, sandy hair. He wore leggings and two bowie knives and two holstered pistols visible from the Rogue Lawman's angle.

Reverend Hawthorne studied his cards and moved his lips as though oblivious to the high jinx of the two hard cases. The other two cardplayers, townsmen by their grooming and dress, fidgeted nervously in their chairs and laughed along with the Two Troughs riders though their hearts obviously weren't in the joking.

Hawk glanced at Saradee. "Keep those two here. Don't kill 'em."

"But they need it so bad," she complained, staring at the two in question.

Hefting his Henry, Hawk took the stairs two steps at a time to the second story and lightened his stride as he moved down the hall, looking around, half expecting to see

Claire out here somewhere, dead. The hall was empty, however, and flooded with shadows in spite of the window at the far end. No candles were lit.

Hawk heard a man grunting, saw Claire's door standing partway open, the lock torn out of the frame from which splinters hung. The door itself was cracked down the middle and showed the indentation of a man's spurred boot heel.

The grunts continued, as did the squawks of rusty bedsprings, the thrashing of a corn-husk mattress. A girl sobbed. Hawk used the barrel of his Henry to nudge the door open wider and stepped into the room.

The bed was against the right wall. A naked man was on the bed, toiling away between a naked girl's spread knees. Hawk couldn't see either of their faces, but he knew who they were.

Moving closer, Hawk saw Claire lying with her head back against her pillow, squeezing her eyes closed against the pain of the man's savage hip thrusts. Like Cassidy, the girl had a split lip, and both her eyes were turning a sickly yellow-purple. She was naked except for a camisole bunched around her waist beneath her pale breasts.

Brazos Tierney's fringed, deerskin breeches were bunched down around his boots, the steel-tipped toes of which hung over the end of the bed as the man thrust his hips against the sobbing, moaning girl.

Suddenly, Tierney stopped thrusting. He stared down at Claire. He was a big, savage-looking man with knife scars on his pasty white back and thick shoulders. His short, brown hair was sweat-matted close to his skull, showing the lines of his funnel-brimmed hat, which was on the floor near Hawk's feet.

Brazos turned his broad, square head toward Hawk. Long sideburns ran down nearly to his mouth corners. His eyes were even more savage than the rest of him. They were the eyes of a soulless, murdering brute. His fat upper lip curled in a sneer, and then the gray-yellow eyes moved to the rifle in Hawk's hands.

Hawk stared grimly down at the man, flexing his fingers against the Henry's fore- and rear stocks. It took a lot of control not to turn the barrel toward the man's face and pull the trigger. Brazos seemed about to say something, but then the sneer dwindled from his chapped, wet lips as his eyes met Hawk's and apparently read the bitterness there — the raw red rage and barely bridled fury.

"Hold on." Brazos swallowed, gestured at

the girl lying beneath him and now staring up at Hawk, as well, beseeching in her pain-racked eyes. "I ain't finished yet."

Hawk took one lunging step toward the bed, dropping the Henry's rear stock and gritting his teeth savagely as he swung the stock's brass butt plate up until it smacked resolutely against the underside of Brazos's chin. The outlaw's jaws snapped together violently, making a sound like a branch being broken over a knee, and there followed the thuds of the man's muscular body bouncing off the wall on the other side of the bed and then dropping to the floor at the base of it, out of sight.

Hawk glanced at Claire. She was up on her elbows, curling one knee over her other leg and looking down at Brazos, still sobbing — worried, frightened. Her tangled hair obscured her face, blood trickling from her lip and down her chin.

Hawk ran a hand down his face in frustration. "Claire, I'm sorry."

The girl closed her hand over her mouth then turned onto her side, away from Hawk, and drew her knees toward her bare breasts. Hawk drew the quilts and sheets up to her shoulders. He'd heard heavy footsteps in the hall, and he turned now to see Reb Winter looking shyly in at him, the boy's watch cap in his hands.

Softly, he said, "Hiya, Gid . . ."

Hawk tossed his head toward the wall to his left. "Can you get someone to haul him over to the jail? Don't worry about clothing him first." He glanced over his shoulder at Claire, recrimination racking him for not being here when Brazos rode into town and sparing the girl the outlaw's abuse.

Biting back a curse, he added to Reb, "It's a warm day."

"I'll get him over there, Gid."

Hawk left the room and went downstairs, hearing a man's groans and angry curses emanating from the side of the house in which the other two hard cases had been playing cards. He walked past three frightened-looking, scantily clad whores who hurried up the stairs behind him to see to Claire.

Hawk looked into the room that served as a formal parlor and gambling den, where Saradee was bent over the outlaw J. T. Hostetler. She was on one knee, wrapping a velvet curtain tieback around the outlaw's wrists, which he held behind his back while pressing his belly to the floor.

He held his head up, and blood ran down from a nasty gash in his temple.

"You bitch, oh, you fuckin' bitch!" he

howled. "You're gonna live to regret this — I promise you!"

The reverend and the other card players stood on the far side of the table, loose-jawed with shock as they watched the beautiful blonde in the rough men's trail garb expertly tethering Hostetler's wrists together. The other Two Troughs rider, "One-Eye" Willie McGee, was down on his knees a few feet away, hands crossed over his crotch and bobbing his head and shoulders as though doing Eastern prostrations though it was obvious the man was in dire pain.

Between grunts and groans, he muttered as though in near-silent prayer. Finally, he fell slowly sideways onto his shoulder and drew his knees to his chest, whimpering and clutching his balls.

"Bitch," he grunted, stretching his lips back from chipped, crooked, black-edged teeth. "Ah, Jesus . . . where the blue-blazin' hell'd . . . *she* come from . . . ?"

"You're close," Hawk told him.

Seeing that Saradee had set the men's guns and knives atop a piano bench that stood against the far wall, under an oval-framed photograph of a young Mrs. Ferrigno and a well-dressed man, Hawk looked out one of the front windows. A dozen or so men stood around the burning gallows with water buckets. They swung their heads this way and that to see which way the sparks were drifting. A couple had moved up in front of the brothel and were tossing their bucketfuls of water onto the porch, which meant the wind must be from the north.

A few women had gathered there, as well, having been drawn to the fire, which was always a real threat in a town built from mostly wood that had dried out in the hot sun and arid wind. One of the women was Regan Mitchell. The schoolteacher stood near Mayor Pennybacker and Learner, who'd been joined by Carson Tarwater wearing a green apron over his suit vest. More men came up from the direction of the town's well a block east of the Venus, water sloshing over the rims of the wooden buckets in their hands.

Hawk returned his gaze to Regan. She was staring back at him through the warped window glass. She seemed to have something on her mind.

Hawk turned away from the window. Saradee had one of her pearl-gripped .45s out and was ordering Hostetler to his feet. She'd also tied McGee's hands behind his back, and she ordered him up, too, though he was on his knees again and grinding his forehead into the floor, cursing so loudly that his voice broke on the high notes.

"Don't be a crybaby," Saradee said. "It was a love tap."

McGee lifted his head, and his ruddy face was swollen with red fury in sharp contrast to the black patch over his left eye. "That was no love tap, sugar!"

"Maybe not, but I bet you'll never ogle a girl's tits again so freely."

"I was admirin' 'em!"

Hawk stepped around behind McGee and began hauling him up by his tethered wrists. "Stand up."

"Who the fuck are you?"

"New law in town."

"Who's she?" Hostetler wanted to know.

"My next fever dream!" quipped one of the townsmen who'd been playing cards. He'd retaken his seat with the reverend and the other man, all three of whom now seemed to be enjoying the show before them, the reverend hastily refilling each of their whiskey glasses.

Saradee cowed the man with a look, and Hawk gave One-Eye McGee a shove toward the doorway opening onto the foyer, McGee still groaning and sucking air through his teeth. There were many loud thumps from the hall before him — the sounds of two men carrying something heavy down the creaky stairway. A few seconds later, Hawk saw big Reb Winter backing through the foyer, heading toward the front door, his arms hooked under Brazos Tierney's bare shoulders.

Reb gave Hawk one of his ludicrous grins as he continued shuffling backward, Brazos batting his eyes and spitting bits of broken teeth along with blood over his lips and down his chin and neck and onto the rough wooden floor. When Reb had disappeared from Hawk's view, the man at Brazos's other end appeared — an Indian even bigger than Reb and with a long braid hanging down the back of his striped blanket coat.

He had his hands wrapped around the semiconscious hard case's ankles. He did not turn his head toward Hawk before he passed the doorway and continued on out to the whorehouse's front porch, the screen door slapping shut behind him.

"Holy shit in the nun's privy," remarked One-Eye McGee in a pinched voice. "When Brazos realizes what you done to him, and when his old man Blue Tierney realizes what you done, Mr. Lawdog sir, you're gonna be one sorry badge-totin' son of a bitch!"

Hawk rammed his rifle butt against the

hard case's back, shoving him out into the foyer before prodding him out the front door. Saradee hazed Hostetler along behind Hawk. As the Rogue Lawman followed the two men carrying Brazos at an angle across the street and around the burning gallows, heading for the jailhouse, the flame-engulfed platform gave a loud belching sound, and then it suddenly collapsed in on itself.

The crowd that had gathered around it, water buckets ready, lurched backward. The fire gained intensity as it swallowed up the last of its fuel. Quickly, however, it lost that intensity, and the roar of the blaze dropped several octaves though the green wood continued to pop and snap, sometimes sounding nearly as loud as pistol shots.

Grateful the fire was dying without having involved any of the structures around it, the crowd seemed to give a collective sigh of relief. Hawk nudged One-Eye on ahead, tracing a broad arc around the east side of the fire, but he stopped again when he saw Regan standing a few feet to his right. The teacher had her arms crossed on her breasts, and she switched her troubled, vaguely curious gaze from Hawk to Saradee behind him, and back to Hawk again.

"I was coming to see you, Sheriff," she said tonelessly. "I have something to discuss." She glanced at Brazos Tierney's naked, bloody form being carried on around the gallows by Reb and the Indian, and said crisply, "I see you're indisposed at the moment. It can wait."

Hawk stared at the woman, who now stared back at him. He was aware of Saradee behind him, and having the two women here together made him feel like he had a sticky coating of wheat chaff under his shirt, though he wasn't sure why.

He nodded to the teacher and continued prodding One-Eye around the burning gallows, through the crowd that opened to let Reb and the Indian pass. Hawk glanced behind to see Saradee exchange oblique, vaguely challenging gazes with the teacher, and that itch under Hawk's shirt got worse.

17.
"Dangerous Doings, Mr. Hawk"

Hawk opened the door to the cell block, then stepped back as Reb and the Indian started through the door with Brazos Tierney, who glanced up at Hawk, his mouth and chin bloody, furling his thin, light-brown brows over his deep-set, bleary eyes.

"Hey," he drawled, his words distorted by the blood and broken teeth, lifting a heavy hand to point accusingly at the Rogue Lawman. "You . . . you're the bastard that busted my chops!"

As Reb and the Indian carried him off, his voice echoed around the cavernous, stone-walled cell block. "You just wait till my pa, Ole Blue, hears about this!"

"Yeah," One-Eye McGee said as Hawk shoved him through the door behind Saradee and Hostetler. "You just wait!"

When Hawk had the three men locked up in the same cell nearest the cell block door, Reb and the Indian slouched on out of the jailhouse to go see about the burning gallows. Hawk locked the cell block door. Saradee doffed her hat and ran a gloved hand through her thick, blond hair, tossing it back off her shoulders. "You're gonna need a jailer, lover. Maybe I'd better stick around a while. Think you can keep your hands off me an' act professional . . . while we're on duty?"

"Don't do me any favors." He walked over to the open front door to see how the fire was doing. "But if I told you to stay, you'd go, and the other way around."

"Who is she?"

Arching a brow, Hawk turned to Saradee sitting on a corner of the cluttered desk.

"You know," Saradee said, lifting her chin to indicate the street, then setting her hat back on her head carefully with both hands. "The chestnut-haired beauty who was comin' to pay you a visit." Her blue eyes shone deviously above her long, straight nose.

Hawk turned away from her. "The schoolteacher."

Pretending as though mention of Regan had only just now reminded him that she'd wanted to speak with him, though the teacher had been on his mind since he'd seen her out by the burning gallows, Hawk set his rifle on his shoulder and headed on out the door. "I best see what she wanted. Might be important."

"It might at that," Saradee said in a light mocking tone, adding from the doorway, where she leaned a shoulder against the frame and crossed her arms on her breasts, "Might be real important. But don't you expect me to hold the fort down all day, now — you hear me, Hawk?"

He walked on into the street, looking for Regan amongst the slowly dispersing crowd. Most of the men who'd filled water buckets were now emptying the buckets on the gallows, which had burned down now to a modest-sized bonfire. Mayor Pennybacker broke away from the crowd to approach Hawk, who continued glancing around for the teacher.

"Dangerous doings, Mr. Hawk," the mayor said darkly.

He was flanked by Ben Learner and Romeo Pike. Pike was in sleeve garters and wearing a green visor on his nearly bald head. The Poudre River Transport proprietor looked no happier than the other two councilmen. Carson Tarwater stood a ways off, nearer the gallows, with two empty buckets in his hands as he stood gazing toward Hawk and the other councilmen, a dubious smile jerking at his mouth.

"I'm doing the job you hired me to do, Mr. Mayor," Hawk said. "Too late for cold feet."

The small, wild-haired man dressed in a vanilla-colored hat and suit tossed a beringed hand toward the gallows and then toward the jailhouse behind Hawk, where Saradee still stood nicely decorating the doorframe, smiling and pushing her breasts out.

"This worries me, however. I mean Brazos and his men so brazenly entering town just a few weeks after killing the sheriff and his deputy, not to mention the executioner, and terrorizing poor Hawthorne!"

He shook his head wearily. "Of course, we expected them back. But this . . . their burning the gallows, abusing whores . . ." He shook his head. "Maybe we should at least pass a law against citizens carrying guns in our fair town. Maybe that would deter them."

He, Pike, and Learner eyed Hawk hopefully.

Hawk stopped looking around for Regan, who'd apparently left the street. He frowned at the three men before him and snorted. "You're saying you wanna pass a law, disarming the citizens of Trinity?"

"Well, of course, it wouldn't really affect the law-abiding citizens, Mr. Hawk," said Pike. "But any man who enters our town would have to check his weapons with you or be jailed."

"Yeah," said Learner, nodding forcefully. "Stop the crime before it even gets started."

Hawk scowled at the three men. "You got enough laws, gentlemen. If you pass any more, I think you oughta pass one making it illegal for Trinity's fair citizens to walk around *unarmed.*"

The trio frowned in unison, and dangled their jaws, aghast.

"Otherwise," Hawk added, beginning to step away to continue searching for Regan, "it'll only be men like Brazos who *are* armed, and Trinity's citizens will be harmless as sheep in a den of wolves." He turned back to the mayor. "One more thing, Pennybacker. Send over some carpenters to start rebuilding those gallows. Sheriff Stanley wanted a hanging, and he's gonna get one."

With that, he strode away, leaving the three councilmen frowning incredulously after him.

Finding Regan nowhere around Wyoming Street, Hawk headed for her small, neat frame house on the southern side street that intersected Wyoming near the Poudre River

House. As he started down the side street, he met the Venus's madam, Mrs. Ferrigno, and a gruff-looking, gray-haired gent in a tan suit and slouch hat carrying a black accordion medical kit. The madam gave Hawk a hard look as she elbowed the doctor and said, "That's him," in a taut, clipped tone.

Then the odd-looking pair continued past Hawk and around the corner behind him, while he continued to the house he knew to be Regan Mitchell's. He pushed through the gate in the crisp, white picket fence and mounted the front stoop.

There was a screen door behind which was a storm door with a glass upper panel. Rose-patterned curtains were drawn across the door. Similar curtains were drawn across the two large bay windows to Hawk's right, though they'd been pulled behind a potted plant perched on an ornate wooden stand so the plant could bask in the southern sunshine.

Hawk opened the screen door, the springs whining, and tapped on the varnished-oak inside door, making the pane rattle faintly. To his right, the bay window curtains moved, as though someone had parted them to see out, and then he heard a light tread that grew louder until the locking bolt clicked and the door opened.

Regan frowned. "The new sheriff makes house calls?"

Hawk shrugged. "I thought you might be in school."

"It's Saturday."

Her probing eyes made him uncomfortable.

"You gonna invite me in?"

She dropped her eyes quickly, as though considering the question. Then she drew the door wide and stepped back. "Would you like a cup of tea? I just started a pot for myself." She looked up at him, her eyes still looking mildly stricken, as they had back on Wyoming Street. "Seeing the burning gallows was . . . rather chilling. I saw what Brazos Tierney did to that sporting girl."

"Well, he's under lock and key now."

Regan turned the corners of her mouth down, then abruptly turned away. Hawk doffed his hat and closed the door as she moved into the kitchen on the foyer's left side. "That tea sounds good."

His hat in his hands, he glanced to his right, into a neat little living room, simply but nicely furnished, with stairs running up the near wall into the second half story. There was a sofa, a fainting couch, a few small tables with plants on them, the plant stand fronting the bay windows, and two brocade-covered armchairs. Two braided rugs on the floor. A black piano abutted the far wall, between two windows. It was old and worn but glistened with nourishing oil. Probably a family heirloom.

"Nice house you have here."

From the kitchen, where she was scooping tea from a tin can, Regan said, "Please . . . go in and sit down. I'm afraid what I have to discuss with you was more troubling *before* I watched the gallows burn."

Hawk glanced at her, but she stood at an angle that made seeing her face impossible. Her chestnut hair tumbled in swirls down her slender back. She wore a dark red ribbon in it. The ribbon matched the slightly lighter red of her casual but conservative basque, though no dress, however conservative, could conceal the ripeness of the woman's figure.

Curious, Hawk went on into the parlor and sank down in one of the armchairs.

He hiked a boot on a knee and hooked his hat on his other knee, looking around at the house's well-cared-for appointments including framed tintypes and daguerreotypes on the walls, a woven tapestry portraying a bucolic scene with farm workers and hay shocks.

Hawk sank back in the chair, feeling somehow at home here in this house, half consciously finding solace in the sounds of stove lids being manipulated in the kitchen, of china cups being set into saucers and then the cups rattling on the saucers as both were set down on a serving tray.

An icebox door opened with a squawk, then closed with a thud and the click of a latch. A stopper was removed from the lip of a bottle — a milk bottle, probably — making another soft squeaking sound. Hawk did not have to reflect on such sounds to be at home with them, and for them to conjure in him a heartrending homesickness. A longing for that which would never come again. At least, not the home and the domestic life he had once known with Linda and Jubal.

Could another, similar life be waiting for him somewhere, sometime? Was that even possible for the man he had become?

Regan came into the room with a tea service and set the tray on a coffee table fronting the sofa against the room's left wall, under an oil painting of an alpine scene with mountain goats.

"Milk and sugar?"

"Please."

She poured milk into both teacups and

followed it up with teaspoons of sugar from a china bowl. Hawk rose and scooped his cup off the table, holding the saucer in one hand and staring down at the woman as he lifted the cup in the other. The curved handle was too small for his index finger so he wrapped his entire hand around the cup and sipped.

He let his gaze trail down from her hair with its streaks of copper fire to her long, smooth neck, on over the curve of her shoulder and long, slender arm to her wrist and pale hand with long, unpainted fingers and a single, understated ring. He could see the outline of her legs beneath the dress — they were long and willowy, and they kindled a fire down deep beneath his belly as he grappled with the fanciful image of them bare and clamped tightly about his ribs.

She glanced up at him as she sat back on the fainting couch with her teacup and saucer on a knee, and he realized he was staring at her. His sudden, inexplicable yearning for her must have been obvious; her eyes acquired a faint incredulity as she dropped them again to her steaming cup, lifting the tea to rich lips, which darkened as her cheeks flushed.

He swallowed the hot, sweet liquid, feeling his ear tips warm with chagrin.

"I'm not usually a tea drinker, but it's right good. Thanks."

Turning away from her, he went back and sat down in his chair, feeling awkward in this house that looked so neat and scrubbed, and here he was in his trail-dusty, mud-splashed duds that probably still had the smell of gun smoke and death on them. The teacup and saucer resembled small, delicate jewels in his brown, leathery hands.

He composed himself quickly, reaching up to loosen the bandanna knotted around his neck, and said with a businesslike sigh, "Now, then, Miss Mitchell — what was it you wanted to see me about?"

"I'm afraid it's rather embarrassing, Mr. Hawk." She lifted her teacup and sipped, keeping her gaze down.

"Your cat stuck in a tree?" He grinned.

He'd meant it as a joke to lighten the mood and to assuage his own discomfort and goatish lust for the civilized woman, but the only effect it seemed to have on her was to dig three vertical lines into the skin above the bridge of her pretty nose.

She pinned her eyes to him, and he suddenly felt like one of her male students she'd caught neglecting his homework. "It's the Reverend Hawthorne. I've caught him skulking around outside my windows three nights in a row, Sheriff. Caught him out there last week, lurking about my garden. I'd thought he was scrounging for root vegetables, and I let it go, but last night I saw his face in that window right there" — she pointed to the window on the far side of the piano — "and the lamp there lit it unmistakably."

Hawk frowned, remembering the pathetic creature he'd discovered curled up in the cemetery earlier that morning. "Hawthorne?"

"I feel terrible about the man. What they did to him. In some ways it would have been better if they'd killed him as they did the two lawmen and the hangman." Regan shook her head darkly and sipped her tea as if to relieve the troubling reverie. "A man of the cloth, begging for his life while others die around him . . . God, how terrible."

She lifted her eyes to Hawk's once more. "Look, I know he's not right in his head, Sheriff. I know the man that he was a month ago would not be skulking around a woman's windows at night, trying to get a glimpse of her bathing. But he's no longer that man, and frankly, I'm a little afraid of what he might do if he's not warned away from my house."

"I just saw him over at the Venus," Hawk said. "He's probably still there."

"I hear he spends most of his time there these days." She took another sip of her tea, then looked at the curtained bay windows flanking Hawk, narrowing her eyes with worry. "I just hope no other innocent people suffer before this thing is over."

"You mean . . . ?"

"Yes, Mr. Hawk," Regan said, returning her resolute, defiant gaze to his. "Until the Tierneys are either dead or behind bars and you are gone. That you are indeed a vigilante was quite obvious by the condition Brazos was in when Reb and Alvin Gault hauled him out of the brothel."

"Do you know what he did in there?"

"It doesn't matter what he did in there. At least, it shouldn't matter to you. Or to me. Only to a judge and a legally seated jury. You see, Mr. Hawk, I firmly believe that's the only way to bring civilized society to the frontier. What you did was illegal. Every bit as illegal as what Brazos himself did."

"He beat and raped Claire Lang." Hawk felt his heart beating more insistently as his temper began running out to the end of its leash. "Only after he'd beaten and likely raped Claire's friend, Cassidy. She's at the doc's now."

"Was he threatening you when you shattered his teeth?"

Hawk only stared at her.

Regan lowered her eyes to her teacup, her cheeks paling slightly. "Like I said, it shouldn't matter what he did. Your abusing him in the guise of a bona fide lawman only sanctions the man's own lawless ways, and, indeed, those of his father and every owlhoot who rides through this town."

Hawk opened his mouth to speak, but she jerked her head up at him again, the angry flush returning to her face, the fiery anger igniting in her eyes. "Oh, I heard what you did to the bank robbers. Wonderful, Sheriff Hawk. Brilliant performance. Thank you for disposing of such brigands, and bringing the law to Trinity!"

"I don't understand you, Miss Mitchell," Hawk growled, feeling his nostrils flare with fury. "You grew up out here. You know how it is. Or did you forget when you went back East to school?"

"I didn't go that far east to school, Mr. Hawk. Only as far as Omaha, Nebraska. But I did learn something about the law . . . something I learned on top of the experience of watching my father be lynched by hooded vigilantes!"

Her eyes were hard, but tears varnished

them. Her lips formed a straight line, but the upper one trembled as the teacup she was holding clattered in its saucer.

Hawk stared down at his own cup.

Regan said, "He was mistaken for a horse thief on his own claim. Riders from a neighboring ranch found us when we were building a wild horse trap across the entrance to a box canyon. Rustlers had recently passed through the area, judging by the fresh tracks the ranch hands were following, and one of the horses had gotten away from the rustlers and slipped into our remuda."

"I'm sorry," Hawk said, continuing to stare down at his nearly empty cup.

"I'm not finished." Her voice was hard and cold, and it trembled now with fury as well as bereavement. "The men from the ranch had suffered the loss of much of their riding stock, and because the local law couldn't do much about the rustling, they took matters into their own hands. It was easy to mistake my father and me for rustlers, since they considered us 'nesters' on Platte River Range, anyway, and were eager to see us gone. Before either my father or I really knew what was happening, they'd hog-tied me and manhandled Pa onto a horse with a noose around his neck."

Regan dropped her pain-racked eyes and sniffed, brushing tears from her cheek with the back of her hand. "I remember the uncomprehending, last look he gave me before they slapped the horse out from under him."

She shook her head as if in a vain effort to rid the image from her mind. "Then they rode away as a wild pack of wolves on the blood scent, and left me to struggle desperately against the ropes while I watched my father dance in the air before me and, finally, *die.*"

"Christ," Hawk hissed.

He heaved himself to his feet, set his teacup and saucer down and sat beside her on the fainting couch. He set her cup and saucer on the tray, then drew her into his arms. She did not resist him but threw her own arms around his neck and sobbed against his bandanna-ringed neck.

"That was neither the beginning or the end to what those men did out there, Mr. Hawk," she said when her shoulders had stopped jerking, continuing to keep her arms wrapped tightly about his neck, clinging to him as though in fear of being thrown from a boat and into a dark, storm-tossed sea. "In the end, eight men were hanged."

"Were they all innocent?"

"Three of the eight were, including my father." She drew her head back to stare up at him grimly. "But don't you see — what they did was worse even than what they accused the men they murdered of!"

"I do see that," Hawk said, pressing his hands against her sides, feeling her ribs expand and contract beneath his palms as she breathed. "A vigilante gang is an ugly thing. But I'm not a gang, Regan. I am not blinded by passion. I am a reasoning lawman who knows badmen when I see them and who knows from his own personal experience that the laws often only serve the lawless, not the lawful."

Regan shook her head slowly, then reached up and placed her hands on his broad, high-tapering cheeks, her thumbs brushing the ends of his mustache. "God, the pain you must feel, Gideon. Don't you see? I understand it. But we must stand strong against it."

"That's what I've done."

He wrapped his hands around her wrists, gently lowered her hands from his face. He was about to rise and grab his hat and leave, but her eyes held him. So did the warmth of her flesh against his. And her sorrow, the intensity of which nearly matched his own. Suddenly, he pulled her against him once more, found her mouth with his own, pressed his lips to hers.

He was surprised to feel her returning the kiss, tilting her head slightly, parting her lips. She pressed her hands against his back and a barely audible groan of passion welled up from deep in her chest.

Her lips were warm, fleshy, pliant. . . .

Hawk kissed her harder, drew her even closer until her breasts flattened against his chest. She groaned once more. Her breasts swelled. But then she wriggled away from him, breaking off the kiss and pressing her hands against his shoulders. Sucking her upper lip, she turned away, shaking her head.

"No . . ."

"I could love you, Regan."

She'd swung her head back to him before he'd even realized he'd said it. She studied him, her eyes probing, and he wondered what she saw there because he wasn't certain of his own heart. He suddenly felt like a drowning man flailing for a life raft, only the current was too strong, the stormy ocean swells to steep and violent . . .

"Oh, Gideon." Her voice was soft, breathless, hushed. She seemed to be staring right through him, and he hated the sympathy he saw in her eyes.

The pity . . .

"Thanks for the tea." Hawk stood. He grabbed his hat off the floor by the chair he'd been sitting in and donned it on his way into the foyer. The back of his neck was warm with embarrassment. "I'll talk to the reverend."

He went out. Just before he'd closed the door behind him, he heard her call his name.

He did not turn back. He walked out through the gate in the picket fence and lengthened his stride for Wyoming Street. Turning west on the main drag, he saw only a small handful of men standing around the gallows now, pouring water on the steaming, blackened ruins. He was about to head on up to the jailhouse's stoop when he saw Saradee on the street ahead of him.

The pretty blond renegade sat her big white stallion, facing away from Hawk. She was at the edge of town and heading west at a spanking trot. She kicked the stallion into a lope, and the rolling hills absorbed her.

Relief loosened Hawk's shoulders. He was glad to be rid of her.

He glanced eastward, automatically looking to see if Blue Tierney was anywhere near, knowing the man and his desperado band would be coming soon. Nothing that way but several wary-looking locals standing around with empty water buckets, peering toward the jailhouse.

Hawk went into the office to see about his prisoners.

18.
“What Grade o’ Suicidal Fool Am I Lookin’ at Now?”

“Mayor Pennybacker said you wanted to see me, Gid?” said Reb Winter hopefully as he approached the jailhouse, flanked by the big Indian who’d helped him haul Brazos Tierney out of the Venus.

Hawk had checked on his prisoners, all three of whom were for the moment quietly cowed, then took a seat on the jailhouse’s front porch where he could keep an eye on things and watch for the coming of Brazos’s old man.

“I did at that,” Hawk said, holding a smoking coffee cup on his left thigh, along with his fully loaded and half-cocked Henry repeater. “I was figurin’ on putting you to work for a day or two, if you think Mr. Lundy can spare you. I need someone to keep an eye on the east end of town, where the trail comes in.”

“For Blue Tierney?” asked Reb, squeezing his watch cap in his hands and leaning forward on the toes of his scuffed, square-toed boots.

"You got it?"

"Why, sure, sure." Reb's eyes sparkled with boyish delight. "I'm sure Mr. Lundy can spare me for a day or two — maybe even three! — since it's such an important job, an' all. Wouldn't want ole Blue and his boys ridin' in unannounced."

"That's how I figure it."

Hawk glanced at the Indian, who stood off Reb's left hip, his face a massive chunk of eroded granite. He was staring eastward along the street, as though his mind were elsewhere.

"Who's your friend?" Hawk asked Reb.

"This here's Alvin Gault. He tends the depot down at the train station." Reb hooked his thumb to indicate the spur tracks and crude little station on Trinity's southern flank. "There ain't no train due till Monday, and he was wonderin' if he could help, too?"

"Why not?" Hawk dug into his pants pocket and tossed Reb two silver dollars. "How's two dollars sound for the day?" He tossed Alvin Gault two coins, and the Indian caught them against the front of his patched blanket coat. "Two more if I need you another day?"

Reb looked at Alvin, but Alvin kept his hard, black eyes on Hawk. As if some silent council had occurred — or maybe Reb could simply read the Indian's mind by the subtlest change of his physical features, though if there'd been a change Hawk certainly hadn't detected it — Reb said, "Fine as frog hair, Gid! Uh . . ."

"What?" Hawk asked.

"You think there's any chance you might deputize us?" The sparkle in Reb's eyes grew. "Maybe even give us badges?"

For the first time, the big Indian's eyes flung an excited spark of their own.

Hawk snorted. "You know where Stanley kept 'em?"

Reb said he did.

Hawk jerked his thumb toward the office. Reb fairly sprinted inside and there was the raspy bark of a drawer being opened and closed. The big younker returned to the porch, pinning one deputy sheriff's badge on his coveralls and tossing another to Gault. Reb's cheeks were flushed with excitement.

"Fire three quick shots if you see 'em comin'," Hawk ordered.

"Three shots — you got it!"

As Reb and the Indian turned and began making their ways eastward, walking abreast and about ten feet apart, shoulders back and chests out, Hawk said, "Your jobs are done after you've fired those signal rounds, Reb. You remember that!"

"Oh, I will, Gid," Reb said, twisting around to yell behind him, throwing up an acknowledging arm. "Don't you worry about a thing!"

As they drifted down the street, Hawk turned his attention to a wagon moving up a southern side street. There were three men in the wagon, all dressed in carpenter's aprons, and the driver swung the wagon onto Wyoming Street. A big collie dog was sitting atop the pile of green lumber in the box, tongue hanging, an eager, expectant look in the dog's eyes.

The driver, who wore a leather watch cap and a full, cinnamon beard, gave Hawk a wave then pulled the wagon to a stop in the middle of the street fronting the jailhouse, about twenty feet behind the still-smoldering ruins of the previous gallows.

"About here, would you say, Sheriff?"

"Looks good to me."

"All righty, then."

The man set the wagon brake, and he and the others climbed down from their perches in the driver's box. The dog leapt from the top of the wood to the wagon's side panel and from there to the ground, prancing around the wagon and waving its shaggy brown tail like a welcome flag. The men walked around the rear of the box and, donning leather work gloves, began unloading the lumber for the new gallows and piling it on the wagon's far side, the sharp thuds of the boards resounding over the town.

Hawk took a last sip of coffee, then tossed the tepid dregs over the pole railing and returned the cup to his desk inside the office. He closed the door on his way out and locked it. Since he was about to have a new gallows, it was time to call in another hangman.

He knew of one up in Cheyenne.

Hawk walked down to the depot station abutting the railroad tracks that still owned a new-silver shine and filled out a pink telegraph flimsy in pencil at the little shed that housed the Wells Fargo telegrapher, his telegraph key, and a fat tabby cat sprawled on the brick platform in the bright but cool spring sunlight.

A dented tin milk bowl sat off the building's southeast corner.

When he'd finished writing his note, Hawk set down the pencil stub and dug into a pants pocket to pay the nickel-a-word fee. The telegrapher — a stooped gent in eye-shades and spectacles — stared darkly down at the flimsy, snapped his dentures, and shook his head.

"Oh, lordy," was all he said, as he picked up the flimsy and started the key tapping as Hawk strode away. As Hawk's boots thumped and his spurs chinged, the cat lifted its head from the cobble platform, curled its tail, yawned, and went back to sleep.

Back at the jailhouse, in front of which the carpenters had finished unloading the lumber from the wagon and were now dragging out toolboxes and nail pouches, Hawk heard a commotion. He went inside to hear the unmistakable clatter of a tin cup being raked across a jail cage wall. He unlocked the cell block door and shoved it open.

The clatter grew louder, and one of his prisoners yelled, "Git back here, Sher'ff! We got something we need to discuss with you, ya plug-headed son of a bitch!"

Hawk gave a snort, then sauntered a few feet down the corridor and turned to the cage in which Hostetler stood with a tin cup in one hand, his other hand hooked around a flat steel bar strap, and a menacing snarl on his lips. One-Eye McGee sat on the edge of one of the two cots. Brazos Tierney sat on the other cot, one knee up, resting his bloody head against the stone wall behind him. He had a blood-soaked bandanna wrapped beneath his chin and tied in a large knot atop his head.

He looked mean and miserable.

In fact, Hawk thought they all looked about as piss burned as three bobcats chained to the same plank and prodded with sticks.

Hostetler said, "We're thirsty. And hungry. And Brazos needs a doctor to sew his chin up and his tongue back together."

Brazos turned his head to regard Hawk through narrowed eyes, his raw, belligerent face looking ridiculous, framed by the bloody bandanna. He looked like an old lady in a nightcap. "I need a doctor, you son of a bitch! And a shot of whiskey."

Sitting on the cot running along the cage's left wall and clutching his privates, One-Eye McGee said, "My oysters is puffed up so they'd do me as wheel hubs."

"You three bought into the wrong game, comin' back here to trifle with them whores." Hawk bit the end off a cigar. "You'll hang as soon as the gallows are built — day or two. Just like the circuit judge ordered and Sheriff Stanley was about to see to." As he scratched a match to life on his cartridge belt, Hawk grinned with menace. "I don't see any point in wasting taxpayers' money on medical services for three soon-to-be sides of human beef."

Hostetler stared hard at Hawk through the bars. His jaws bulged, and one eye twitched. "Mister, it's you that bought chips in the wrong game. I don't know how much Pennybacker and Tarwater an' them is payin' you, but oh, lord, it ain't enough. Not near enough! You're stackin' trouble up right high for yourself!"

"What about food?" McGee asked. "You gotta feed us."

"You'll have plenty of food," Hawk said, lighting his long, black cheroot. "Plenty of bread . . . and all the water you can drink."

The three glowered back at him. Their fury was like some rancid thing moldering in the air around them.

Finally, Brazos moved his lips and then spit a dogget of blood toward Hawk. Amidst the blood was a tooth, which bounced off the barred door with a small *ping,* then clattered to the earthen floor.

Puffing cigar smoke, Hawk turned and walked back into his office and drew the cell block door closed behind him. He turned the key, locking the door, then hung the ring on its hook, and returned to his chair on the porch where he saw that the carpenters were already framing one side of the gallows, their hammers sounding like echoing pistol shots.

Except for the three sunburned woodworkers and the collie dog lounging in the shade of a building on the other side of the street, Wyoming Street was deserted. Not a soul remained of the scurrying crowd of a few minutes before.

A chill breeze blew, shepherding a dust devil into town from the east. It sputtered this way and that and then died on the Poudre River House's front porch. A small, black dog crossed the street at an angle, disappearing down a gap between a drugstore and a haberdashery, and then there were only the carpenters and the breeze and the napping collie.

Hawk turned the cigar in his lips and smoked.

The three signal shots came later that afternoon.

Pow! Pow! Pow!

They sounded like the carpenters' hammers muffed by distance.

The carpenters had taken a late afternoon break from their pounding and sawing on the replacement gallows and were nowhere to be seen as Hawk, who'd been catnapping on the jailhouse porch, poked his hat brim off his forehead and swung his gaze east along Wyoming Street. There was only one man on the street — he was crossing it, head turned in the direction of the shots. When he was halfway across the street he clamped his bowler hat on his head, broke into a run, and disappeared behind the post office.

Beyond the town, brown dust rose like smoke from a small but growing wildfire. Bouncing human heads rose up beneath it and beneath them rose the heads of galloping horses.

It was another minute before Hawk could hear the thuds of the horses' hooves. He couldn't count the number of approaching riders yet, but they all seemed to be flanking the lead man who rode a cream barb. Long, snow-white hair hung down from the leader's white, brown-banded slouch hat to flop about his shoulders clad in a long, blue greatcoat like that worn by cavalry officers.

The man wore a sweeping mustache the color of his hair, and as he and his followers galloped on into the town, the thunder of their hooves now echoing off the buildings, Hawk saw that his face was as red as old saddle leather, and that he wore two white-handled pistols up high against his belly, over his coat.

Blue Tierney led the gang past the Poudre

River House Hotel, and when they were within seventy yards of Hawk, Tierney held up his left hand, checking down his own horse and ordering his riders to follow suit. He stopped the cream barb after another ten yards, the gang stopping behind him, the horses snorting and blowing and shuffling their feet, lifting dust that glowed in the brassy, late afternoon sunshine.

A long-bearded rider on a white-socked black moved up beside Tierney. He had a long horsey face with a knife scar across his lips, little red eyes, and a battered brown hat with the front brim pinned to its crown. He had two rifles in saddle boots, and Hawk counted three nice pistols visible on his otherwise raggedly attired person.

Like Rance Harvin, a professional killer. Scum.

Tierney stared at Hawk. Hawk stared back at him. The Rogue Lawman slowly gained his feet, set the Henry on his shoulder, and strolled on down the porch steps to stand in the middle of the street, feet spread wide, facing the group. A cold, half-smoked cheroot jutted from the left corner of his mouth.

One of the riders behind Tierney laughed and said something, pointing, and Tierney looked at the charred gallows ruins.

"I'll be damned," exclaimed the bib-bearded Wildhorn, his scarred lips causing a bizarre lisp. "They're already throwin' up another'n!"

Tierney's eyes raked the framework of the new gallows before sliding back to Hawk. The orbs were slitted, but through the slits Hawk could see that they were the color of a frozen lake not yet covered by snow. Hard, cold, and as brute mean as his son's.

Keeping his eyes on Hawk, Tierney turned his head slightly, said something, moving his lips, then rode forward until he sat the barb about twenty feet from the Trinity sheriff.

Tierney filled his lungs with air, and let it out slow. "What grade o' suicidal fool am I lookin' at now?"

Hawk rolled the cheroot to the other side of his mouth and grinned. "That's funny. I was just thinkin' the same thing."

19.
Deep Water

Hawk swung the Henry down from his shoulder and thumbed the hammer back, drawing a bead on Blue Tierney's chest. Tierney's eyes snapped wide in shock and sudden fear as Hawk said, "You and your boys are barred from town. It's illegal for you to be here. Now, if you turn around and ride the hell out of here right now — pronto — I won't arrest you."

Hawk felt his trigger finger tingle with anticipation and the barely bridled urge to drill a hole through the outlaw leader's black heart. The only thing that kept him from following through on the urge was the knowledge that if he killed the man, he'd be starting a war he wasn't likely to finish. He was outnumbered fifteen to one. The gunmen beside Tierney and the other men spread out across the street behind him were as savage and merciless a bunch of killers, not to mention well-armed, as Hawk had ever faced.

And he wasn't prepared to die. Not yet. Not until he'd seen Brazos and his other two prisoners dangling from hang ropes.

If he killed Tierney outright, the others would storm him. Only Tierney himself could call them off. So he'd let the man live as long as he could. He had a feeling he'd have ample opportunity later to hunt the man down and kill him and the whole rest of his gang.

"Christ, you're a crazy son of a bitch!" Tierney said through gritted teeth, blue eyes flashing desperately. "A suicidal moron!" He poked a commanding finger at Hawk and narrowed a flinty blue eye. "You hang my son and One-Eye and Hostetler, they'll be the last three you ever hang, you hear me, mister?"

"I ever see your face in this town again," Hawk snarled back at the man, pressing his cheek up hard against the Henry's rear stock, "I'll give it a third eye."

Tierney stared down, hard-jawed, from his saddle. His broad chest behind the blue wool greatcoat contracted and expanded as he breathed. His left eyelid twitched, and the ruddy, lightly freckled skin above the bridge of his nose wrinkled. "Well, I'll be damned . . ."

"What is it, Boss?" asked the bib-bearded regulator beside Tierney, keeping a tight rein on his black.

"Why, it's Gideon Hawk!" Tierney said with unbridled delight. He leaned against his saddle horn, showing two silver eyeteeth as he grinned. "Mr. Hawk, I've heard a lot about you. A very entertaining character. I hope you believe me when I tell you that I do regret having killed you."

Hawk had heard the faint crunch of gravel to his left, and the even fainter tearing sound, like that of coarse cloth catching on a stone wall. Like the stone wall of the jailhouse, say. Now, in the corner of his eye, he spied movement, and he whipped around so quickly that the man trying to sneak up on him by slipping around the jailhouse's west side stopped suddenly without even raising his rifle and opened his mouth in shock.

Hawk's round took the man through his open mouth. It slammed the man's head back so violently that his gray, high-crowned hat bounced off his chest and hit the dirt as his feet jerked two feet off the ground. He triggered his own Henry repeater nearly straight into the air over Wyoming Street.

Before the man's head and shoulders struck the ground, Hawk had turned back to the gang before him, quickly ejecting the spent cartridge and slamming fresh into the Henry's breech. Every rider that he could see was grabbing or aiming iron, and Blue Tierney was wrapping his hands around the two ivory-gripped gun handles jutting across his belly like twin bullhorns.

Since the fuse of the powder keg had now been lit, Hawk had no reason to spare Tierney. He quickly lined up his sights on the outlaw leader's chest, but just as he squeezed the Henry's trigger, Jack Wildhorn, who'd filled his fists with two long-barreled Colt Navys, snapped off a shot. The slug burned across Hawk's cheek, causing him to jerk his rifle slightly. His own slug tore into Tierney's upper right arm.

Tierney sagged back in the saddle, gritting his teeth, while Hawk levered and fired the Henry again, at the same time that Jack Wildhorn triggered his other Colt. Hawk had shifted his weight just enough that the regulator's bullet screeched past his left shoulder to bark into the street behind him. Hawk's own bullet painted a bloodred hole in the middle of Jack Wildhorn's forehead.

The man grimaced and blinked, and his eyes crossed as he lowered both arms, his black suddenly pitching.

Hawk triggered another shot at Tierney,

but Tierney's cream gelding had curveted sharply, and the errant shot plowed into the face of a man behind him. Blood spurted onto the rider to the face-shot man's left, causing that man's own triggered round to sail wide of Hawk and hammer into a barber pole on the south side of the street.

Hawk held his ground in spite of a half-dozen slugs screaming around and over him, most of them errant due to the pitching and pinwheeling and sunfishing of their startled mounts. One punched Hawk's hat off his head, but the Rogue Lawman continued firing until he'd laid out two more riders in addition to Wildhorn, who'd dropped to the street and was kicked several times by his pitching black.

Staring in awe at Wildhorn's lifeless lump on the street, Tierney neck reined his pinto around sharply, bellowing, "Fall back! Fall back!"

They'd likely expected him, a lone lawman, to hole up in the jailhouse with a rifle and take only potshots at them from windows while they burned him out or starved him out. Or waited until he'd chewed through his ammo. They hadn't expected him to meet them head on and lay his rifle sights on their leader so unabashedly, and then to kill their best shooter outright.

Hawk continued firing the Henry, wounding two more before they'd gotten their horses on leashes and kicked them all back down Wyoming Street in a fog of broiling dust and a din of whinnying, frightened animals and pounding hooves. One of the three they'd left in the street behind him rolled onto his back and, cursing through gritted teeth, began slipping a big horse pistol from a shoulder sheath showing beneath the flap of his wolf coat.

Hawk fired his sixteenth and final round through the man's heart, leaving him grinding his heels and spurs into the dirt as he died. Hawk tripped the lever near the end of the Henry's octagonal barrel to open the loading sleeve. Tierney's riders were a hundred yards away from him now and dwindling quickly into the eastern distance, obscured by a brown dust cloud touched with the salmon lances of the setting sun.

Quickly, heart thudding, knowing they might circle around him and give him a much harder time of it, Hawk slipped rimfire .44 cartridges down the loading sleeve until he had fifteen in the barrel and one in the breech. He stood in the middle of the street, where the dust and powder smoke continued to sift and waft, and stared after the gang, keeping his ears pricked in case they decided to split up and surround him.

At the far eastern end of the street, there was only dust and the darkening land beyond the town. Had they decided to call it a day? Tierney was likely losing too much blood to . . .

Wait.

Hawk strained his eyes as he peered down the vacant street. A figure appeared no bigger than a dust mote. It grew to the size of the tip of his little finger, and he could make out Tierney's snowy hair hanging to the shoulders of his blue greatcoat.

The man held his cream's reins high in one hand, and he turned a full circle as he shouted angrily, his voice sounding crisp and clear on the high, dry air: "Good folks of Trinity, if my son is not released by sundown tomorrow, I'll burn the town to the ground! I'll kill your men and rape your women! I'll leave your children wandering the countryside as *orph-annnzzzzz!*"

The threat echoed over the tall false facades.

Tierney jerked his horse around once more, batted his boots against its flanks, and lunged away. In seconds, he was heading off down the curving eastern trail, his blue figure atop the cream mount diminishing quickly until it was swallowed by the piñon-studded knolls and hogbacks.

Hawk lowered his rifle. Up and down both sides of the street, men were moving cautiously out from the shops and saloons. Both the Laramie and the Four Aces were down that way, near the Poudre River House. The men shuttled weary glances after the gang and then to Hawk and back again.

Footsteps sounded behind Hawk and he turned his head to see Carson Tarwater strolling toward him, as much as a wooden-footed man could stroll. He wore his customary, bemused grin that set him apart from all others. His bowler hat and his lack of an apron said he'd closed up his tack and feed store for the day.

"That's Blue Tierney — fire and brimstone fury. They say his pa was a Baptist preacher." He clamped a Denver newspaper under his arm and stared down at the three dead men in the street.

"I'll be damned," Tarwater mused aloud, nodding at the dead regulator lying twisted on his side, tongue poking out from between the man's scarred lips, long beard bent under his chin, his eyes wide and staring at the ground. "Tierney's really got himself outfitted. Must be stealin' horses from the bigger outfits around."

Tarwater started past Hawk, stepping with a grunt over Wildhorn. "Believe I'll see how cold they're servin' the beer over at the Four Aces."

As he walked east, Hawk saw Reb Winter strolling west. The big odd-jobber was a block away and closing, giving Tarwater a shy nod, then lowering his gaze to the blood staining the street around the dead men. The deputy sheriff's badge glinted on Reb's coverall bib.

"Appreciate the warning, Reb."

"Ah, it weren't nothin', Gid. A blind man coulda seen the dust cloud them boys was lifting. Holy shit — is that Jack Wildhorn?" Reb was aghast.

"That's what I'm told."

Hawk heard more footsteps behind him, and he turned to see Hy Booker and a young man about fourteen or fifteen, Booker's sullen son, heading toward the fresh carrion. "Do me a favor, will you, Reb?"

"What's that?"

"Mind the store. Don't let anyone in. Or out." Hawk clamped a hand on the big kid's heavy shoulder. "You see any trouble, give me that three-shot signal again?"

"I'd be right happy to do that, Gid. I'm your deputy, now, remember?" Reb rose proudly on his boot toes. "Where you goin'?"

"I'm tired. Think I'll take a bath and a catnap so I'm fresh for tonight and tomorrow."

"Gid?"

Hawk had started walking east. Now he turned and looked back at the young man. "What're you gonna do if Blue Tierney makes good on his threat?"

"It wouldn't make much sense to burn the town till he gets his son out of the jail — now would it?"

Hawk winked at the younker and continued walking away. Reb stared after him, his normally optimistic gaze now cast with apprehension.

Hawk felt the eyes of half the town on him as he pushed through batwings of the Four Aces Saloon. The conversational din in the place could be heard in the street until all faces swung toward Hawk. Then most of the mouths stopped moving, and the silence settled so that a man could have heard a mouse scratching beneath the floorboards.

A craggy-faced oldster dressed in ragged prospector's garb bunched his lips disapprovingly and pulled his weather-stained canvas hat down low on his forehead.

The dozen or so drinkers and gassers

swung their gazes to track Hawk as their newly appointed sheriff walked over to the long, elaborate, L-shaped bar that ran along the saloon's right wall. Carson Tarwater stood at the bar, his wooden foot propped on the brass rail that ran along the floor.

From the far side of the saloon, a man said in a hushed voice barely above a whisper, "He made fast work of them holdup men, but I'd like to see how he's gonna handle *this.*"

"Shoulda steered clear o' the Tierneys," another man groused as the conversations around the saloon began rising gradually once more so that Hawk could clearly hear another man complain, "I don't care who he is — you poke a stick at a wildcat like Blue Tierney, you're gonna get bit. Gonna git the *whole town* bit!"

Tarwater turned to the last man who'd spoken — a stocky man sitting about ten feet from the bar and with his back to Tarwater and Hawk. "Yeah, hell, they were just a couple whores that got knocked around," the councilman said with mild sarcasm, smiling at Hawk. "Ain't that right, Arlin?"

The stocky gent glanced over his shoulder. His face flushed with chagrin as he slid his small eyes between Tarwater and Hawk. Then he jerked it back toward his tablemates and sort of hunkered down over his beer.

The bartender had come over to stand in front of Hawk, an expectant gleam in his eyes over which his mussed, dark brown hair hung at an angle so that the left eye was nearly hidden behind it.

"Bourbon," Hawk said.

"Old Kentucky?"

"There another kind?"

The barman plucked a shot glass off the pyramid standing on a clean, white towel. He splashed bourbon from a bottle and slid the shot glass in front of Hawk. "On the house. I do appreciate what you're doin', Mr. Hawk." He smiled grimly. "Though I got a feelin' you ain't gonna be amongst the living much longer. And most of us prob'ly ain't, neither."

As the apron headed down the bar to serve a couple of punchers who'd just come in, Tarwater raised his beer. "To the beginning of the end of lawlessness in Trinity."

Hawk arched a brow at him.

"Those were the words, roughly paraphrased, that Sheriff Stanley began his last speech with."

"Here, here." Hawk threw back half the bourbon shot.

He stood holding the glass on the bar in

his hands, inspecting the room via the polished back bar mirror. There was a sparse crowd, but he knew from his experience in other towns that when there was pressing business to discuss, like the business of the three dead Tierney men in the street, a larger crowd even than usual for a Saturday night would soon be gathered. The gestures of the men in heated conversation around him were forceful, passionate, and as he watched he saw more than one head bob in his direction, indicating the subject of their discussion.

"What're you gonna do, Hawk?"

He glanced at Tarwater regarding his dark visage in the mirror. Turning to the actual man, who then turned to him, Hawk said, "The carpenters promised to have the gallows built by the end of the day tomorrow. I intend to hang Brazos, Hostetler, and One-Eye as soon as the hangman gets here. I'm hoping he arrives on Monday's train, though I haven't heard back from him yet."

He threw back the last of the shot.

"That's a mighty deep creek you're wading," Tarwater said with a sigh.

"I've waded 'em before. But I'm not fool enough to believe I won't need a hand crossing this one." Hawk refilled his glass from the bourbon bottle, turned to Tarwater, and rested his right elbow on the zinc bar top. "Any lawman's only as good as the town he's protecting. How badly do you think these people want to see law and order brought to Trinity?"

Tarwater sipped his beer then licked foam off his clean upper lip. "Speaking for myself, I have an old English Enfield gathering dust in my broom closet. The British sent the damn things too late to help the Confederacy, but I'd hate to not put it to some good use."

"I figured I could lean on you in a pinch, Tarwater." Hawk glanced at the gradually growing crowd to his left. "How far would the rest of the town go to save their town, their families from Tierney's riders?"

Tarwater looked over the men involved in passionate conversations. Some looked angry. Others afraid. The way they kept glancing at Hawk, he wasn't sure he knew whom they were most angry at or afraid of — Hawk or Tierney.

Turning back to the Trinity sheriff, Tarwater said, "I suspect a few would grab their old army sabers and pitchforks. Hard to know for sure until someone started spreading the word to 'em, started 'em thinking about it, building their nerve."

Hawk threw his entire second shot back

and ran his sleeve across his mustache. He grabbed his rifle off the bar. "Start passing the word that they might be needed, will you? But only those who can shoot, and those willing to shoot to kill if I go down or if Tierney sets fire to the town, need consider it. I don't want fence straddlers."

Tarwater spread his lips and nodded. Then he furled a dubious brow. "Aren't you afraid, Hawk?"

Hawk thought about that, probing his own heart. He was mildly surprised at what he found there. Both his brows wrinkled, and his eyes dropped uncertainly as he said, "Yeah."

He turned and started heading for the batwings and the darkening night beyond. "Yeah, I reckon I am." He chuckled as he pushed through the doors. "Imagine that."

20.
"No Blondy"

At the Poudre River House, Hawk ordered a bath and a bottle to be brought to his room, and then he went up and shucked out of his clothes. The Chinaman, Baozhai, brought both the bath and the bottle, and when he'd finished filling the tub, he regarded Hawk sitting in a chair by the window, clad in only a towel while prying the cork out of the fresh bourbon bottle.

"Where blondy? No blondy?" Looking disappointed, Baozhai raked his hands down his shoulders to indicate long hair.

"No blondy." Hawk flipped the man a tip.

"No blondy — thas too bad!" The Chinaman shuffled off with two empty buckets, Indian moccasins rasping across the rug, and opened the hall door, laughing. "She settle you down good, huh?"

Laughing, he shuffled out of the room and closed the door behind him.

"Yeah," Hawk grunted, dropping the

towel. "She settle me down good."

He stepped into the steaming tub. It was that cool, damp time of the year when the mountain weather penetrated the very marrow of your bones and took root there. As directed, Baozhai had made the bath hot enough to scald a chicken, and the hot liquid crawled slowly up Hawk's lean, rugged frame as he eased himself into the tub.

The water bit like a dog's sharp teeth until he'd let it settle over him; then it felt as welcoming as embryonic fluid, and he rested his head back and napped in it before waking, refreshed, and scrubbed himself clean with the long-handled scrub brush and unscented soap cake provided.

He'd climbed out of the tub and was just starting to shave in the mirror over the washstand when someone tapped on the door. Hawk dropped his freshly stropped, bone-handled straight razor into the porcelain basin, and grabbed his Russian .44 from its holster hanging from a bedpost.

"Who is it?"

Silence. Then, haltingly: "Miss Mitchell."

Hawk dropped the Russian back into its holster, toweled the shaving cream from his face. He tightened the towel around his waist and opened the door.

She stood facing him in a form-fitting

brown dress with a fur collar. Her freshly brushed hair was down, and she held the handle of an oilcloth-covered wicker basket hooked over one arm.

"To what do I owe the pleasure?"

"I came to check on you. I heard the shooting, of course, as did nearly everyone in the county, and" — she held up the basket from which emanated the succulent aromas of a home-cooked meal — "I had a feeling you probably hadn't bothered with supper yet."

Hawk took the basket. "Much obliged."

He figured she'd leave, but when she stood there, averting her eyes from his bare torso, making no move to retreat down the hall, he pulled the door open wider and stepped back into the room.

"Come in."

"I shouldn't." She glanced around him at the tub. "Obviously, you're . . ."

"Come on in anyway, Regan."

She looked around skeptically, then stepped haltingly into the room.

"Perhaps you could put some clothes on?"

Hawk gave a wry snort as he set the basket on the dresser. The room had come equipped with a privacy screen, and he'd grabbed his black denim trousers and was moving toward the screen when she said, "Wait."

Hawk turned to her.

She'd moved over to the bed, and she slumped down to the edge of it now, wrapping one hand around the fingers of the other, and sort of twisting them, closing her front teeth down on her lower lip.

Hawk felt the back of his neck warm with blood. He tossed his pants onto a chair and walked over to her. She did not look up at him though he stood only a foot in front of her, until he reached out and lifted her chin with the first two fingers of his right hand.

Her eyes met his, her lips slightly parted. A flush had risen in her cheeks, and her breasts, half-revealed by the dress that was lower cut than any other that he'd seen her wearing, rose and fell heavily. Hawk dropped to his knees before her, leaned toward her, placing his hands on the edge of the mattress on either side of her, propping himself on his outstretched arms, and pressed his lips to hers.

She responded hungrily, running her hands up and down his arms that bulged with muscle and corded tendons, wrapping her arms around his waist, raking her fingers up and down his back. The tip of her tongue pressed against his lips, and he sucked at it, then mashed his own tongue against it, rising up and wrapping his hands around her slender back, drawing her even closer as he kissed her.

She groaned, digging her hands deeper into his back, her fingernails gouging the flesh just above his hips.

After a time, he pulled away from her, lowered his face to her corset, and pressed his lips to the valley between her breasts. Blood surged through him, and he lifted his head suddenly to begin unbuttoning her dress. It took both of them to remove her whalebone corset. When it was on the floor behind him, he brushed her hands away from the straps of her camisole and removed it himself, then slid her pantaloons and pink underpants down her long, slender legs, kissing the smooth flesh as he exposed it.

He lingered down there for a long time, until she was arching her back and keening like a wildcat in heat. Then he rose up off his knees, leaving his towel on the bed, and mounted her, silencing her mewling, desperate cries with his own mouth.

After an hour's worth of scrambling around beneath the sheets, she'd somehow gotten on top of him, and Hawk lifted his head and shoulders to catch her as she sagged backward toward his ankles, sweaty and spent, her hair damp and disheveled. He eased her over to the other side of the bed, and she stared up at him as though through an opaque second lid.

A strand of hair was pasted to her cheek, the end touching the right corner of her mouth.

Hawk smoothed the hair back and kissed her long and tenderly. When he pulled his head back, she wrapped her arms around his neck, grunting and frowning impishly, trying to draw him back down to her.

"Hell, I gotta go," he grunted, prying her hands off his neck, letting her arms fall back down to the rumpled bed. "I left Reb with the prisoners."

"Tierney won't be back tonight," she said. "I heard you wounded him. He won't send his men alone."

"Just the same . . ." Hawk dropped his feet to the floor and started to rise.

"Gideon?"

He sat back down on the edge of the bed.

"I could love you, Gid."

He met her soft gaze. A bittersweet smile quirked the corners of her long, ripe mouth that had turned redder with their lovemaking. Her hands were folded on her pale, flat belly, beneath her breasts that were lightly chafed from his hands and mustache.

Hawk gave his own bittersweet smile, then leaned down and kissed her belly button, nuzzled her fingers before she lifted her hands and ran them brusquely through his still-damp hair.

Hawk pushed away from her, kissed her hand once more. "You best head out the back stairs. You were here alone in the new sheriff's room longer than what most would see as proper."

She nodded, curling the corners of her mouth down slightly, sadly, and nodded as though at what he hadn't said as much as what he had.

Hawk dressed, feeling her eyes on him as she lay on her side, head resting on the heel of her hand, though he didn't look back at her. He couldn't look at her. He felt a hard knot in the pit of his belly, knowing he would never be the man for her, beyond what they'd been for each other for a few hours this afternoon.

She'd had a taste of him. He, of her. That had to be enough.

He buckled his cartridge belt around his waist, donned his hat, and went to the door. He stopped, his hand on the handle, and looked over at her.

"You didn't eat your supper." She lay on her back now, staring at the ceiling. In the dim room, her naked breasts rose and fell slowly.

Hawk shook his head. "I'll heat it up later, when I really need it."

He went out and took the stairs to the hotel lobby where Mrs. Lundy was checking in a well-dressed couple with luggage on the floor around their expensive shoes. The woman wore a long fur coat, and her picture hat was adorned with ostrich feathers. Stage passengers, likely. The stage was parked out front of the hotel.

"That's him, there," said Mrs. Lundy to the man and the woman, both of whom swung around toward Hawk.

"You're the sheriff?" asked the bespectacled man in a new but dusty beaver hat. Fresh off the coach.

Hawk paused, looked at the pair.

"Do you know that the trail just outside of town is being haunted by ruffians?"

Hawk studied them. Anger and fear shone in their eyes.

"You don't say."

He went on outside where the man who was obviously the stage driver was standing around with his shotgun messenger and five townsmen, just off the coach's right front wheel. One of the townsmen indicated Hawk with a tilt of his head, and the shotgun messenger — a big man coated in dust from the crown of his battered yellow Stetson to the toes of his scuffed boots — turned to the new lawman of Trinity.

"Badmen outside town, Sheriff. Blue Tierney."

"How far?"

"A couple miles. They were millin' around the trail as though they were waitin' for us. I thought they'd rob us, as they'd robbed us before. Only, this time they had a warning. A warning to be delivered to you."

Hawk waited.

"No one gets in or out of town until you've released Brazos Tierney. That goes for the train."

"That won't do, Sheriff," said a man dressed in the billed watch cap and blue jacket of a postal clerk. "The U.S. mail is due to arrive on train fifty-nine from Denver on Monday morning, and the mail must not be held up. I have several men awaiting tax receipts from cattle they sold in Chicago. Not to mention freight for the mercantile and the other businesses here on Wyoming Street."

Hawk raked his eyes across the men shrewdly. "What are you suggesting?"

The men looked at each other.

"That you release your prisoners," said

the postal clerk. "You're only one man, for crying out loud! You know what he did to Sheriff Stanley and Deputy Freeman. The whole town is at risk here!"

"And what about the next time Brazos comes to town to kill and beat up more whores?" Hawk waited. The men just stared at him, hard-eyed. "You mean, you'll knuckle under? Let him do what he wants because you're all afraid of him?"

Hawk shook his head. "I suggest you men arm yourselves. When I hang Brazos Tierney Monday morning, you're likely going to need a good rifle if you want to see that your homes and businesses don't get burned. If you want the train to make it into town, you ride out there to where the tracks come in and make sure it does."

"What about you?" asked the stage driver, scowling with exasperation.

"My priority is to see that Brazos and his partners hang, as Stanley intended. When and if Tierney shows himself again — which he hasn't yet except trying to put the fear of god into a few sheep — I'll move on him as best as one man can. Remember, though — this is your town. It's up to you to stand up for it."

Hawk pinched his hat brim and stepped down off the boardwalk fronting the Poudre

River House and began tramping eastward along Wyoming, along which flares and oil pots had been lit. There was only a little streak of green over the purple western ridges. Ahead, Reb was stepping out away from the jailhouse, his old rifle with its rope lanyard on his shoulder. A pink paper fluttered in his hand.

"Everything all right?" Hawk felt chagrined at having left the kid alone so long. But he couldn't have turned Regan away if the town had been burning around him.

"It was, Gid." The big younker was looking high over Hawk's right shoulder, while absently extending the pink telegraph flimsy. "Till now, I reckon."

Hawk didn't turn to look where Reb was looking, however. Something had caught his eye on a high, flat-topped bluff northeast of town. The bluff was cloaked in purple shadows clearly showing a fire burning at the top of the formation, with the silhouettes of men milling around the flames. Hawk turned to peer in the direction Reb was still staring, and his eyes hooded darkly.

On another formation — this one a broad mesa shelving downward on its north side, and called Trinity Ridge — another fire about the size of a bonfire burned. A couple of more man-shaped silhouettes were moving around the fire, tossing large branches on top of the leaping flames.

Startled murmurs rose eastward along Wyoming Street. Others had seen the fires. Men were standing in the street, some with beer mugs in their fists and skeptical expressions on their faces, swinging their heads from southwest to northeast. Burning oil pots on the boardwalks fronting the saloons and the hotel limned their faces in eerie red light and shadows.

"Tierney," someone said. "Tryin' to get our goats!"

Hawk turned to Reb, who'd turned his own head to see what some of the others were gazing at in the northeast. He shoved his billed watch cap back on his sandy-haired head and whistled. "Well, now — w-would ya look at that!"

Hawk read the flimsy, and his chest lightened with satisfaction. The hangman he'd cabled had agreed to come. He'd be here on Monday's early train.

Hawk let the breeze take the flimsy and started walking past the kid. "Fetch some bread and water for my prisoners — will you, son? We're gonna have to keep 'em alive till Monday." He flipped a ten-dollar gold piece in the air, and Reb wrapped a big hand around it. "Then get yourself a beer. You've earned it."

"Wow." Reb stared down at the coin, for the moment distracted by the perplexing fires. "I do thank you, Gid."

"Like I said, boy — you earned it."

Hawk started up the jailhouse's porch steps, glancing once more at the growing bonfire that he could see over the building's shake-shingled roof.

"What you suppose them fires is all about, Gid?" Reb asked behind him. "Just old Tierney tryin' to bedevil us."

"Yep." Hawk looked up and down Wyoming Street where more and more men were gathering. Even a few respectable women and whores. "Looks like he's doin' a pretty good job of it, too."

Hawk looked at the gallows between the jailhouse and the well-lit Venus brothel, glad to see that the carpenters had a good third of it erected. They'd likely finish easily by tomorrow noon. Come Monday, there'd be a hanging.

And Sheriff Stanley could rest a little easier.

Hawk went into the jailhouse to see about his prisoners.

21. "That Son of a Bitch Answered My Pleas and Let Me Live"

Later, Hawk inspected the area around Regan's house and the doctor's frame house beside it. He wasn't expecting to find Pastor Hawthorne lurking around out here tonight of all nights, but as he walked on down the center of the side street, a rustling sounded from the gap between the church and an old adobe-brick hovel, across the street from the teacher's place.

Hawk cocked the Henry and turned toward the dark gap, the half-ruined hovel and the roof of the white, steeple-fronted church glistening in the starlight. There was a coyote-like whoop from one of the ridges. Ahead of Hawk, a man gave a startled grunt.

Hawk stopped. A dark figure moved in the shadows. Hawk pressed the butt of his rifle against his cartridge belt, aiming straight out from his right hip. If it had been Tierney's men, he'd have seen a gun flash by now.

"Hawthorne?"

A rheumy chuckle. There was a gurgling sound, like that of a bottle being tipped, and then a man coughed.

"Go on home, Reverend," Hawk said, keeping his voice low. "Go home, get a hold of yourself. It's Sunday tomorrow. Don't you have a sermon to write?"

The reverend's tall, lean figure separated from the dense darkness of the gap between the buildings as the man stumbled slowly toward Hawk. The starlight flashed off the collar at the man's neck, the bottle in his hand. Hawk could smell the rancid whiskey sweat on the man before he could see his eyes — two dark spheres above his aquiline nose.

"You think I was gonna go try to see the teacher again, don't you?" Hawthorne moved up to within three feet of Hawk.

The Rogue Lawman's eyes burned from the stench. "Wasn't that where you were headed?"

Hawthorne stared at Hawk, his eyes fierce in their deep sockets.

"No." The minister shook his head. "I was headed away from there. She's retired, apparently, her windows dark. But why shouldn't I look at her? She's beautiful."

Suddenly, the man's broad slash of a

mouth showed the white teeth behind the lips. "You know she's beautiful. I know where she was today — for nearly three hours this afternoon. I know what she was doing up there with you. If she hadn't been sinning in unwedded bliss with the new sheriff of Trinity, she wouldn't have had to leave by the back stairs."

"Go home, Reverend."

"How was it, Mr. Hawk? How was it, having such a beautiful, innocent creature writhing beneath you?"

Hawk shook his head. "What the hell happened to you, Hawthorne?"

"What do you mean — what happened? A man of the cloth begged for his life while others died." With the same hand holding the bottle, he pointed toward the fire atop the northwestern ridge. "And that son of a bitch answered my pleas and let me live. He should have put a bullet in me!"

Revulsion flowed through Hawk like a wave of black tar. Gritting his teeth, he lowered his rifle and grabbed the man's collar with his free hand. He pulled Hawthorne up close to his own face despite the death-like stench of his breath.

"We all gotta save ourselves, Hawthorne. In our own way. Now, it's your turn. In the meantime, stay away from Regan. The next time I see you out here, I won't kill you, but I'll have you prayin' again right quick!"

Hawthorne gritted his teeth as Hawk tightened his grip on the man's shirt collar. He grunted and struggled, knees buckling. Still, he managed ribald laughter. "Come on, Hawk," he hissed. "Tell me how she was! How did her breasts feel in your hands?"

Hawk let the man sag to the ground. Hawthorne fell forward, dropping his bottle and cursing. Hawk moved back out of the mouth of the gap, and looked at Regan's house on the far side of the street. Her place behind the white picket fence was dark, the leaded glass window inserts reflecting the stars and the orange fire on Trinity Ridge.

Hawk glanced once more at Hawthorne, who had scrambled to a sitting position in the brushy, trash-strewn gap and was holding his bottle up to see how much whiskey remained. He was chuckling softly.

"Remember what I told you, Reverend." Hawk headed on out of the gap, turning toward Wyoming Street.

Behind him, glass shattered. The preacher's chuckles turned to desperate sobs. "Son of a bitch!"

Ten minutes later, Hawk stopped near the new gallows, poked his hat brim off his forehead, and stared over the false facades along Wyoming Street's south side. Last time Hawk had checked the time, it was one thirty a.m., nearly the darkest hour. The fire atop the shelving mesa still licked its flames at the sparkling, star-dusty sky.

He turned to the north.

The other fire burned, as well. Both were about the same size — large enough to roast a pig on. Occasionally over the course of the night, Tierney's men had fired gunshots and howled like crazed coyotes. They hadn't kept up the din, as they likely wanted to conserve their ammo as well as their voices, but they'd give a howl or trigger a shot at one of the rooftops of Trinity just to nudge awake those few in the town who were beginning to drift asleep.

Terror tactics. Hawk remembered that both his own Union side as well as the Rebs had used them to great effect during the War Between the States.

A rifle cracked.

Hawk felt his own nerves tighten like drawn piano wire. Even his nerves that had become so accustomed to strain. He could imagine the effect that it had on the rest of the town — men and women lying awake in their beds, staring at the dark ceiling above their beds. Or, having given up on sleep, sipping coffee in their parlor chairs or at their kitchen tables.

Bastards. Oh, well, they were just testing Trinity's mettle. Hawk himself was curious about how hard the town would dig in when Tierney and his pack of hired gun wolves came calling. Which they would most certainly do sooner or later, either before Hawk hanged Brazos, Hostetler, and One-Eye, or later. Whenever they came, they'd be too many for Hawk to take down alone. He'd need help. And, like he'd told Pennybacker, a lawman was only as strong as the town he was sworn to protect.

Hawk caressed his rifle's hammer as he looked around.

All the saloons were dark. Even the Venus had let its oil pots and flares burn out. No one was in the mood for drinking or patronizing the whores, it seemed.

The last of the saloon patrons had stumbled off to the livery stables or flophouses several hours ago. Now, most of the town was dark, though on his rounds Hawk had seen a few dim lantern glows. Most of the citizens, like Regan, had darkened their windows to render their houses less compelling targets for Tierney's potshooting cutthroats.

The town was quiet, but it wasn't a serene

quiet. It was like the quiet Hawk remembered before the start of the skirmishing at Chancellorsville. A heavy, tarlike quiet. The silence that precedes and follows an explosion.

He walked up the jailhouse steps, unlocked the office door, went in, and turned up the wick on the lantern he'd left burning on the same post that held the main key ring.

"Hey, Hawk," Brazos shouted from the cell block, his voice muffled by the stout door and heavy stone walls. "What's it like out there. Them coyotes getting close?"

Brazos laughed.

Softly, One-Eye McGee started singing "Bringing in the Sheaves," while Hostetler and Brazos snickered mockingly.

"Better have a pot of coffee boiling for Pa!" he shouted after a while, as Hawk sat in his desk chair and slowly rolled a quirley. "He's gonna be mad if you don't have the coffee on when he comes."

More laughter. Hawk ignored it. They were wanting his goat. While they were annoying, and he'd like to indulge in a catnap, they were not accomplishing their task. The shooting from the ridges and the coyote-like howls strained his nerves momentarily, but mostly he was filled with a fateful calm.

Whatever was going to come would come. He was ready. There was no point in whipping up fantasies of himself and Regan. What they could have had together, they'd had in his room at the Poudre River House. No, he was no longer afraid of what would happen to him here in Trinity. He was just wondering how the rest of the town would meet it when it came.

He got his answer the next morning, after Reb had spelled him in the jailhouse and he'd gone back to his hotel to wash up and grab a quick breakfast. He was sitting on the steps watching the carpenters dutifully putting the finishing touches on the gallows while casting him skeptical glances, when he saw Mayor Pennybacker and Councilmen Pike and Learner walking toward him from the direction of the hotel. The three looked grim.

Hawk sucked a pungent lungful of tobacco smoke, then rose and flicked the stub into the street as the three men approached.

"Gentlemen," Hawk said. "You don't look all that well rested."

Pennybacker said nothing. Neither did the other two until the rotund, olive-skinned Pike gritted his teeth and said, "Who could get any sleep with those wolves prowling the ridges!"

Behind the three, a small group of other townsmen had gathered, all looking wary, tentative, expectant. Hawk saw Regan, as well, striding slowly up the south side of the street from the east. She wore a heavy cape over her dress; the soft morning light shone in her hair. She stopped at the front of the town's drugstore and stared toward Hawk with an oblique expression.

Hearing footsteps behind him, Hawk saw Carson Tarwater moving toward him from the west. Tarwater was flanked by Hy Booker and several other businessmen from that end of the town. Pastor Hawthorne came up from a gap between two buildings on the street's north side to press his back to the side of a blacksmith shop, hands behind him, grinning fatefully.

If it was possible, the preacher looked worse than he'd looked the night before. He'd likely spent the night in the cemetery again, after Hawk had kicked him off of Regan's street.

Tarwater limped up to the sheriff's office and stopped at the bottom of the porch steps. His cheeks were flushed, his eyes fervent.

"I just want you to know, Hawk — I'm against it. Dead set against it."

Hawk felt a worm flip in his belly. He

looked from Tarwater to Pennybacker, Pike, and Learner, all three of whom looked desperate but vaguely chagrined.

"Dead set against what?" Hawk growled, though he knew what it was.

"Sheriff," Pennybacker said, removing his spectacles to clean them on a crisp linen handkerchief with his initials monogrammed in a corner, "the town council and several select citizens met informally in the schoolhouse at the crack of dawn."

Hawk glanced at Regan, who continued to stare across the street at him with that queer, sullen, vaguely defiant expression.

"And . . . ?" Hawk knew what the man was going to say, but he wanted him to say it.

"And . . ." Pennybacker glanced at Pike and Learner, then at Tarwater before sliding his gaze up again at the county sheriff standing on the second porch step. "And we feel it's in the best interest of this town and this county to free Brazos Tierney, One-Eye McGee, and J. T. Hostetler. Our county prosecutor, Mr. Devlin, reopened the case against them and decided that the way you handled the situation . . . assaulting these men without provocation . . . is grounds for their dismissal."

Hawk ran his wry gaze from face to face

and curled one corner of his mouth.

"Without provocation?" Tarwater exclaimed, scowling with exasperation. "You men are cowards — it's as simple as that!"

"This is a law matter, Mr. Tarwater," Learner reprimanded his fellow councilman. "I suggest you restrain your high-strung Confederate emotions."

Tarwater laughed. "Well, I'll be damned. That's the first time any of you have ever brought up the fact that I wore Confederate gray during the War of Northern Aggression. Here, I thought we good citizens of Trinity were all integrated!"

Learner flushed, as did Pike, who looked down.

"This isn't about us, gentlemen," Pennybacker interjected. "Let's all just settle down. This is about the future of Trinity." He looked at Hawk. "Sheriff . . . ?"

"Anyone over there at the school vote against this decision?" Hawk asked, glancing at Regan, though it was clear by her faltering gaze now which side she was on.

Pennybacker glanced over at the young schoolteacher, as well. Regan turned and, head down, began walking back along Wyoming Street.

Pennybacker looked at Hawk. "It didn't come to a vote. On the move to acquit placed before the Trinity Town Council by Prosecutor William G. Devlin. . . ."

The mayor glanced at one of the better-dressed dudes standing in the street behind him and the other councilmen, at a man with trimmed muttonchops and a black derby, who was holding a beer schooner in one fist and a cigar in his other hand.

Pennybacker puffed up his little chest and continued, ". . . I gave the order on the authority that Judge Lewiston P. Tecumseh Price has vested in me in his absence. If and when the judge decides to reinstate the charges, he may do so, and, if so, at that time Mr. Tierney, Mr. McGee, and Mr. Hostetler will be rearrested and given a new trial."

Pennybacker had let his voice fade during that last officious sentence, because, having had enough of the rancid bullshit being spewed by these dapper cowards, Hawk had turned and walked on up the porch and into the jailhouse.

Pennybacker and the other councilmen stared after him, listening to the jingle of the key ring and then to the ratchety scrape of the key in the lock of the cell block door. They continued to listen, hearing Hawk's boot thuds diminishing inside the cell block.

Carson Tarwater let a devious smile tug at

his mouth.

Pennybacker, Learner, and Pike shared apprehensive glances, worry suddenly sharpening their eyes. All three men gave a simultaneous, startled jerk as a scream peeled out of the cell block, and Pennybacker lurched forward.

"Oh, god, no!"

22.
Quiet Sunday

Mayor Pennybacker stopped short of the front porch steps when the scream he'd heard from the cell block transformed abruptly into a victorious howl that grew even louder, echoing around the cell block and leeching into the street.

The howl was followed by two more as all three prisoners rejoiced. Several sets of boots thudded amidst the mocking laughter, and as the three men moved out of the cell block and into the main office, Brazos Tierney said with a definite, halting lisp, "The wheels of justice do grind slow, but I was just certain the good folks of Trinity would see it my pa's way!"

More laughter.

Pennybacker and the other men stepped back as Brazos moved out the front door, his hat cocked at a rakish angle, strapping his gun and shell belt around his waist, just below a wide leather belt studded with leather conchos. The whang strings on his deerhide breeches fluttered as he sauntered onto the porch, clicking his boot heels across the puncheons and ringing his spur rowels.

His jeering grin showed the stubs of his broken teeth and torn gums. Dried blood smeared about his mouth gave him a heightened look of psychopathic savagery.

Laughing and shooting their pistols, the three went running down the porch steps and up the street in the direction of the livery barn. The clusters of onlookers gathered on either side of the street lurched back in fear. Hawk came out to stand atop the porch, staring bemusedly after his three freed prisoners and biting the end off a black Mexican cigar.

"Mr. Hawk," Pennybacker said, looking a little constipated. "I hope . . . I hope there are no hard feelings."

"You did what you figured you had to do." Hawk plucked the sheriff's badge off his vest and flipped it over the porch rail and into the dust at the councilmen's polished boots.

"You're leaving?" Pennybacker asked.

"Nah, I'm just quittin'." Lighting his cigar with a stove match, Hawk started down the porch steps. "I believe I'll hang around town a while, in an unofficial capacity. Just for the hell of it."

As he moved past the councilmen, he glanced at Carson Tarwater, who stared at Hawk with a fateful expression, and shook his head slowly, darkly from side to side. Hawk continued into the street, angling past the gallows and Reb Winter and his silent Indian friend, Alvin Gault. Reb looked at Hawk, the younker's eyes sharp with exasperation as he twisted his cloth watch cap in his big hands nervously.

"Where you gonna go, Gid?" Reb slid his eyes toward the livery barn from which the laughter of the three freed prisoners could still be heard. "What're you gonna do?"

"I'm gonna have a beer. Then I'm gonna go up and catch me some beauty sleep." Hawk scratched his two-day growth of beard stubble and continued walking between the clusters of tense-looking onlookers, toward the Four Aces.

An especially large crowd was gathered in front of the saloon, including the county prosecutor, who averted his eyes from those of the former Trinity sheriff as Hawk passed him and abruptly threw back the last of the beer in his heavy schooner.

The street gradually cleared. Most folks went back about their Sunday business, whatever that entailed since there were no church services in Trinity these days. Hawk ordered a beer and sat down at a table facing the front window, polishing off half the beer in a single draught, then sitting back in his chair and sipping the rest as he took long, thoughtful pulls on his cigar.

Whoops and hollers sounded from the west. Horse hooves pounded. Hawk tipped his schooner to his lips and watched over the rim as Tierney, Hostetler, and One-Eye McGee galloped past, popping their pistols into the air above their heads and yammering like crazed coyotes.

Quickly, the din died. Smoke from the gun blasts faded, and the dust of the trio sifted over the sun-bathed street. Sunday quiet prevailed once more over Trinity.

Hawk took another sip from his beer, then set the glass back down on the table, near the butt of the Henry he'd set on the scarred tabletop, as well, within easy reach. Nearly every muscle in his lean frame was drawn taught as freshly stretched Glidden wire. A fist-sized knot burned in his belly.

There weren't too many people in the saloon. Most of the saddle tramps and punchers who'd been stranded in town by Tierney's threat had pulled out. Now Hawk watched the stage pull out away from the Poudre River House, as well, the driver whipping the reins over the backs of his fresh team and the shotgun messenger holding his double-barreled Greener up high across his chest. The carriage rocked back on its thoroughbraces and wheeled to Hawk's left and out of view from the dusty windows, heading west to the little mining towns of Calumet and Manhattan roughly forty miles away, at the foot of Cameron Pass.

Carson Tarwater had been walking into the Four Aces as the stage was pulling out, and he stood between the batwings now, watching the stage as it dwindled away. Turning forward, holding a newspaper in one hand and a briar pipe in the other, he moved into the saloon. He wore a wool jacket against the chill, and a bowler hat.

As he angled over to the bar, his eyes found Hawk in the shadows, leaning back in his chair with his empty beer schooner before him. Tarwater sidled up to the bar and ordered a beer from the Sunday waiter, a thin, bald, somber-looking gent in a bow tie. While the apron pulled a beer, Tarwater hiked an elbow on the counter and arched his brows at Hawk.

"Maybe it was for the best, after all."

Hawk continued to stare into the near-vacant street where a few crusts of snow lined the walks. The snow glistened in the sunlight that was slowly melting it. Smoke from stoves hung in thin, blue clouds over the street.

"Maybe."

"Buy you a beer?"

"No, thanks."

Tarwater slid a couple of coins across the bar top, then lifted his beer and sipped. He smacked his lips, and in a dark tone, he said, "You don't think they'll leave us alone, now, do you?"

Hawk hadn't even started to respond when the thunder of a distant shotgun blast sounded in the far distance. He held still in his chair, staring out the dusty windows at the sunny street.

Tarwater swung his head toward the batwings. "What the . . . ?"

He let his voice trail off as distant gunfire crackled. It stopped as suddenly as it had started. Tarwater turned to Hawk, who continued sitting his chair, still as a statue, staring out the windows. The other men in the Four Aces had fallen silent, and they too were staring darkly toward the street.

A man's shout sounded from the same direction as the gunfire — west. He shouted again, and Hawk reached forward to wrap his right hand around the neck of his Henry.

At the same time, hooves drummed. The thuds grew louder and were soon joined by the clatter of iron-shod wheels.

Hawk lifted the Henry off the table, the knot in his belly doubling in size, and kicked his chair back as he stood and donned his hat. A worried murmur rose around him as did the men themselves.

Hawk strode toward the batwings, followed closely by the limping, shuffling Tarwater. Behind him, chairs raked the scarred floorboards as the other drinkers gained their feet and headed toward the batwings, as well.

Hawk pushed through the doors and, swinging his head toward the west, stepped out into the street. He stopped, his auburn brows furling. The stage was heading back toward him, the pullers shaking their heads and twitching their ears, their eyes white-ringed with anxiety.

Only the burly driver sat in the driver's boot. The messenger was nowhere to be seen. The driver himself had lost his hat, and he rode slumped forward, wincing and fumbling with the ribbons as though he was barely able to maintain a grip on them.

When the stage had drawn to within a block or so of the saloon, the jehu lifted his head suddenly, throwing himself against the seatback, and gave a loud groan as he raised the ribbons high and pulled them back hard against his chest.

Hawk started taking long strides toward the coach that kept coming toward him until the driver finally had the team stopped, and the horses jumping around nervously in the traces. The man threw the brake and dropped the line to the floor of the driver's box. Then he slumped forward, crossing his arms on his belly, which, Hawk saw as he closed the distance between him and the coach, was bright with blood.

The seat beside the driver, where the messenger had been sitting, was also splashed with blood.

Several men ran up from the cross streets on both sides of the coach but stopped when they saw the driver's condition. Other men moved out from alley gaps. Most of the stores were closed, but a few men and women working overtime stepped out of their shop doors or peered through windows. The driver continued to slump forward until he turned a somersault over the dashboard and hit the ground behind the wheelers, causing the horses to pitch and whinny.

Hawk snapped his rifle up.

He snugged the butt against his hip as he

swung wide of the skitter-stepping team where he could get a good look at the side of the coach. The deerskin shades were drawn, but he could hear no one moving around inside. He moved toward the door, keeping his ears pricked for sounds of the passengers. When he was two feet away from the door, he stopped, set his boots, and reached for the door handle.

Faintly, he heard a sound from inside. A muffled click.

Suddenly, he pulled his hand back from the door. Wrapping his left hand around the Henry's barrel, he seated a round quickly in the rifle's breech and fired. The slug tore a ragged hole in the door.

From inside, a man screamed.

Hawk fired and continued firing until he'd punched six holes through the door and the dusty, umber-painted sides of the carriage housing, in the old "smokehouse" pattern. There was a thud. The coach rocked. The horses were kicking up a cacophony now, but the brake and their training was holding them.

Ejecting the sixth spent cartridge, Hawk wrapped his hand around the handle and jerked the door wide, lurching forward and poking his rifle through the opening.

He released the tension in his trigger finger.

Inside, two men were on the floor between the seats — both dressed in deerskin leggings and leather vests, with holsters thronged on their thighs. One was on his back, a bloody hole in his chest. The other man, a black man with a feathered hat, lay over the first, chest down over the first man's face. The second man wore a sheepskin coat that had a hole in it, over the man's left shoulder blade, and the hole was gushing thick red blood with every beat of the man's fluttering heart.

The man lifted his shaggy head and turned his face toward Hawk, gritting his teeth and trying to bring up the cocked Schofield in his left fist. Hawk raised the Henry to his shoulder, sighted down the barrel, and fired, snapping the man's head back against the far-side door.

Hawk had just started turning around when something hot and heavy slammed into his upper left arm. The thundering rifle boom reached his ears a half-second later.

As his knees buckled and he starting going down, he glimpsed the shooter, J. T. Hostetler, aiming a smoking rifle at him from the side of a high-jutting roof facade.

Hostetler grinned as he levered his Winchester, ejecting his spent cartridge casing and seating a live round in the chamber.

23.
Gallows Express

Blood welling from the hole in his arm, Hawk dropped to his knees beside the coach as Hostetler fired again from atop the roof. The slug screeched so close to Hawk's head that he could feel the curl of the wind against his right ear before the .44-40 round hammered the side of the carriage.

As the horses squealed and pitched and jerked the coach forward, Hawk raised his rifle from his knees, drew a bead on the figure standing beside the tall false facade, and fired. Hostetler had been raking a fresh round into his Winchester's breech.

Hawk's slug took the bushwhacker through his chest, causing the man's head to bob and his arms to be thrown out to his sides. As he sagged backward, he looked down at the hole in his denim jacket, and his eyes grew wide. He staggered, momentarily regained his footing, then, dropping his rifle, pitched forward over the lip of the store's roof. He turned a complete somersault, screaming, before he slammed through the brush ramada below and landed on the boardwalk in a rain of wood and dirt.

Hawk gritted his teeth against the pain in his shoulder as he ejected the spent cartridge from the Henry's breech. The stage team had torn the stage free of its brake and was lurching eastward along Wyoming Street, dust rising with the clatter of the churning wheels. Behind Hawk, a familiar whoop sounded, echoing around the street from which the stunned crowd that had gathered around the stagecoach was now fleeing, an anxious din rising.

From the direction of the hotel, Reb Winter was running, bounding out of the path of the runaway team.

Hawk waved him back. "No, Reb!" he shouted. "Stay there!"

A rifle barked. Grit blew up at Hawk's boots.

Through the coach's sifting dust, he saw another gunman — Brazos Tierney — peeking out from behind the red false facade jutting above the hotel. Hawk bore down on the man, firing two quick rounds from his shoulder. His slugs merely hammered the side of the facade as Brazos gave a mocking whoop and bolted back behind it and out of the path of Hawk's bullets.

Thunder rose as Hawk squeezed off another futile round, and he jerked his head to his right, dread filling his belly like bile when he saw the riders galloping toward him. More hoof thuds rose to his left, and swinging his head in that direction, he saw more riders hammering toward him from the west.

Cursing, Hawk lowered his Henry's butt to his right hip and began firing and levering, scattering the western riders, causing them to turn their pitching mounts toward the boardwalks or to carom into alley mouths. Hawk's fusillade slowed them, but they continued to come, smoke and flames stabbing from the rifles and pistols they triggered over their horses' bobbing heads.

Bullets screeched around and over the Rogue Lawman.

Hawk spun around and sent a spray of .44 rounds to the east, scattering those riders as one man jerked back in his saddle, screaming, and another showed his teeth as he clamped a gloved hand over his left shoulder.

The Henry's hammer gave an eerie ping, and Hawk threw the empty rifle aside. He crossed his arms over his belly and clamped his hands over the handles of his Russian and his Colt .44, but he had the pistols only half raised before another shot barked from atop the feed store.

The hot, screaming slug slammed like a ball-peen hammer into Hawk's left temple. It chewed a dogget of flesh and bone from his skull, then plunked into the street near Hawk's right boot, shredding a pile of fresh horse apples and splattering the manure with blood.

He groaned as the violent blow spun him half around.

With the forceful thrust of two brutal arms, the blow shoved him to his knees as he inadvertently triggered the Russian into the street, blowing dust up over his ankles. He ground his molars against the railroad spike of agony hammering through his temple and into his right eye. His head swam; nausea flooded him.

The thunder of the oncoming riders grew louder.

Hawk growled, bearlike, as he lifted his head and tried to bring his pistols up, as well, though the guns now felt like lead anchors in his fists. He blinked as he stared eastward, saw the first horse of that bunch of hard cases gallop within ten yards of him, its broad chest crossed by a concho-studded breastplate.

He squinted as the single horse separated, became two horses as the railroad spike was hammered farther into Hawk's brain, giving him double vision. Unable to lift his pistols from a sitting position, Hawk gave another growl as he heaved himself up off his boot heels.

Staggering, he had the Russian only half raised before the closest eastern rider bore down on him. Hawk tried to lurch out of the horse's path, but then he saw two rifle butts swing toward him, until he could see the grain in the weathered wood, though he felt only one club slam into the side of his head.

He heard himself groan, saw the dusty street spin around him. The ground came up to slam viciously into his left shoulder and hip, ratcheting up his misery.

Darkness washed over his eyes, but he remained conscious enough to feel the ground pitching beneath him like the deck of a ship caught in a hurricane. The gunfire ceased. Hooves clomped around him.

"No!" shouted Brazos Tierney. "We ain't killin' him. Not yet we ain't!"

Hawk lolled on his back, his guns useless in his paralyzed hands. He managed to open his eyes a crack and stared as if through three feet of water at the riders milling around him, several staring down at him with savage looks on their bearded faces. Pistols or rifles were in their hands.

He felt a sharp bite of pain as a horse hoof clipped his left ankle. In the periphery of his vision he could see a few townsfolk standing around, watching from boardwalks or alley mouths, though his overall sense was that, excepting the Tierney gang, the street was deserted.

Suddenly, Brazos Tierney was staring down at him. The sharply glinting predator's eyes dropped closer to Hawk's as the killer squatted over him, grinning and poking his hat brim up off his high forehead.

Blue Tierney's face appeared above and to the right of his son's, long gray hair nudging the shoulders of his blue greatcoat. The old man and the son had similar features though Blue Tierney's eyes were hard and blue and sunk more deeply in their wizened sockets.

The man's voice was garbled in Hawk's ears, but the Rogue Lawman could make out the words: "What you wanna do with him, son? I reckon he's yourn."

"Hang him." Brazos plucked the pistols from Hawk's hands as he continued to grin down at him. "Express ride to the gallows he done had built in our honor!"

He straightened, drew a foot back, and slammed the boot against the side of Hawk's jaw, increasing the pain in Hawk's thundering head. A couple of his back teeth cut into his cheek, and he felt the cool, copper-tasting blood dribble down along his jaw and trickle out the corner of his mouth.

Hawk saw Blue Tierney's mouth move, but he couldn't make out the man's words.

"Why, sure," said the outlaw leader's son. "We'll do him like we done them rustlin' Sioux up on the plains. A nice, slow hangin' . . . till the blood's runnin' out his ears and he's beggin' we shoot him!"

He reached down and lifted Hawk's head by his thick, dark brown hair and one arm. "Let's go, boys!"

"No!" a woman screamed. "You can't do this."

"For god sakes," said a man's voice, a familiar one though Hawk's foggy brain couldn't identify it until he saw Carson Tarwater and Regan Mitchell enter his field of swirling vision.

"Christ," Hawk groaned. "Get the hell outta here," he barely heard himself mutter, his cheek in the dirt. "Both of you."

"What do we have here?" Brazos said, grinning across Hawk's slumped body at the two newcomers. "Or, I should say, *who* we got here?"

"Stop this," Tarwater pleaded. "This man was only doing his job. We hired him. Let him go. You and your friends are free, Brazos. Why cause any more trouble, huh?"

"I wasn't talkin' to you," Brazos said, as the other men in his gang — there had to be a good nine or ten of them — gathered around Tarwater and the young schoolteacher.

Hawk felt an even worse sinking feeling as he stared up at the men surrounding the pair. He wanted to scream but didn't have the energy.

"I'm Miss Mitchell," Regan said, taking one step back from Brazos but backing into a big, shaggy-headed hombre who'd come up behind her. "The schoolteacher."

"Hot damn!" Brazos intoned. "If I'd o' known they made schoolteachers like you, I might've done some schoolin'!"

"Regan," Hawk grunted, barely able to make his voice audible. "For god sakes, get the hell outta here. . . ."

Tarwater stepped between the teacher and Brazos. "Please. This isn't about her."

"Mister," Brazos said, "is that a southern accent I hear in your voice?"

Tarwater stared at the man darkly. "That's right. I fought for the Confederacy under

Hood. I don't know what that's got —"

Hawk had seen the knife flash as if from nowhere in the young killer's right fist, and he'd tensed his body to try to stand. A futile effort.

"Gnahhh!" Tarwater said as he bent suddenly forward over the pig sticker that Tierney had just buried in his gut.

Regan screamed and jerked back into the arms of the man behind her. She tried to twist away from the man, and as she did so Hawk somehow managed to climb to his feet though the ground continued to pitch and sway and nearly exchange positions with the sky. As the big, shaggy-headed man lifted Regan up off her feet, nuzzling her neck, Hawk funneled the last of his strength into his right fist, tried a swing at Brazos's head. He wasn't sure why. Probably, it was the only thing he was in any condition to do.

One of the other men warned young Tierney, and Tierney managed to pull his head back just enough that Hawk's knuckles merely grazed the side of the killer's head, knocking his hat off. Brazos glared at Hawk, eyebrows arched, face brick red and swollen with exasperation. His eyes shone a murky yellow-gray.

"Why, you . . . !" With that, he buried his

right fist into Hawk's belly.

The street came up to slam into the Rogue Lawman's knees. He dropped onto his side to see Carson Tarwater on the ground beside him, grinding his forehead into the dirt and holding his arms across his belly. A thick pool of blood grew in the fine-ground dirt and horseshit below the councilman, staining the knees of his brown broadcloth trousers.

"Ah, Christ," Hawk heard himself groan beneath Regan's horrified screams that quickly diminished as she was carried away.

Then everything went as black as night at the bottom of a deep well. He was faintly aware of his hips aching, as though more railroad spikes were being driven through his midsection. The top of his head burned. Then it pounded.

His mouth came open — he could feel a draft on his tongue. He closed it, but it seemed desperate to stay open.

There were more sounds and more sensations, but they seemed to Hawk to be emanating from deep inside a distant cave. They were anxiety-provoking sounds, and when he was finally able to identify them, he realized that one was a piano being played badly. So badly that a man commented on it, shouting words that Hawk couldn't quite make out.

"I told you!" a girl screamed in fury. "I don't know 'The Battle Hymn of the Republic'!"

"Anyone who knows how to play the piano knows 'The Battle Hymn of the Damn Republic,' so play it!" the man retorted, his words clearer. "Any *real* Texan fought for the *North!*"

"I'm from Kentucky!"

"Goddamnit, you think I don't know that, girl? I also think you know how to play 'The Battle Hymn of the Republic' — so play it or I'm gonna send you back to Ole Kentuck in itty-bitty pieces in a croaker sack!"

The girl screamed defiantly.

A gun exploded. The girl screamed again. The scream was clipped by two more pistol shots.

Hawk opened his eyes with a start. He blinked as he found himself in an upside-down world, the facades he recognized as belonging to the shops around Wyoming Street all inverted.

Hawk blinked. Shook his head. Ropes raked his wrists and ankles, bit into the tender flesh.

No, the world wasn't upside down. He was.

Beneath his head lay unpainted whipsawed

pine boards. He frowned and then his heart twisted in his chest as he realized that he was hanging upside down from the gallows. It was late in the day, with a chill in the air and shadows angling over him and across the street around him.

The girl's voice he'd heard had belonged to Claire.

Hawk twisted his body slightly and looked around again, desperation flooding over him, and he tried to move his feet and arms. Neither would budge because his feet were tethered to two nooses of the three nooses that had been intended for Brazos Tierney and the other two prisoners. Hawk's wrists were tied to two steel spikes that had been driven into the gallows floor, about four feet apart.

The more he struggled, the deeper the ropes dug into his wrists, causing fresh blood to ooze out from beneath the blood that had already oozed and crusted.

He twisted his head, getting a look at Wyoming Street around him. By the angle of the sun, it was around five. There was no one on the street bathed in salmon-touched light. Dust motes twinkled in it. To his right he could hear a girl's muffled sobs.

Cassidy?

Hawk turned his head in that direction.

The Venus was there on the south side of the street. Hard-faced men milled on the porch. Tierney's men. Laughing, drinking, smoking. The shaggy-headed man who'd hauled Regan off sat there on a chair, at the edge of the porch. Holding a double-bore shotgun across his stout legs, his buckskin pants tucked inside high-topped, mule-eared boots, he stared toward Hawk. The breeze tussled his shaggy, curly hair.

He grinned as though with carnal satisfaction.

As Hawk hung upside down from the gallows, like a dressed out deer carcass, he jerked again at the knotted ropes and knew a frustration as bitter as any he'd ever known.

Shadows grew. The light dwindled, turning coppery, then brown edging toward gray.

The chill wind blew against Hawk, who hung there in mute agony, miniature hearts pounding in both eyeballs, a heavy hammer whacking his head in several different places. His wounded arm was numb. His blood-engorged hands and feet ached with a throbbing pain.

Blood had crusted on his temple, down his left arm, down the side of his face, and on his lips. Drops had dried on the floor of the gallows beneath him.

Inside the Venus, another man shouted. Another girl screamed. The girl whom Hawk had heard sobbing before now sobbed louder. "Claire," Cassidy cried. "Oh, Claire!"

Someone began playing "The Battle Hymn of the Republic." Better than the person who'd been playing it before. The shaggy-headed man smiled again at Hawk.

"Hey, Sheriff," the shotgun-wielding killer said in a thick Spanish accent. "You wanna join the party? We're just getting warmed up." Slowly, he shook his head. "No . . . I don think so, amigo."

24.
"When Have I Ever *Not* Been with You, You Son of a Bitch?"

"Gid?"

The voice sifted like faint wood smoke into the prism of Hawk's tormented half consciousness. In fact, he seemed to smell the voice as much as hear it. It reeked of the malty-sour odor of beer.

Hawk recoiled at the hand that closed over his shoulder. Every nerve and muscle in his pain-racked body was poised for battle, which is the one urge that held at bay the half wish for death to steal over him and abolish his misery.

He wanted now, as much as ever, to kill.

The voice was closer, the beer stench stronger, warm against his left ear. "Hey, G-Gid, you s-s-still kickin'?"

Reb Winter's voice.

Hawk opened his eyes. Reb hunkered down beside him atop the gallows. Beyond Reb hunched another large man-shaped figure on the ground near the gallows steps.

Alvin Gault held a Winchester carbine in his hands across his heavy, striped wool coat. The big Indian's breath frosted in the air before him, touched with torchlight emanating from the Venus.

Hawk glanced at Reb once more, anxiety pricking him like cactus thorns. He swung his head toward the Venus. None of the hard cases were milling on the porch. The chair in which the shotgunner had been sitting was still there, facing the gallows, but the shotgunner himself was gone. His shotgun lay across his chair, however . . . as though he were maybe only using the privy or something, and would return soon.

Hawk looked at Reb. "Get the hell outta here, fool! They'll gun you down like a dog. Both of you."

Reb shook his head and grinned, showing his large, square upper teeth front and bathing Hawk once more with the cloying beer stench. He and Gault had obviously buoyed their bravery with some suds prior to risking a visit to the gallows. Reb lifted a large skinning knife in his gloved right hand; his left hand was wrapped around the forestock of his old Spencer repeater with its dangling rope lanyard.

"Gonna cut ya down. Me an' Alvin been waitin' across the street." Reb grunted as he began sawing into the tough hemp binding Hawk's left wrist to the pin embedded in the gallows floor. "Think all Tierney's gun wolves are inside with the girls or gamblin'. Some're likely passed out. They been hittin' it hard all day."

As Reb continued sawing into the rope and, after all the malt he'd consumed, likely into Hawk's wrist as well, the Rogue Lawman turned another anxious look toward the well-lit Venus. Shadows of men and women passed behind the lit shades drawn over the windows.

"Well, hurry up, then," Hawk growled, continuing to stare, his heart thudding eagerly with the prospect of getting free and also getting his hands on his guns. "I'd right admire if you wouldn't cut my damn wrist off in the . . ."

He let his voice trail off as a shadow slithered out the front door and onto the porch. It was followed by a big, hatless, shaggy-headed man. Hawk sucked a breath. "Shit. Hold on."

Just then he felt his left wrist come free of the pin with only a slight kiss of Reb's razor-edged knife. The wrist and hand were mostly numb, anyway. He stared hard at the big man who moved slowly out to the near edge of the porch, staring toward the gallows. Hawk silently prayed that the man didn't see his visitors, but it was too much to hope for.

"Hey, who's over there?" he grunted, cocking his head to one side and then moving toward the shotgun lying atop his chair.

Hawk jerked his head toward Reb. "Skedaddle!"

"I-I ain't l-leavin' you here, Gid!"

"Move!" Hawk hissed. "You can help me later."

As the big man moved down the porch steps, wobbling slightly as though from drink, he lifted the shotgun straight up. Flames stabbed from one barrel. The great thundering boom rocked the night.

Reb jerked with a start, almost falling backward. "Shit!" He rose to a crouch, swiveled around, and leapt off the platform, wheezing, "Come on, Alvin!"

"Hey!" the shaggy-headed killer shouted, breaking into a shambling sort of run and slanting the shotgun across his chest. "You two gonna die bloody!" he shouted as he continued running on past the gallows.

Reb and Alvin hightailed it westward down Wyoming Street. From his inverted position, Hawk saw both men slant northward, cutting toward the jailhouse that sat hunched and dark under the velvet sky awash with milky starlight. The Two Troughs rider stopped at the corner of the gallows, set the shotgun's stock against his shoulder, and canted his head against it.

The second barrel flashed crimson. Another boom rocked the night, evoking more shouted exclamations from inside the Venus. As the thunder echoed hollowly around the street, Hawk saw the twin lumbering figures of Reb and Alvin angle past the front of the jailhouse and then dart behind its far wall.

As the din continued to rise inside the Venus, the shaggy-headed man turned to Hawk, his flat face rigid with fury. "Who was that?"

Holding his freed left hand down against the stake, Hawk said, "Go fuck yourself, scumbag."

The big man started toward Hawk but stopped when a man called in a drunk-heavy voice from the Venus's open door, "What's the shootin', Farina?"

Hawk turned his head to see the elder Tierney, Blue, standing in the doorway in just his hat, socks, and white longhandles, a jug in his hand. Another inquiring face or two stared from over his shoulder.

"Someone sneaked up to the gallows."

"Where the hell were you?"

Farina glanced at Hawk dubiously, then looked back at Tierney. "I was where I was s'posed to be, boss. In my chair right there. How do you think I ran 'em off?" He grinned unctuously.

Tierney turned around, gave a dismissive wave with the bottle, and started back into the bowels of the brothel.

Farina started back toward the Venus without so much as another glance at Hawk, who was glad his severed left bindings hadn't been discovered, and yelled, "When am I gonna be relieved?"

"Ya ain't!" Tierney shouted over his shoulder and then staggered on into the Venus and out of sight.

Farina cursed.

He breeched his shotgun and, shambling toward his chair, plucked out the spent wads, tossed them onto the ground, and replaced them with fresh from the bandoliers crisscrossed on his chest. Hawk watched the man, wanting to use his free hand to try to work the ties loose from the other one. But Farina had obviously been rousted back into action, and as the big man sagged down in the creaky chair, he set his shotgun across his stout legs, a knife poking up from one boot well, and directed his glum gaze toward the gallows.

Hawk hung there, his eyes feeling as though they had filled long ago from all the blood that had rushed to his head. Silently, he cursed. One hand was free. How was he going to get the other one and both ankles free, as well? He had to find a way. Poor Claire. Likely dead. She'd have to be avenged. Hawk hoped he wasn't too late to save Regan and Cassidy. . . .

He looked at the shotgun resting across the big man's lap.

He almost wished Reb hadn't cut the left one loose. It only put an even sharper edge on his rage and desperation.

How he would love to get his hands on that gun!

The night wore on. Farina remained in the chair, still as a statue, staring straight out from the porch at Hawk. The Rogue Lawman managed to work enough slack into the bindings on his right wrist that more blood seeped into his hand, easing the pain and numbness.

His feet, however, he could no longer feel. He drifted into semiconsciousness, waking now and then to stare up at the gradually wheeling stars fanned out in a vast bowl above the gallows.

Waking from one such half-asleep state, he turned toward the Venus. The torches had all gone out and the oil pots merely flickered. Most of the windows were still lit, though an eerie quiet had descended not only over the brothel but over the entire town.

He could see Farina's silhouette seated in the chair atop the porch. The man's head appeared to be dipped toward his chest. Hawk had no sooner made the observation and had begun tugging at the ropes at his right wrist with his free left hand when a shadow moved on the brothel's far right side.

Shit. The shaggy-headed Mexican was about to be relieved.

Hawk watched the silhouette mount the porch and walk toward Farina. Hawk felt scowl lines cut into his forehead when he saw the newcomer lean forward and walk quietly on the balls of his boots.

The newcomer, a slender figure in a long duster mostly concealed by the porch's thickening shadows, slipped around behind Farina. Black-gloved hands reached around from behind the man. One hand jerked the man's head up suddenly. A blade winked in the starlight as the other hand made a quick slicing motion across the shotgunner's throat.

There was a garbling sound. Farina tried

to stand. He dropped the shotgun, and the slender silhouette managed to grab the gun before it could land atop the porch floor. As Farina half gained his feet, the newcomer gave the man a kick from behind. Farina turned a somersault over the front porch rail and disappeared in the dark street below with a thud and a clipped groan.

Hawk winced, hoping the sounds hadn't been heard from inside.

The silhouetted figure moved nearly soundlessly off the porch, and as the girl walked toward him, Hawk could see starlight silvering the long blond hair on her shoulders and the two pearl-gripped Colts thronged low on her well-turned thighs clad in tight, black denim. Saradee's long, black leather duster flapped out away from her legs as she not so much walked as floated toward him. She'd removed her spurs, so as she began setting her heels down again, there was only the soft ticks of her light tread in the dust.

Hawk had never thought he'd be happy to see the blond killer, beautiful as she was. But he had to admit he was happy to see her now. As she approached, he cast quick, anxious glances at the lit windows behind her. The Venus was eerily quiet.

Saradee walked past him with her long,

saucy stride. Keeping her hands on the handles of her twin Colts, she mounted the gallows steps, setting her boots down again lightly. Atop the platform, she came over to Hawk, slipped a bowie knife from a sheath belted behind her back, and squatted beside him.

She leaned across the left pin, glancing at him briefly, silently, to cut the ropes binding his right wrist to the spike. When she'd freed his hand, she glanced coolly at him once more, her blond hair framing her face and starlit blue eyes, then walked over to where the ropes at the ends of both nooses were tied off, near the handle that would have opened the trapdoors.

"Catch yourself," she said tonelessly as, having cut the first noose free so that Hawk was dangling precariously, she cut the second one.

She cut through only about three-quarters of the second rope, then walked over to where Hawk was slowly falling from the crossbeam as the rest of the strands frayed. She grabbed his buckskin vest in both her fists and drew him toward her. Just then, the remaining strands of the rope broke, and Hawk fell three feet to the gallows floor, landing relatively softly on his back and shoulders.

Hawk sucked air through his teeth as the blood flooded back out of his right hand. The pain was worse than before — both hot and cold and prickling, as though he'd fallen in a cholla patch. His feet tingled painfully, as well, as blood rushed back into them.

"You ready to pull your picket pins?" Saradee said snootily as she cut his left ankle free of the noose, grunting with the effort.

"No."

Hawk kicked free of the ropes and, sitting up on his rump, legs stretched straight out in front of him, held his right hand across his belly as he flexed it, trying to work blood back into it to regain the feeling. It was swollen and purple, but the nearly unbearable pain meant it was still alive.

Saradee arched a blond brow at him. "This town hung you out to dry like a pair of washworn underwear on a cold wind."

"I'm not finished here." Hawk looked at the brothel, noting a sudden flash of orange light in an upper-story window, behind the balcony rail. "I still got some rabid dogs runnin' off their leash that needin' shooting. When that's done" — Hawk glanced at her — "then I'll leave."

Inside the brothel, a man screamed.

A pistol popped once.

Saradee turned toward the Venus, then glanced again at Hawk. "I used to think I was the craziest person I knew."

Hawk used his left hand to draw her toward him. He was too desperate to resist her. He kissed her lips, then pulled back to stare into her eyes that regarded him obliquely. "My right hand's likely shot. I'm gonna need help in there." He hesitated. His pride was a large, jagged bone lodged in his throat. He tried to clear it. "You with me?"

Inside the Venus a girl screamed. Another pistol barked. The window in which the light had flashed was now bright with a flickering orange glow.

Saradee grabbed a fistful of Hawk's chambray shirt collar and pulled him toward her. She kissed him hungrily, twisting his collar until it chafed his neck. She turned her head and entwined her tongue with his. As she drew away, she gave his lower lip a nasty nip.

She gritted her teeth and hardened her eyes as she stared into his from six inches away. "When have I ever *not* been with you, you son of a bitch?"

25.
"THINGS ARE HEATIN' UP"

Inside the Venus, men were yelling and stumbling around, drunk and wondering what the screaming and yelling on the second floor was about and probably smelling the smoke from the fire that Hawk could see ever brightening the second-story window.

Saradee handed the Rogue Lawman the double-barreled Greener she'd taken off of Farina after cutting his throat.

"We best get moving," she said, nodding at the fiery window. "Things are heatin' up."

Hawk heaved himself to his feet. His right hand was still aching, but he had enough feeling back in it that he thought he could pull a trigger or two.

"Let's go."

Breeching the double-bore, he limped down the gallows steps. Saradee striding up beside him as he winced and strode tenderly on his swollen feet, he moved across the street to the Venus. Behind the windows, figures were moving, some in the shapes of men jumping around as they dressed. Suddenly, two men pushed out the front door and onto the gallery, coughing. They both had revolvers in their hands.

As smoke slithered out the door behind them, they swung around to look up at the second-story windows. One caught a glimpse of Hawk and Saradee and turned full around to face them — a slender, curly-haired, bearded gent in checked trousers, suspenders, and underwear shirt. His gun belt was in his left hand, a long-barreled Remington in his other.

"He's mine," Hawk growled to Saradee as she and he continued toward the porch, not slowing their pace a bit though Hawk was limping on both feet.

"Rather territorial, ain't ya?"

"Hey!" the man shouted, raising his Remy as, narrowing one eye, he stared into the dark street at the two coming toward him.

Hawk triggered the shotgun's right barrel.

Ka-booommm!

The curly-haired man was lifted two feet off the porch and thrown straight back into the Venus's gaping front door through which more and more gray smoke sifted. The second man had already swung around, bringing up a Schofield and clicking back the hammer.

Ka-booommm!

The shotgun's second barrel blew him back through the window behind him in a screeching clatter of tearing curtains and breaking glass. Hawk tossed aside the empty gut shredder and continued up the porch steps.

"I want my prisoners alive," he told Saradee, walking along behind him. "Hostetler's dead but I want Brazos and One-Eye McGee alive!"

"That might be a tall order. Would half alive do?"

"It'll do."

Hawk crouched to scoop from the porch floor the big Remy of the first man he'd shot. When he'd grabbed the second Remy from the second holster on the man's shell belt, he strode through the smoky doorway. Saradee had gone in ahead of him and turned through the door opening off the foyer's left side, into the parlor. Upstairs, several shots had already been fired, and a man was screaming.

"Downstairs!" shouted a woman's voice. "Hurry — get downstairs!"

Hawk stepped over the first dead man and saw a bulky figure on the foyer floor, to his right. The Venus's madam, Mrs. Ferrigno sat against the wall, stubby legs stretched out before her. Her head was tipped towards one shoulder, and her eyes were open and staring toward the front door as though wishing she could get up and walk through it.

Dried blood dribbled down from the bullet hole in her forehead.

As more guns popped in the direction Saradee had gone and more men started shouting and girls screaming, Hawk spied movement on the steps rising at the back of the foyer. A man materialized from the gray smoke gushing down from behind him, running, one hand on the rail. In his other hand he held a pistol.

When the man jerked his head toward Hawk, he stopped so suddenly that he almost fell and raised his pistol. Hawk raised his own Remy and shot the man through his chest, sending him down and back against the steps. The man dropped his gun with a loud clattering thud and rolled on down the steps to the foyer.

More screams emanated from upstairs.

There were more pistol shots and men's yells from the direction in which Saradee had disappeared.

Hawk stepped over the dead man and

started up the steps just as a blazing fireball blew out of the second story at the top of the staircase, a man screaming inside it.

Hawk stepped back. The fireball came down the stairs, waving its arms and pumping its knees.

Inside the leaping flames and swirling smoke, Hawk saw the man opening his mouth and widening his eyes in horror as the flames turned his flesh black. The fireball swept past Hawk, leapt the dead man at the bottom of the stairs and the other dead man near the front door, and bounded outside and into the night, burning.

"Hawk!" Saradee shouted from the doorway leading to the other half of the house, thumbing shells from her cartridge belt and through the loading gate of one of her pearl-gripped .45s.

Hawk spun, raising the Remy. At the top of the stairs, Cassidy screamed and held a crooked arm in front of her face, as though to stop a bullet. Two more girls were behind her — all only about one-third dressed.

Hawk lowered the pistol and beckoned the girls down the stairs. Hawk grabbed Cassidy's arm. The girl's face paint was badly streaked from tears.

"Claire?" Hawk said.

More tears gushed down the brunette's face but her voice was low and fateful. "Brazos killed her."

When the two doves had hustled out behind Cassidy, Hawk went up the stairs, taking the steps two at a time in spite of his aching feet. As two men stumbled toward him from above the second-story landing, heading down from the third story, a gun barked in the lead man's hand.

The slug thwacked into the railing to Hawk's left.

Hawk pivoted to look up the second set of stairs, raised the Remy, and drilled one pill through the chest of the first man, whose knees buckled. He pitched forward, hit the stairs facedown, turned two somersaults, and piled up on the landing at Hawk's boots. Hawk raised the Remy to the man who'd been thundering down the stairs behind the first. The man tossed his gun over his shoulder and lifted his open hands in front of his face in supplication.

"I give up!"

Hawk fired three times, watched in grim satisfaction as his bullets punched through each of the man's palms and into his forehead. Hawk turned into the second-floor hallway as the second dead man rolled down and over the body of the first man, one of his hands brushing Hawk's left ankle.

Amidst the thick smoke produced by the flames at the far end of the hall, Hawk spied a body on the floor to his right. A naked man with a fish-belly-white paunch and long, thin, blue-veined legs. Long, gray hair lay in a wild nest beneath Blue Tierney's head. The man clamped his hands to the wound in his lower left side. Blood oozed through his fingers, dribbled over his hip and onto the floor.

"Pa?" a man shouted from down the hall.

The smoke was so thick that Hawk could just barely make out the outline of a man's head in a half-open doorway on the hall's left side, opposite the open door from which flames leapt and smoke gushed.

"Hep," Blue Tienry groaned, just loudly enough for Hawk to hear. The man's pale eyes stared up at Hawk with dire pleading. "Hep . . . hep me."

"The crazy bitch gutted Willie Wilbur and set him on fire!" Brazos shouted from the half-open door. "Brained me from behind. I can't see nothin', Pa. You out there?"

Blue Tierney lifted his head and tears dribbled down his cheeks. "She kilt me, boy! That goddamn schoolteacher . . . she done kilt me!" He squeezed his eyes closed and arched his back as he shouted at the ceiling.

"Avenge me, boy! If it's the last thing you do — *avenge me!*"

"I can't see!" Brazos screamed, stumbling out into the hall. He was ass naked. His pale skin glistened from the sweat of the heat in the place. He held a gun low down in his right hand. He held his other hand to the back of his head. "She clubbed me . . . bitch wrecked my vision! I'm blind, Pa!"

"Avenge me, Brazos, you chickenshit son of a bitch!"

Brazos stumbled toward Hawk. "Where is she?"

"Avenge me, boy!" Blue screamed at the ceiling, arching his back and making the cords in his neck stand out like steel cables.

He looked up at Hawk, slid his hand toward a Smith & Wesson pocket pistol on the floor beside him. When he had his hand on the gun, Hawk set his boot down on top of it hard, grinding the man's hand into the weapon.

Blue Tierney screamed.

Brazos Tierney stopped six feet from Hawk, and raised his pistol, his eyes wide and unseeing. "Who's there?"

Hawk moved up in front of Brazos. "Your executioner."

Brazos's chin fell as his mouth opened in shock and horror, and as he fumbled with the hammer of his uncocked pistol, Hawk grabbed the gun with his left hand, jerking it out of the killer's grip.

He stepped to one side, placed his hand on the back of the man's bloody head, and gave him a savage thrust down the hall and onto the landing, where Brazos piled up on top of the two dead men already sprawled there.

Brazos screamed, flailing with his hands while Blue Tierney continued to demand that his son avenge him. Glancing back at the flames that were chewing along the walls on both sides of the hall and leaving very little oxygen, Hawk started up the stairs, heading for the third floor.

"Regan?" he shouted, taking the steps two at a time.

At the top of the stairs, he stopped suddenly. Regan stood before him. She wore only a torn, bloodstained camisole. Her disheveled hair was streaked with blood. There were scrapes and bruises on her face, and her lips were cracked and swollen.

She held a cocked Colt pistol straight out in her left fist, the barrel aimed at Hawk's head. Her teeth were gritted, her eyes hard, savage in their determination.

"Regan?" Hawk said, softer.

Glancing behind her, he saw two more

men lying dead in the hall.

She stared at Hawk, the light of recognition gradually growing in her eyes. The gun sagged by inches, and then she lowered it.

"They're all dead up here," she said, pausing before adding in the same matter-of-fact tone. "I killed them all."

Hawk extended his hand to her. She did not take it but only stepped around him and started down the stairs, one hand on the rail to her left. In the other hand she carried the cocked Colt.

She went down gradually, lifting each bare knee in turn, setting her feet down gently on each step. Hawk followed. When she came to the landing where the dead men lay one atop the other — Brazos was no longer there, but Hawk could hear him screaming out on the street — she found a small, clear spot between them and stepped onto it.

She stopped and turned her head toward Blue Tierney still lying where Hawk had left him. The outlaw leader was no longer screaming, but his chest continued to rise and fall sharply as he cupped his hands over the bloody wound in his side.

Regan slowly raised the pistol, aimed, and fired.

The bullet tore the tip of Blue Tierney's

nose off.

He'd begun screaming again before Regan cocked the pistol, fired again.

This time her bullet punched through the side of the man's head, whipping his face toward the wall. His long hair covered his cheek like the wing of a scruffy white dove.

His chest rose once more, heavily. It fell once more and lay still.

Regan lowered the smoking Colt. Her lips were cracked and puffy, one eye badly bruised. Tierney's men had done a job on her, before she'd gotten the upper hand and taken several of them out. Apparently, in the dustup, someone had knocked over a lantern. Now Regan stepped over the legs of one of the dead men and started on down the last stretch of stairs. Hawk followed her through the foyer and out onto the porch. As she continued down the porch, Hawk stopped there and looked around.

Saradee had Brazos Tierney and One-Eye McGee on their knees before the Venus, their hands behind their heads. Tears dribbled down McGee's cheeks, and he ground his jaws painfully as blood oozed from bullet wounds in his shoulder and upper left thigh. Brazos Tierney stared blankly at the brothel, the second story of which was now almost completely engulfed by flames. The fire shone in his strange, now-blind gray eyes.

Behind Saradee and the outlaws, the doves who'd survived the Tierney gang's occupation stood around, arm in arm, some sobbing, some staring in shock at the burning building before them. Cassidy knelt over Claire's naked, bloody body.

Behind them, the gallows stood dark and silent. Waiting . . .

Hawk walked down the porch steps and into the street. He stopped before the two remaining Tierney riders.

"What're you gonna do with 'em?" Saradee glanced at the two men — both of whom looked as bewildered as the young whores — she held one of her cocked .45s on.

Hawk looked over at Claire. Then he looked at Cassidy, who returned his gaze.

"Gonna hang 'em." Hawk cleared the emotion from his throat, wedged his Remy behind his cartridge belt. "Just like Sheriff Stanley intended."

He turned toward where he'd last seen Regan. She was walking away from the burning brothel, moving with her head down through the sparse crowd of onlookers and men running around to begin forming a bucket brigade. Regan had dropped her gun in the dirt and was heading toward a gap between two buildings that would lead her back to her house.

"Regan?"

Hawk took one step toward her and stopped. She did not look back. Her slender, pale, dirty figure in the torn camisole turned into the dark gap between the buildings and disappeared like a figure in a dream.

Hawk groaned and expelled a long, held breath. "I'm sorry, Regan."

He turned to Saradee. She was watching him expectantly, a faint smile lifting one side of her upper lip.

"You wanna hang 'em now?" she asked, gesturing at Tierney and McGee with her pistol. "Then you and me light a shuck out of here and get a decent drink somewhere?" Her lip rose a little higher. "A decent bed?"

Hawk slipped his gun out behind his cartridge belt and cocked it as he aimed it at his prisoners. "Back to jail, fellers."

"Like hell," One-Eye growled.

Hawk triggered a slug into the dirt at his knee, blowing dust up over his thigh. McGee jerked back with a start then, staring warily up at Hawk, slowly gained his feet. Hobbling on his bad leg, he turned and headed across the street toward the jailhouse.

"You, too, Brazos," Hawk ordered.

"I'm blind," Brazos sobbed. "Bitch blinded me!"

"Get movin', or I'll gut shoot you."

Still sobbing, Brazos gained his feet. Hawk prodded him with his pistol barrel toward McGee's limping, diminishing form. Saradee watched all three men climb the porch steps and head on into the jailhouse where a light soon shone in a window.

She shook her head, glanced once more at the burning brothel. "Well, I need a drink."

She pushed through the growing crowd of scurrying, bucket-bearing men and headed toward the Four Aces.

Epilogue: Yep, Might Just Marry the Girl . . .

Hawk set one lilac-blue crocus atop each of the three graves fronting the granite headstone chiseled STANLEY, then stepped back, doffed his hat, and hooked a thumb behind his cartridge belt. The paper flowers he'd laid atop the baby's grave had blown away, but someone had planted a four-foot ponderosa pine sapling a few feet beyond the headstone. A bowl had been dug around the evergreen, and the freshly churned soil in the bowl was still dark from a recent watering.

Whoever had planted the tree obviously intended to care for it.

Who?

Hawk looked around as if the planter might still be around or had left some sign of his identity. There were only the stone and wood markers slanting shade as the morning sun continued to kite above the eastern horizon. The ground was still damp from the night's frost, and the air smelled clean and fresh. Robins flitted, and meadowlarks cooed. Mountain bluebirds were vibrant and fleeting splashes of periwinkle blue against the dun grass still matted and torn from the winter snows.

Spring was coming to Trinity.

Hawk returned his gaze to the Stanley graves. He studied each cold, rocky mound until his eyes came to a rest on the sheriff's. Holding his hat in his hand across his belly, he drew a deep breath and fingered the bandage the doctor had wrapped around his head late last night, after Hawk had jailed his prisoners and the fire had been contained by the bucket brigade. Laudanum had done wonders to quell the pain in his head and arm, but it made him foggy-headed and weak-kneed.

Not too foggy-headed to feel some satisfaction for what he had done, however.

"Your prisoners are due to be hanged, Sheriff." Hawk drew another breath, ran his tongue across his upper lip. "Hangman came in on the morning train. He's outfitting the gallows now, rigging the nooses and adjusting the sandbags. You can rest easy." He ran his gaze across the other two mounds humped with red stones of all shapes and sizes. "You can all rest easy."

Hawk donned his hat and turned away from the graves.

He walked out through the cemetery's dilapidated gate and started down the hill toward the town over which a blue morning smoke haze hung. He could see between the roof of the jailhouse on one side of the street and the black mound of what remained of the Venus on the other side that a small crowd had gathered around the gallows. Hawk's prisoners were on the platform while Reb Winter and Alvin Gault held shotguns on them from behind.

Hawk stopped suddenly as he drew his eyes to a wagon parked at the foot of the cemetery, on the narrow horse trail that wound down the shoulder of the hill and on into the town. Saradee sat in the driver's boot, the reins of the big mule in her hands. Both her cream stallion and Hawk's grulla were tied to the wagon's tailgate. Neither was saddled, only bridled.

Buffalo robes had been laid across the floor of the box, making a bed between the heaped mounds of saddles, saddlebags, and other sundry trail provisions including burlap bundles of food.

Saradee narrowed an eye at him hopefully. "Where to?"

Hawk stared back at her for a time, trying

to draw some shred of strength up from the bottom of his soul, enough with which he could resist her. Her golden hair fluttered about her shoulders, and her teeth were white between her red, fleshy lips.

And he couldn't find a single strand of fiber with which to stand against her.

He gave a dry chuckle and looked into the distant hills rolling out away from Trinity, wheat blond with grass and mint green with sage and rabbitbrush as they climbed toward high, purple ridges mantled with the grays of old winter snows.

"I think I'd like to head back Nebraska way."

"Got a couple graves of your own to tend there, eh, Hawk?"

"Somethin' like that."

Hawk eased his battered body onto the tailgate and scooted himself up onto the robes Saradee had laid out for him. Damn, he should give second thought to shooting the girl and think hard on marrying her. . . .

"Maybe I'll take up farming."

Saradee chuckled. "Plenty of whiskey back there. Doc gave me extra laudanum, too, for all your sundry scrapes and scratches. Some salted beef and sausage. Help yourself."

"Don't mind if I do," Hawk chuckled,

leaning back against the head of the box and squinting up at the buttery sun, enjoying the warmth on his face and the deep hides beneath his weary ass and legs. "Don't mind if I do. . . ."

Yep, might just marry the girl.

He stretched his arms out across the top of the panel behind him and stared out over the tailgate as Saradee clucked the big mule on down the hill and into the town, swinging east when she hit Wyoming Street. The wagon rattled and swayed. Hawk's grulla and Saradee's cream clomped along behind, heads down.

The jailhouse passed on Hawk's right. The gallows appeared on his left, a small gathering of townsfolk gathered around it, including Mayor Pennybacker and councilmen Learner and Pike. All three glanced at Hawk quickly, then looked away, faces flushing slightly with chagrin.

Cassidy was there, too, with several other doves, all wrapped in blankets.

Regan was nowhere in sight. Hawk hadn't expected to see her here.

Reb Winter and Alvin Gault stood behind the hooded, doomed men standing atop the trapdoor, nooses just now being tightened by the hangman who'd come in from Laramie on train seventy-nine before dawn.

The sheriff and deputy sheriff's badges glinted on Reb and Alvin's chests, respectively, and for only a second Reb switched his expression of serious, official duty to grin and wave at Hawk before adjusting his grip on the big shotgun in his hands and returning his hard-eyed sheriff's stare at the back of Brazos Tierney's hooded head.

Hawk saluted Trinity's new sheriff before his gaze caught on the black-clad, white-collared minister standing on the ground, facing the gallows and reading from the Good Book open in his large, pale hands. Reverend Hawthorne's blue-gray hair was slicked back, still showing the marks from a recent combing, and his dark broadcloth coat and trousers were new and crisp. His jaws had been scraped of their steely stubble.

As he read a prayer to the doomed prisoners, the reverend glanced at Hawk over his shoulder, gave a cordial nod, then returned his eyes to the open tome and to Tierney and McGee standing in grim silence above and before him.

Hawk reached inside his sheepskin vest to dig a cheroot out of his shirt pocket. "Well, I'll be damned."

Hawk and Saradee were a block beyond the gallows when the reverend closed his book and lowered his head. The hangman lowered his own head somberly as he pushed forward the brake-like handle bristling from the side of the gallows. Brazos Tierney's last scream echoed shrilly as the doors beneath the gallows opened, and he and McGee dropped straight down and started dancing the short-lived dance of the hanged.

The crowd clapped and cheered.

Saradee clucked to the mule, picking up the pace.

The wagon rattled and squawked. Soon, they were in the countryside, Trinity under its cap of wood smoke growing small behind.

"How you doin' back there, Hawk?" Saradee asked.

Hawk bit off the end of the cigar. "Me?"

Hawk pushed Regan out of his mind and fired a match on his shell belt.

"Hell, I'm fine," he said, puffing smoke and looking around. "Nice day for a ride. Damn nice day."

ABOUT THE AUTHOR

Peter Brandvold was born and raised in North Dakota. He's lived in Montana, Minnesota, Arizona, and Colorado. A full-time RVer, he writes Westerns under his own name as well as his pen name Frank Leslie, spending his summers in the mountains of western Colorado and his winters traveling around the Southwestern deserts. Send him an email at peterbrandvold@gmail.com.

The employees of Thorndike Press hope you have enjoyed this Large Print book. All our Thorndike, Wheeler, and Kennebec Large Print titles are designed for easy reading, and all our books are made to last. Other Thorndike Press Large Print books are available at your library, through selected bookstores, or directly from us.

For information about titles, please call:
(800) 223-1244

or visit our Web site at:
http://gale.cengage.com/thorndike

To share your comments, please write:
Publisher
Thorndike Press
10 Water St., Suite 310
Waterville, ME 04901